KU-463-426

Whiskey
and
Water

ALSO BY NINA WRIGHT FROM MIDNIGHT INK

Whiskey on the Rocks

Whiskey Straight Up

Whiskey and Tonic

YOUNG ADULT BOOKS BY NINA WRIGHT

Homefree

Sensitive

Whiskey
and
Water

A Whiskey Mattimoe Mystery

Nina Wright

MIDNIGHT INK
WOODBURY, MINNESOTA

Whiskey and Water: A Whiskey Mattimoe Mystery © 2008 by Nina Wright. All rights reserved. No part of this book may be used or reproduced in any manner whatsoever, including Internet usage, without written permission from Midnight Ink except in the case of brief quotations embodied in critical articles and reviews.

First Edition
First Printing, 2008

Book design and format by Donna Burch
Cover design by Lisa Novak
Cover art © 2007 Bunky Hurter
Editing by Connie Hill

Midnight Ink, an imprint of Llewellyn Publications

Library of Congress Cataloging-in-Publication Data
Wright, Nina, 1964–.
  Whiskey and water : a Whiskey Mattimoe mystery / Nina Wright. — 1st ed.
      p. cm.
  ISBN 978-0-7387-1216-1
  1. Mattimoe, Whiskey (Fictitious character)—Fiction. 2. Women real estate agents—Fiction. 3. Michigan—Fiction. I. Title.
PS3623.R56W475 2007
813'.6—dc22   2007047432

This is a work of fiction. Names, characters, places, and incidents are either the product of the author's imagination or are used fictitiously, and any resemblance to actual persons, living or dead, business establishments, events, or locales is entirely coincidental.

Midnight Ink
Llewellyn Publications
2143 Wooddale Drive, Dept. 978-0-7387-1216-1
Woodbury, MN 55125-2989 USA
www.midnightinkbooks.com

Printed in the United States of

MORAY COUNCIL LIBRARIES & INFO.SERVICES	
20 26 41 72	
Askews	
F	

DEDICATION

For Coach, my genuine Mississippi blues man in Michigan.

And for everyone who truly loves dogs,
from the big to the itty-bitty.

ACKNOWLEDGMENTS

Thanks and a rousing round of whiskey to all my usual suspects—I mean, friends: Teddie Aggeles, Kate Argow, Pamela Asire, Bonnie Brandburg, Linda Jo Bugbee, M. K. Buhler, Paul Epstein, Rebecca Gall, Danita Hiley, G. Neri, Richard Pahl, Nancy Potter, Tom Rychlewski, Barbara Sayers, Dennis Taylor, Rita Thomas, Diana West, and B. P. Winzeler.

Hugs to my favorite four-leggers, who come in all sizes and a couple of species: Elivia, Flame, McKenzie, Scruffy, Spike, Sir, Oreo, and Flannery.

ONE

"Whiskey! Look what Prince Harry can do!" Chester's delighted laugh reached me from the beach below.

I didn't have the energy to open my eyes... much less sit up—or, god forbid, get up—to investigate the antics of my young neighbor and his pup. The June sun was seductive. Lying on the chaise longue on my deck, I wanted to unwind all the way. To sleep, to dream... perchance to tan. I wouldn't move so much as an eyelid.

"Quick, Whiskey! He can't hold this pose much longer!"

"Describe it to me," I yawned. Which is what Chester was doing when I nodded off.

The next thing I knew I was dreaming, and it wasn't an especially sweet dream. Some man was shouting at me. For neglecting my kid and his dog. It had to be a dream because I don't have a kid, although I do have a dog. A big dog. A big nightmare of a diva dog no one would want to wake up to.

1

That was part of the dream—Abra the Afghan hound's wet nose in my face. I pushed it away. She put it back. When I pushed it away again, she stuck her nose in my ear. I rolled away from her, my eyes still shut.

Then I felt the man in my face, so mad that he spat as he spoke. "You're laying here asleep on your fancy deck while the little boy and his pup almost drowned!"

"You're in the wrong dream," I said.

Then Chester piped up, sounding just like he did when I was awake. "Don't blame Whiskey. She's not a child-care provider. And she can't handle dogs."

"*Whiskey*?" the man echoed. "Is she drunk?!"

He grabbed my shoulder and shook me. Hard. I opened my eyes. The sun was much lower in the sky than it used to be. Chester and Prince Harry, both wet, shivered under an army blanket. And Chester, who's always pale, looked blue. Not blue, depressed—blue, the *color*. I sat up so fast my wide-brimmed hat fell off. Abra grabbed it in her teeth and sauntered away.

"Chester, what happened?" I said.

"Riptide," the angry man announced. In his late sixties, he was weather-beaten, bald, and not inclined to like me. His fishing vest was festooned with hooks and lures. They gleamed like merit badges. "Carried him and the dog a mile down the shore."

He sniffed my breath and told Chester, "I don't smell whiskey. Maybe she slept it off."

Teeth chattering, Chester recounted his adventure. While he and Prince Harry were practicing "Coast Guard maneuvers," inspired by my step-grandchildren's ex-military nanny, they'd paddled out farther than usual. The next thing Chester knew, they couldn't come back in. A powerful current was pulling them along.

"I've read about riptides," Chester said. "So I know you have to go with the flow. I held onto Prince Harry, and away we went. Mr. Gamby was fishing from his boat. We waved at him as we floated by. He pulled up anchor and came after us."

Glaring at me, Mr. Gamby said, "The only thing *you* did right was make sure the kid had a life jacket."

Actually, Chester had made sure he had a life jacket. But he didn't take credit for it. And I was too mortified not to.

"I'm glad you're okay," I told him. Prince Harry barked to remind me that he was okay, too. "But why did you have Mr. Gamby bring you here instead of home?"

Chester looked uneasy. "Because my mother's ... busy."

"Thank god *you're* not his mother," Mr. Gamby snapped.

Had he met Cassina, he might have preferred me for the job. She couldn't focus on motherhood, being too "busy" composing, recording, and touring—when she wasn't fighting with Rupert, her on-again, off-again manager and paramour. Rupert was also Chester's ineffectual father. I seldom saw Cassina and almost never saw Rupert. Cassina hired people to perform many odd jobs, including looking after her son. Unfortunately, she fired them so often she sometimes forgot to replace them. Cassina frequently left town with Chester locked out of the Castle, their villa just north of my place. Guess who ended up babysitting? My dog Abra more often than me. And Abra was less maternal than Cassina.

I looked around for Prince Harry's mother. The blonde Afghan hound had retreated to a shaded corner of my deck where she contentedly munched my hat. Since she rarely chewed other people's possessions—preferring simply to steal them—I knew she was acting out.

Mr. Gamby said, "Aren't you going to take that away from her?"

"What's the point? She'll only go steal something else."

"You're completely irresponsible! I should call Children's Social Services."

"I'm not Chester's legal guardian," I reminded him. "Or his nanny. I just live here."

A squirting sound got everybody's attention. Prince Harry was relieving himself against the leg of my chaise longue. As we watched, he peed and peed. I wondered how much of Lake Michigan he'd managed to swallow. Mr. Gamby glanced from the peeing puppy to his chewing mother to shivering Chester—and then shook his head in disgust.

I felt at that moment like I'd failed my gender. Or at least my mother. She had taught me so many things—cooking, cleaning, diaper changing, shopping, grooming, flirting—yet all I really knew how to do was buy, sell, and rent real estate. And use the occasional power tool.

At age thirty-four, I was still an excellent swimmer, although I'd just slept through my best opportunity to prove it. I was fast on a bike, too, and I remembered most of what I'd learned as captain of my high school volleyball team. You might not think I'd have much need to cover the net. But you'd be wrong. During the fourteen months since my husband died and left me his kleptomaniac canine, I'd often been grateful that I was quick, strong, and six feet tall.

"Whiskeeeeeey!" I winced at the sound of my least favorite voice coming from up the hill, behind me. "Watch the kids while I'm out! I need a freakin' break!"

Without turning around, I understood that my stepdaughter, Avery Mattimoe, was about to jump ship, leaving me in charge of her seven-month-old twins, Leah and Leo. The only thing worse than taking over for Avery was living with Avery, which I was currently doing. Long, sad story. For me.

"I thought you weren't a nanny," Mr. Gamby said.

"I'm not. The nanny is away at a conference. I'm the scapegoat."

That made Chester laugh. Although he looked six, he was actually eight and sometimes seemed wise enough to be forty. Too bad he couldn't introduce me to a real man that age. I urgently needed a shoulder to cry on, and to burp a baby on.

"Their diapers need changing!" Avery hollered. "I've had enough shit for one day. Why is Chester wearing a blanket? It's like eighty degrees! Hey—there's a truck blocking me in. *Move!*"

I wished Avery would move ... far, far away. Hugely pregnant and estranged from her family, she had come home to roost after her father died. Avery's sense of entitlement made me crazy. Still, I knew my late husband would have welcomed any adult child of mine.

A few months ago Avery moved in with the man who thought he was the father of her twins. That was a strange time for me. Though relieved to be free of Avery and brood, I found myself disconcertingly attracted to handsome Nash Grant. He was closer to my age than hers, and I had been celibate a whole year. A superficial charmer, Nash only wanted proof that he wasn't shooting blanks. When a paternity test revealed the twins weren't his, he told Avery to get out and take her spawn with her. The trio landed back at my house, just in time for the start of my busiest season—and just in time for Deely Smarr, the "Coast Guard nanny," to head overseas. I was struggling to hold things together till she returned.

"Better move your truck," I advised Mr. Gamby. "Avery's having a bad day."

"She trusts *you* to look after her *babies*?" He was appalled.

"I may be incompetent, but I work for free."

"Don't worry," Chester told the fisherman. "As soon as I put some dry clothes on, I'll come back here and help."

"That girl's sticking her tongue out," Mr. Gamby observed. I still hadn't turned to face Avery.

"It's nothing personal," I told him. "Just her tic."

That was true; Avery flicked her tongue at everyone. Any wonder I didn't want to look? She must have been holding the back door open. I could hear either Leah or Leo starting to howl.

"If I don't get outta here," Avery shrilled. "I'm gonna lose my mind. Somebody move the damn truck!"

Prince Harry finished peeing. Chester pulled him under the blanket, no doubt for additional body heat. Abra, oblivious to everything except my straw hat, gagged on the grosgrain ribbon.

I stood, rising at least four inches over Mr. Gamby. "Well . . . thanks so much for saving Chester. And for driving him home. He'll tell you how to get to his house." I offered my hand. Mr. Gamby didn't take it.

"I still think I should turn you in," he muttered, "before you lose any more kids."

———

Changing diapers is like riding a bike in the snow. Once you've learned how to do it, you can always do it. But you'll never like doing it. Avery had left me with two stinky diapers on two cranky babies. Leah, Leo, and I all felt better after I'd cleaned their bottoms. I felt better yet after I'd drunk a goblet of Pinot Noir.

It was dinner time when my doorbell rang. I assumed that was Chester, keeping his promise to come back and help with the twins. Really, he was such a sweet kid. A pettier person—or a less lonely one—might have avoided me after I'd let him almost drown.

It wasn't Chester, however. Not bothering to check the peephole, I opened my front door to his celebrity mom. Cassina had every right to be mad. Hell, she had every right to sue me. She was a pop music superstar. She could afford to sue anyone.

"I am so sorry!" I exclaimed.

Since Cassina was wearing Jackie O-style sunglasses, oversized and darkly tinted, I couldn't read her expression. But the rest of her, as usual, appeared to have just arrived from outer space. Cassina wears only white. That evening, she was swathed in what looked like a pigment-free, pure cotton body wrap that concealed everything except her face, her feet, and a few wisps of scarlet hair. All ten toes sported gold and emerald rings.

I gushed, "I've lost a lot of sleep since Avery and the twins came back, and Deely went to her animal rights conference in Amsterdam. So when I finally got an afternoon off, I just wanted to relax in the sun! I didn't mean to fall asleep! I didn't know there was a riptide!"

For a long moment, Cassina stared at me. Or so I assumed since I couldn't see her eyes. Finally, in her famously breathy voice, she said, "Whiskey, who gives a fuck? Are you going to let me in?"

Of course, I let her in, bowing and scraping. Although she left her dark glasses on, I could tell she was scanning my foyer for any sign of Abra. Cassina doesn't "do" dogs. Chester managed to keep Prince Harry only because the Castle, at twenty thousand square feet, offered enough rooms to hide a puppy in. Even so, he sometimes stashed Prince Harry over here.

"Just so you understand," I said, "I never meant to be negligent."

"How sad for you," Cassina said. "I love being negligent. It makes life worth living."

"So … you won't sue me?"

"Why the hell would I do that? I've got enough hobbies."

At that point I wondered if Cassina even knew about her son's near-death experience. It didn't seem in my best interest to ask. Cautiously, I inquired as to what had brought her to my door.

"I need a favor," she said. "But first, I need a drink."

Although Cassina's performance persona was that of an ethereal fairy-like creature who whispered romantic ballads as she strummed her harp, in real life she usually seemed strung out. Her entourage and her son insisted that she had given up drink and drugs. I proceeded carefully.

"What would you like?"

"Well … anything with your name on it would be welcome."

Ah-ha. I invited the diva to sit while I poured her a scotch. My nickname notwithstanding, I rarely drink the hard stuff, but I do keep a well-stocked bar. I'm a red wine kind of gal. My husky voice earned me my moniker, way back in junior high. Jeb Halloran chose it for me; I kept it long after I divorced him and discarded his last name. The nickname was an improvement over the name I was born with—Whitney Houston.

Not sure how Cassina liked her whiskey, I brought it in a tumbler with ice on the side. She waved away the cubes, downed the whiskey in one toss, and handed me back the glass for a refill.

"Oh—while you're at it, you might want to send someone out to get the package I left in your driveway," she said.

Unlike billionaire Cassina, I didn't keep a staff of gofers to fetch for me. That hadn't occurred to her, however.

"You left a package in my driveway? May I ask why?"

"Get the whiskey and I'll explain."

I returned with no ice and a nearly full bottle, which I let Cassina pour for herself. After downing a second tumbler, she delicately licked her lips.

"I left the package in your driveway because I didn't know if you'd be home. Also, I didn't know if I'd want you to know that I left it. But I've decided that I do."

"Okay …" This sounded like a game of Twenty Questions. "Is it … bigger than a bread box?"

Cassina, who was pouring her third very large drink, said, "Just have your man bring it in."

Rather than explain that I didn't have a man—of either the hired or desired variety—I went out to retrieve it myself. I doubted that Cassina even noticed I had left. Sure enough, there was a box in my driveway, about ten feet from her Maserati. I was relieved to see she had a driver; he and I exchanged waves. At least I wouldn't have to worry about getting the singer home—just into her car. And the driver looked strong enough to help. The box was small, or I might have asked him to help me with that. No bigger than a bread box, it featured several rows of holes. And the ominous label LIVE ANIMAL. As I stood there, staring at the box, it jumped.

I jumped, too. I may also have let out a little shriek because the driver rolled down his window.

"He can't hurt you. He's just a wee thing."

The driver had what I thought was a Scottish accent. Convenient. He shouldn't mind the smell of scotch whiskey sure to accompany Cassina on the ride back to the Castle.

"What is it?" I asked the driver, pointing to the container, which now rocked from side to side.

"I don't know. He's a cutie, though."

So were most babies, but I wouldn't want to find one in my driveway. Gingerly, I picked up the box. It couldn't have weighed five pounds. From inside, I heard panting. As far as I knew, the only thing that size capable of panting was a puppy. I put the box down.

The driver motioned me over. "Here's the thing," he began and handed me a certified check for one thousand dollars. I handed it back.

The driver said, "Miss Cassina and Mr. Rupert are having a row, don't you know. He gave her this pup to win back her love, but she's leaving the country for a month at a Tuscan spa. She knows you have a dog, so ... here's another one."

Did he honestly think that made sense? He produced a second check, this one made out for two thousand dollars, and gave it to me, along with the first one.

"For the charity of your choice," he said.

"No!" I said and gave both checks back.

"Think of your nanny," he pleaded. "How she loves dogs and all creatures. How would she feel if you left this little one out here in your driveway?"

He pulled an exaggeratedly sad face.

I said, "First of all, I'm not going to leave him in my driveway. I'm going to give him back to you! Second of all, this isn't my nanny's house. It's my house. And I already have one dog too many!" … which reminded me I hadn't seen Abra since the hat-eating incident on my deck. I made a mental note to look for her. Later.

The driver reached into the front-seat console and removed yet another check, this one made out for five thousand dollars.

"No!" I shouted. "I am not taking a bribe!"

"Just think, Ms. Mattimoe, of all the good works Fleggers could do with *eight thousand dollars.*"

I shuddered. He was referring to Four Legs Good, the animal rights advocacy founded by my nanny and my vet—and the very reason Deely wasn't here to help me right now. Fleggers asserted that *all* animals were created equal and should be so recognized under the law. An alarming credo. I shared my life with a felonious Afghan hound who already had more clout than I did.

"Absolutely not!" I declared.

"I see," the driver said. He turned his gaze straight ahead and contemplated Lake Michigan. "In that case, how about a lucrative real estate listing? Miss Cassina owns a five-thousand-square-foot 'cottage' twenty miles up the coast. She sometimes goes there to …"—he cleared his throat—"work. But she's bored with the place and wants something new. She's asked me to find her a realtor."

He presented a manila folder, which I opened. It contained the paperwork required to list a property. Plus four photos showing a magnificently secluded three-story cedar-sided home in the dunes.

"A comparable property sold last month for three-point-three million," he said, dramatically rolling his Rs.

"Are you an agent?" I demanded.

"I was, back in Glasgow. MacArthur's the name. I'm studying now for my Michigan license. Are you hiring?"

I tucked the folder under my arm and told him to call me at the office. Then, against my better judgment—and all reasonable standards of sanity—I scooped up the rocking box and carried it into my house.

TWO

I found Cassina sprawled on my living room couch, half my scotch gone and most of her cotton body wrap unraveled.

"Whiskey, don't be so damn cheap," she slurred. "Crank up your air conditioner!"

Yards of flame-red hair fanned out across my ivory jacquard pillows. Since her sunglasses were still in place, I couldn't tell if Cassina was on her way to passing out or simply in position to contemplate my ceiling. She had spilled most of her current drink on her now exposed white teddie … and my couch. Hey, I had no right to complain. She wasn't going to sue me! What are a few whiskey stains between neighbors?

She ignored the LIVE ANIMAL box I set down on the coffee table next to her shoulder. The box, or rather its contents, had progressed from panting to whimpering. A moment later, it graduated to yipping.

"Cassina?" I inquired. "Do you hear that?"

"Yes, and I wish you'd turn it off."

"This is the box you left in my driveway. Can you please explain it?"

She lifted her head just enough to suggest eye contact. "You of all people should know what a dog sounds like."

"But why *this* dog at *this* time in *this* place?"

"I don't have time for riddles," she moaned, letting her head fall back onto the pillows. "I have to go to a spa in Tuxany!" I assumed she meant Tuscany and wondered if "spa" was code for "rehab."

"Why, oh why, does Rupert torture me like this?" she wailed. "He knows I hate dogs, and Chester loves dogs. So he gives me a dog, and now I have to get rid of it without Chester knowing I got rid of it."

Cassina crooked a finger and motioned for me to come closer, presumably so that she could share a secret. "Chester wants a dog. But he can never, ever have one because I won't have one. So you have to take this one. And you can't tell Chester. Ever."

"But—"

"It's just a little dog," Cassina insisted. "You can hardly even see him."

Apparently Cassina hadn't seen Prince Harry although he'd been living at her house for months. Three cheers for Chester. But I had no intention of keeping this pup, however cute he might be. The truth was I didn't like dogs one bit more than Cassina did. I had inherited mine and felt obliged by my love for my late husband to keep her. When Abra's criminal tendencies became clear, I briefly hoped she would land in jail, and I'd be free. It turned out, though, that the courts held me responsible for what my dog did.

A foul stench blasted through the breathing holes of the box into my living room.

"Whew!" I cried. "What did he do in there?"

"Shat a shitload, probably," Cassina said. "That's why they call 'im a shitzapoo…"

"A what?"

She didn't answer and didn't look inclined to speak again anytime soon. Cassina was unconscious.

"Technically, he's a *shih poo*. Says so right here." I turned to see MacArthur the driver standing in my foyer, reading from a small card. "A cross between a shih tzu and a toy poodle. A sissy breed, but he's sweet."

"Did you ring the bell?" I asked.

"Sorry, no. Miss Cassina paged me."

"No she didn't."

"You're right. Sorry. We have … an arrangement. If she goes in somewhere I know she can get a drink, and she doesn't come out in fifteen minutes, I go in after her. Generally, I dispense with formalities like doorbells and knockers. I found this card, by the way. It was supposed to go in the box with the dog."

Fanning the air, I said, "Good thing it didn't. By now we wouldn't be able to read it."

Then he delivered the card, which gave me an opportunity to watch him cross the room. A too-brief visual treat. MacArthur the driver was a hunk. Alas, Cassina the singer was a drunk. The ethereal harpist-singer snored like a bull elephant.

"So you're not really a driver," I said. "I mean, you were hired to … do more."

"I was hired by Mr. Rupert to get Miss Cassina where she needs to go. And right now she needs to get on a plane to Tuscany. But first let me help you with the pup."

I could hardly believe my ears. A tall, handsome stranger was standing in my living room, and he was willing to take care of shit. True, he had delivered two problems, but he was going to make them both better. If the real estate lead he'd given me was legit, I stood to earn a six-figure commission. And if he wanted to train as an agent, he would enhance the scenery at Mattimoe Realty.

MacArthur suggested we adjourn to my laundry room to clean up the pup. Good plan. I don't deal well with the gross and stinky—including the twins' diapers. Body excretions in any form (except sweat) make me sick on a scale from light-headed to nauseated to passed-out flat. Managing the shitzapoo was no exception. As soon as I lifted the lid, I felt woozy. Fortunately, MacArthur was there with a steadying hand and a box of baby wipes, plus disinfectant spray and lots of paper towels. He took over while I stepped back to admire his work. Well, his ass. He looked just as fine from behind as he did from in front. Six-foot-four, solid, and trim. When he turned around again, I fixed on his sparkling blue eyes. How did a gorgeous guy from Glasgow end up babysitting an American superstar? I had to know.

MacArthur said, "I knew Rupert, back in the day, and he owed me one."

That further stirred my curiosity, which I would have to satisfy later. For now I was grateful that the tiny black dog and his box were clean. MacArthur set the creature on the floor. It immediately started circling my ankles and whimpering.

"Adorable puppy," I said insincerely.

"He's older than he looks," MacArthur said. "About a year, I think."

"He's … full-grown?" My innate distaste for small dogs kicked in hard. This one was barely six inches tall. Although I can't handle the big ones, the little ones make my teeth itch. Especially when they whine. This dog was getting louder.

"Teacup-size, they call them," said MacArthur. "By now his personality's probably fully formed, too. He's a tad needy. Name's Velcro."

The little guy peered up at me, whimpering. Framed by curly black fur, his dark brown eyes shone like buttons. And his little stub of a tail wagged hopefully. Oh, sure, he was cute … in the same way ladybugs are cute: in moderation. We were almost past that point already.

How I wished Deely were here. I'd have to get through almost twenty-four more hours on my own—with two dogs, two babies, and one whacked-out stepdaughter. My eyes lighted on the doggie door that Deely installed last winter. Gently I picked up Velcro and pushed him through it. His whining became a piercing howl. Although he was probably too small to push his way back in, I wasn't taking any chances. I seized the partition and slid it into place, rendering the in-and-out flap useless. Even through a solid wall, the dog's "*yay-yay-yay*" was nerve-shattering.

"He has remarkable lung power," MacArthur observed. "And energy. He can keep going and going … speaking of which, I've got to get Miss Cassina to the airport. There's a private plane waiting in Grand Rapids."

"You can level with me," I said. "Is she really going to a spa?"

"She's really going to a spa."

"No way! Rupert hired you to keep her sober, but it's not working, which is why *you* want to get back in the real estate game."

He smiled. "I want to get back in the real estate game because I like making money. I also enjoy this job … because I like making money. I intend to do both jobs and make lots and lots of money."

I had to respect that, especially if he signed on to make money with me. "But a 'spa' in Tuscany? Come on. What's the story?"

"Sometimes, Ms. Mattimoe, a spa is just a spa."

MacArthur excused himself to prepare Cassina for departure. I was impressed by the delicate yet professional manner in which he "rewrapped" her, managing—or so it looked from my angle—to touch neither her sheer silk teddie nor her exposed alabaster skin. A lesser man might have copped a feel. Then without so much as a grunt, he hoisted the unconscious singer over his shoulder fireman-style and bid me adieu.

"When you're ready to show that property, the key is under the wood-nymph sculpture near the side door. So's the alarm code. I'll call your office when I get back."

"You're going to the spa, too?"

"My job is to hand her off, then I return. Rupert has more work for me."

I couldn't imagine what that might be. As far as I knew, Rupert's only work was to manage Cassina. MacArthur wished me luck with the wee dog and left. Listening to Velcro's earsplitting howl, I knew I'd need way more than luck. I'd need Deely and Chester and probably a case of Pinot Noir. I poured a second goblet and tried not to guzzle it; I had another dog in my life, her current location unknown. Not that I minded losing Abra. I often fantasized about her staying lost, yet she always turned up. The problem was what she turned up with. In the past it had ranged from a priceless tiara to a missing finger. I quaffed the last of my wine just as the doorbell rang.

Who could that be? If MacArthur hadn't rung the bell before, he wouldn't ring it now. And Avery had her own key. That meant I either had a friend at the door who for some reason hadn't called first, or I had a stranger, whom I had no desire to see. If it had been Girl Scout cookie-selling season, I wouldn't have hesitated. Love those Thin Mints.

When the doorbell rang a second time, I decided to use the peephole. Chester—dry, dressed, and no longer blue—stood on my front porch, waving up at me. I opened the door.

"Where's Prince Harry?" I said.

"Playing along the fence line with that little black dog."

Now I would have to explain Velcro. Where could I say he'd come from? Chester knew me too well to believe I'd adopt another dog, even at gunpoint. Should I admit that I'd done it for a real estate commission ... and to stave off a lawsuit?

"He used to be at my house," Chester said.

"You ... know this dog?" I tried to keep my voice neutral.

"Rupert forgot that Cassina doesn't like dogs. We couldn't keep him, but I'm glad you've got him now. He and Prince Harry can play every day!"

Chester beamed a big smile up at me, pale eyes shining behind thick lenses. His resourcefulness amazed me, especially his talent for recasting Cassina and Rupert's behavior so that it passed for normal.

"How are the twins?" he asked. "Need help changing diapers?"

I told him I was managing so far, but appreciated having him around. Velcro's yips had stopped. Maybe Prince Harry as playmate was the answer. Not that I wanted a *third* dog around to keep a *second* dog happy. That reminded me ... where was the *first* dog? Trying to sound casual, I mentioned to Chester that we should probably look for Abra.

"You lost her? Again?" he said.

"I never 'lose' her. Abra tends to take off without filing a flight plan."

Maybe I was as good at denial as Chester. He was better with animals than I was, especially with that one. Abra adored Chester. She liked Deely and our vet Dr. David, too, and a few other folks. But she was indifferent to most people and openly rude to me. She and Avery had that in common. They both deeply missed Leo, Abra's first owner and Avery's father. Although Abra couldn't say it, and Avery hadn't said it yet, I knew they both wished I had died instead of Leo.

"Which way did she go?" Chester shaded his eyes against the sun setting over Lake Michigan. I admitted that I hadn't seen her since she ate my hat.

"She doesn't usually consume what she steals," I said. "So either she needs more straw in her diet, or she's pissed off."

"I vote for pissed off," Chester said. "What did you do to her?"

I mentally replayed my day. What had I done that might offend Abra? Other than allow a riptide to carry off her son and her favorite human. Abra had showed zero interest in Prince Harry since weaning him, but Chester she would have missed. Still, she knew he was fine, so punishing me seemed petty. Especially after she'd had the pleasure of watching Mr. Gamby chastise me.

"Maybe Abra resents having Avery and the twins back again," Chester said.

"Not half as much as I do," I muttered.

"I mean, maybe Abra resents you for giving them so much attention."

"Like I have a choice?"

Maybe Chester was onto something. From April to early June—except for a brief invasion by about forty stray cats—it had been just Abra and me here at Vestige, my country home by the lake. Perhaps she'd gotten used to being the only one I cursed at. Perhaps, in her world, all attention was good attention, and now she was getting less. Could that explain her eating my hat? Or were more sinister forces at work? Abra had a history of consorting with criminals. But what kind of sick mind would train a dog to consume fashion accessories?

My thoughts stopped abruptly when Chester shouted, "There she is!" I followed his pointing finger and saw what he saw: At the water's edge, down the bluff from my house, my blonde bimbo Afghan hound rolled ecstatically in the wet sand. Probably on a dead fish. She stopped long enough to make sure we got a good picture; then she resumed rolling. From here, her pleasure looked sexual. Obscene. I wanted to cover Chester's eyes.

"I'll go get her!" my young neighbor volunteered, his enthusiasm compelling.

As the adult in our duo, and the legal owner of that dog, I felt obliged to help. Prince Harry, already bored with Velcro, tagged along. Stuck in my side yard, the teacup dog howled inconsolably.

It wasn't a dead fish that Abra was rolling in. It was *two* dead fish and half a dead tern. I suspected Abra of deliberately compiling a stack of stinky things for her own erotic pleasure. But when I scanned the beach, I noticed much more flotsam than usual. Chester must have made the same observation.

"Maybe another riptide rolled in," he said. "I've read that they churn up lots of debris and then dump it on beaches. They're cyclical, you know."

When I was eight, I don't think I knew the words "debris" or "cyclical," and I certainly couldn't have used them in a sentence.

"I'm just glad the riptide didn't churn you up," I said. Watching Prince Harry join his mother in a smelly somersault, I added, "or your dog, either. I'm sorry I fell asleep."

"It's all right, Whiskey. I know you're doing the best you can within the framework of your own limitations."

That sounded like Noonan-speak, i.e., the lingo of Noonan Starr, our local massage therapist and New Age spiritual counselor. I knew for a fact that Cassina kept Noonan on retainer, so Chester was often exposed to her aphorisms.

"Thanks," I said. "Now how about doing the best we can with these dogs?"

"You're going to need a lot of help with Velcro," Chester sighed. "He's smaller than Abra, but even more high-maintenance."

From the direction of my yard on the bluff above us came the sustained high-pitched howl of an itty-bitty dog.

THREE

CHESTER WAS PROBABLY RIGHT about Abra resenting Avery. Hell, I resented Avery, and I could appreciate how cute her kids were.

Almost every time I held little Leah or Leo, I thought about how their grandfather and namesake, my late husband, would have adored them. He'd died before finding out Avery was pregnant. No question, Leo would have been a fabulous grandpa. That explained why I felt I should do what I could to help the babies— even though I couldn't stand their mom.

So I was frankly relieved when Chester asked if he could spend the night. Between the twins and the two canines, I needed all the help I could get—even if Chester came with an additional dog, Prince Harry. By the time I heard Avery return in her usual huff, the twins were snug in their cribs, Chester had bedded down with the hounds, and I was hiding in my room.

Chester didn't have a parent or guardian to go home to, anyhow. Cassina had left the country, and Rupert's current whereabouts were unknown. A few months earlier, Chester had discovered a bizarre triangle of estranged maternal grandparents. But they weren't as convenient as I was. One was incarcerated, another had just been paroled, and the third lived in Iowa.

Fortunately, the ex-con grandfather was now a good guy. He worked as a part-time handyman for Mattimoe Realty. Still, I lived close to the Castle, and I needed Chester as much as Chester needed me. I had hired him shortly after Leo died to be Abra's official keeper. Even though Deely now handled that, I continued to rely on Chester for back-up. In his own way, he was a handyman, too.

The next morning I slipped out of the house before anybody else woke up. I had a real estate empire to run. Ahead of me loomed twelve hours with business issues only—no Avery, no babies, and no dogs.

As usual, my star real estate agent, Odette Mutombo, was already in her cubicle and on the phone making deals. Originally from Zimbabwe, Odette spoke a mellifluous version of English that rendered most prospects unable to say anything but yes. After concluding her pre-breakfast business, Odette rapped on my open door. She was holding a shopping bag.

"I bought something for you to give Avery," she crooned. Her skillfully marcelled waves gleamed under my office lights. Even at this ungodly hour, her makeup was flawless. I never saw Odette re-apply her crimson lipstick, yet it always looked fresh.

"I'm already giving Avery more than any sane person would," I replied.

"Exactly why you should give her this. It's the gift that keeps on giving and especially satisfies the giver."

"What is it? A whoopee cushion? A headache? A venereal disease?"

Odette handed me the shiny bag. I pulled out its tissue-wrapped contents. "A … guest towel?"

"A *personalized* guest towel."

The towel bore this inscription, stitched in delicate script on fine white linen: *"Do not mistake endurance for hospitality."*

"That might be too subtle for Avery," I said.

"And too bold for you. That's why I attached this reminder."

Odette had pinned instructions to the towel: *Hang in Avery's bathroom. Immediately!*

"If you can't find the balls to throw her out, at least make sure she knows she's unwelcome," Odette declared. "Last I checked, you were certified to run a realty, not a daycare center for kids and canines."

My unfortunate sideline wasn't limited to *day*care, but that didn't seem a point worth making. I changed the subject.

"This morning I'm going to inspect the new North Side property. If the renovations are finished, I should be able to rent it immediately. Two spacious units, and the timing is perfect. We have a long waiting list for rentals in that price range."

Odette nodded with complete indifference. The North Side of Magnet Springs was a low-rent neighborhood she would never willingly set foot in. I, however, believed in diversified holdings. Following in the footsteps of my late husband-slash-business partner, I made sure Mattimoe Realty did more than broker high-end sales. We also owned and/or managed rental properties for virtually all income brackets. In my humble opinion, the North Side was on its way up. And in the meantime, it was still a place to make a buck.

"Speaking of rentals, I've found someone to sublet Nash Grant's house," Odette said, referring to the rental property suddenly abandoned by Avery's ex. "The new tenant will assume the full rent starting this month. Most of Magnet Springs thinks you'll be thrilled to have Jeb back in town."

I said, "Since when can my ex-husband afford that kind of rent?"

Jeb Halloran was an itinerant musician long on charm and short on cash. Whenever he passed through Magnet Springs, he stayed for free with one of his many cousins. But not before he tried to spend the night with me.

"Since he landed an open-ended contract playing five nights a week at the Holiday Inn in Grand Rapids," Odette replied. "And received a handsome check for signing with a new recording label."

"What's he singing these days?" I asked without curiosity. "Country? Celtic? Canine?"

I meant the last option as a joke; Deely and our veterinarian Dr. David had recently discovered that Jeb's voice calmed cats and dogs. My ex was a gypsy—forever shifting musical styles and performance venues in search of an audience.

Odette said, "He's playing oldies but goodies at the Holiday Inn and promoting his new *Animal Lullabies* CD."

"Fleggers came through with the cash?"

I was stunned. Last I'd heard, Deely and Dr. David were brainstorming a plot to sell Jeb's tunes to affluent owners of hyperactive pets. Except, according to Fleggers, there are no "pets"—just four-legged "people equivalents" who lack conventional credit.

"Fleggers has deep pockets," Odette said. "And a formidable marketing plan. Deely and Dr. David are in Amsterdam negotiating European sales for Jeb's CDs."

"I thought they were in Amsterdam for a Fleggers convention!"

"Wake up, Whiskey. Deal-making is the real business of Fleggers," Odette said. "It's everybody's real business. Your nanny learned to negotiate in the Coast Guard."

"She learned damage control in the Coast Guard," I argued. "That's why I hired her to work at my house."

———

Thirty minutes later, I was making the short drive to the new North Side duplex. As usual, I had put property manager Luis Regalo in charge of renovations, which in this case included extensive remodeling of bathrooms and kitchens in addition to painting and replacing flooring throughout both units. Since Luis had assigned Roy Vickers—my best recent hire and Chester's newly discovered ex-con grandfather—to finish the job, I expected to find Roy on site.

And I did. Roy stood in the repaved driveway talking to my new tenant from the tiny house next door. Twyla Rendel was a mousy young woman whose best feature was the bright smile she rarely flashed. About five-foot-six with lank dishwater-blonde hair, hazel eyes, and an anemic complexion, Twyla tended to slouch whether standing, sitting, or tending her two small kids.

The previous week, she and her children had moved into the nine-hundred-square-foot yellow clapboard cottage. Newly hired as cashier at Food Duck, our local grocery, Twyla couldn't offer local references or much of a work or credit history. Ordinarily I might have turned down her application. But I felt hopeful about Twyla. She'd come from Flint, Michigan—on the other side of the state—where she'd worked a series of short-term unskilled jobs since graduating from high school. Her most recent gig had been as receptionist for a dentist who'd inconveniently dropped dead while extracting a wisdom tooth. That had left Twyla jobless in an economically depressed town. She claimed she'd decided to move to Magnet Springs after spotting an article about our charming burg in a travel magazine that the dentist kept in his waiting room.

"It sounded like a nice place to raise kids," she told me.

Nice and expensive, I could have told her. Ours was a tourist town. Great views, fabulous restaurants, quaint shops, and stellar real estate. Lots of pricey services available, too, but not many career opportunities for someone with only a high school diploma. During our brief interview, Twyla volunteered that she had no husband and no family beyond her two-year-old son and one-year-old daughter.

"That's a lot of responsibility," I commented. Not that I wanted to hear her sad story, but I was intrigued by her stony determination to single-handedly give her kids a better life. I recalled my mother's accounts of our Irish immigrant ancestors who moved to America with only the clothes on their backs. At least they'd had family.

Twyla shrugged and stared at her feet. "I'll figure it out," she said. "I always find a way to get by."

Then her eyes met mine, and she flashed a quick, shy smile that touched my business-hardened heart. She was emotionally damaged, no doubt about it. But I sensed a solidness in her that I attributed, with respect, to the School of Hard Knocks.

Also, I couldn't help but compare Twyla and Avery. They were both single moms, close in age, with two tiny kids. Unlike Avery, Twyla didn't have a trust fund. Or a stepmother with survivor guilt and a couple extra bedrooms.

In short, I found myself rooting for Twyla. Starting over is never easy. Maybe she had more reasons than a dead dentist and a magazine article for moving to Magnet Springs. Reasons like a surly ex or a string of sad memories in Flint. Twyla didn't have to confide in me. In fact, I preferred to know nothing about my tenants' private lives. They were part of my business, not my circle of friends. As long as they honored their leases, I liked them just fine. But this one—this one got to me. Just a little.

Now, as I pulled into the recently redone driveway that served both my new duplex and the house Twyla rented, the young mother's face turned ashen.

I knew why. The last time she'd seen me, I had Abra at my side. And Abra had ripped a shiny plastic bangle right off Twyla's wrist. She'd run away with it, too. My dog left no teeth marks, but she did rattle nerves. She was an incorrigible thief. If it glistened or moved, Abra had to have it. If it glistened *and* moved, you'd never see it again.

"I left Abra home!" I called out in lieu of hello.

"Thank you," said Twyla, smiling weakly. "It's not that I don't like your dog. It's just that she scares the crap out of me."

"Abra scares the crap out of me, too," I said cheerfully. "How's it going here, Roy?"

At age seventy, Mattimoe Realty's handyman didn't look a day over fifty-five. And we're talking a very fit fifty-five. Roy Vickers was strikingly tall, with military bearing and bulging muscles. His hairline, like his waistline, could have belonged to a much younger man. Only the network of deep lines and broken veins around his bright blue eyes betrayed Roy's history as our town drunk. People rarely mentioned that history, least of all the chapter that had earned him nine years in the slammer. In an alcoholic rage, Roy once stabbed a man. Fortunately, that man had survived … to marry me and teach me about real estate. Leo Mattimoe forgave Roy, and so did I.

"I'm almost finished here, Whiskey." Roy detailed his remaining tasks, which involved removing tools and other equipment and then sweeping up.

"So we'll be move-in ready by next week?" I asked.

"By the weekend."

That's why I liked working with Roy. Oh, I'd had qualms when I hired him. But Noonan Starr had built an awesome, guilt-inducing case for helping Roy find "karmic balance." She'd insisted that to rebuild his life after jail, Roy needed to do good works where he'd once done damage. Leo would have agreed. So I'd found a spot for Roy on my payroll, and I was glad that I had.

Twyla excused herself to go check on her kids in the house. As soon as she left, Roy whispered, "Something's not right with that gal."

"Did she say so?" I asked.

"Not straight out, but the Seven Suns of Solace tells me so."

I resisted the urge to roll my eyes. The Seven Suns of Solace bugged the hell out of me. Next to Avery and Abra—and a few other annoying locals—it was one of the major downsides of living in Magnet Springs. A fuzzy New Age philosophy, the Seven Suns of Solace was embraced by most of my hometown. Roy had studied it in prison and gave it credit for saving his mind. Noonan practiced it along with her massage therapy and gave it credit for saving her business.

Over the past year, she had built a lucrative practice as a New Age telecounselor, advising former tourists by phone how to stay in touch with their "higher selves" after their vacations ended. Noonan also counseled dozens of locals face to face. That portion of her clientele included our acting mayor and purveyor of fine coffee, Peg Goh, and my acting-out stepdaughter and squatter, Avery. In terms of results, I could only observe that Peg remained as cheery as ever, while Avery was her usual sulky self. Still, there was no question that Roy had come out of prison a reformed man, so the Seven Suns of Solace must have shone on him.

"What's up with Twyla?" I asked Roy. "Besides her natural fear of Abra?"

He frowned thoughtfully. "I think she's harboring deep anxieties that have nothing to do with your dog. Something's blocking her karmic flow."

That's the kind of statement you're likely to hear in Magnet Springs. One of the oddities of our small town is that many residents lay claim to "insights." A touch of clairvoyance or other unexplained talents. Odette, for example, can sometimes predict what prospects look like on the basis of their telephone voices. Noonan's wide-ranging psychic talents are downright alarming. And then there's our police chief, who, when riled, can channel the town's magnetic fields.

I smiled at Roy, one of the few men in Magnet Springs I literally had to look up to.

"Well, let's hope Twyla's just having a bad day." More important, I thought, let's hope she keeps her problems to herself. A quiet, compliant tenant was my favorite kind of tenant. So far, Twyla fit that bill.

Roy and I walked through both units of the new duplex, reviewing my checklist. He was right. Everything that needed doing was done, save the final clean-up. When I headed back out to my car, Twyla's ten-year-old Ford Taurus was gone. And the unofficial neighborhood guardian was waving at me from across the street. Correction: she was waving me over to her side. Urgently.

Sixty-six-year-old Yolanda Brewster was the self-appointed Boss of the North Side. "Boss Bitch" according to some of her neighbors, but I knew she meant well. During the warm months, she and her portable TV spent most days and evenings on her front porch. During the rest of the year, she parked her gleaming wheelchair in the living room by the picture window. Neighborhood dramas interested her far more than her favorite soap operas and talk shows. As a North Side property owner and Yolanda's landlord, I appreciated her vigilance. She did more to keep crime off the streets than our local cops did. But then our local cops consisted of one full-time chief, one full-time canine, and one part-time officer who wanted to be an art historian.

"Where's that big dog o' yours?" Yolanda called out as I crossed the street toward her.

"Home ... I hope."

Yolanda knew only too well my chronic inability to keep Abra in check. Last spring she had helped me and the police locate my missing canine after Abra committed a felony in plain sight of two hundred people.

"How are you, Mrs. Brewster? Any chance I can get a glass of your famous iced tea?"

"I'm good, I'm good, Miz Mattimoe," she replied. "Of course you can get you some tea. I brewed a fresh batch cuz I knowed you be coming. I seen Roy carrying paint cans outta that house this morning. That mean you be showing up soon. Come on in!"

I held open the front door for Yolanda—not that she needed me to—and then followed her wheelchair through the house to her spotless kitchen. None of my tenants kept a cleaner house than Yolanda. And none of my other tenants was wheelchair-bound. I didn't know how she managed. Her sweet iced tea was another mystery. Flavored with mint, honey, and ginger, it was the best version of that beverage I'd ever tasted. I sipped it gratefully, waiting for Yolanda to say what was on her mind. I didn't have to wait long.

"I seen you talking to the Rendel girl," Yolanda began. "You know what's up over there?"

I shook my head. Although the tea felt good going down, my stomach tightened. Roy had gotten weird vibes from Twyla, and now Yolanda had news to share.

"Let me ask you this, Miz Mattimoe: how many kids you think she got?"

I held up two fingers. In response, Yolanda held up five.

"No way," I said. "I met the kids."

Yolanda continued to display five fingers. "Best I can tell from here, she got three boys and two girls. Real close in age."

I understood Yolanda's concern. And I wasn't happy, either. That house was zoned for very limited occupancy. Although technically it had two bedrooms, the second one was the size of a modest walk-in closet. Where could Twyla put five kids?

I opted for denial. "She can't have five kids," I said. "She's only twenty-three."

If I'd paused to think, I would have seen my own stupidity. Yolanda kindly pointed it out. She herself had had five babies before she reached that age, giving birth for the first time when she was sixteen.

"Here's my worry," Yolanda said. "I don't see how that girl can take care of those babies. She got no family to help. I hear 'em crying all day and all night."

FOUR

ALL THIS TALK ABOUT babies reminded me of the two at my house. I thanked Yolanda for her concern and returned to my car to check my cell phone. It was down to one battery bar. In last night's confusion, I'd failed to plug it in. And in my rush to flee home this morning, I'd forgotten my charger cable.

En route to the office, I played back my voice mail, which contained a higher-than-usual number of Vestige-based messages. Mostly from Chester. With mostly helpful reminders about replenishing my supplies of human and canine essentials.

Failing to keep fridge and pantry stocked ranked high on my list of notorious shortcomings. Another reason I needed Deely Smarr. She was a whiz at making the house seem to run itself—an illusion, I realized, but one that I happily paid her well to sustain. Deely was more of a personal assistant-slash-housekeeper than nanny, and I compensated her accordingly.

If Deely had been on duty today, I wouldn't have had to hear the other three voice mail messages from home. They were Avery's, noting that I was out of dog food, people food, and toilet paper. Not in that order. And not without hostility.

But there was one message missing. The one from Avery screaming about the new little dog. Where was that message? Amid her many complaints about my household, she hadn't even mentioned Velcro. Now that I thought about it, neither had Chester. Maybe I'd dreamed the dog? Nah. I hardly ever had nightmares.

There was one message from the office. A mellifluous voice said, "I saw what's on your desk, and I know it's worth three million dollars."

Leave it to Odette to snoop while I was out in the field. She'd found the folder for Cassina's "cottage." Based on its location, size and amenities, I figured the property was worth all of that—before we factored in "star power," the built-in prestige of its famous current owner. That should add a few hundred thou to the ticket.

I knew Odette would have peeked at my schedule and then parked herself in front of Mattimoe Realty with Cassina's folder, ready to accost me when I came back. She was there, all right, and she wasn't alone. Tina Breen, my disorganized office manager, fidgeted by Odette's side, wringing her hands. As soon as she caught sight of me driving toward them down Main Street, tiny frizzy-haired Tina jumped and waved. I felt like the pilot of a medevac helicopter swooping in to save the day. Only I had no idea what was wrong, and I didn't want to find out. In fact, I considered driving right on by.

Odette's face wore its usual bland expression. She just wanted to go make money, which was my goal, too. I decided to stop so that she could get in and help me.

"Vivika Major has been calling you all morning!" Tina whined as I powered down my window. "Why isn't your cell phone on?"

"It's always on," I said, quickly checking. *Oops*. The one bar had become none. "Sorry. I didn't recharge. Who did you say has been calling?"

"Vivika Major. She needs to see you."

The name still wasn't resonating.

"Your first multimillion-dollar sale," Odette said helpfully. "They say you never forget your first. But maybe *you* do."

I remembered. Four years ago, with a little help from yours truly, Vivika Major had bought a small inn on the shore of Lake Michigan for her fabulous second home. Her fabulous first home was across the lake, in a rich, out-of-sight Chicago suburb.

"Ms. Major is 'tired of this side of the lake,'" Tina quoted. "She wants you to sell Druin for her—and she wants you to get the highest price the market will bear. As soon as humanly possible." Tina's voice buzzed like one of those remote-controlled toys you desperately want to step on.

I sighed, both pleased and annoyed. I always got the highest price the market would bear. But my definition of "as soon as humanly possible" might not jibe with Vivika's. She had given me the same orders, in reverse, four years earlier: "Find me the most incredible place, at the most incredible price, as soon as humanly possible." I had met that goal by discovering the perfect unlisted property and convincing the owners to match Vivika's numbers within Vivika's time frame. It hadn't been easy, but it had proved worthwhile.

"You're on your way to see her now," Odette informed me. "I'm along for the ride—and my share of the commission. I'll get this deal done."

Of course she would. That's how Odette and I worked: I put the package together; then she put the people together who could buy the package.

Vivika Major was an Internet marketing genius. Though hardly a household name, she had started several spectacularly success-ful online businesses, including one that most families used every day. Nobody who clicked on a certain search engine had any idea they were making Vivika Major even more obscenely rich than she already was.

"This could be the luckiest week of your life," Odette cooed. "Two mega-rich divas are bored with the shore and ready to un-load high-end homes."

My luck did look incredible. If you didn't count the return of Avery, the absence of Deely, and the arrival of Velcro. Or the il-legally expanding family of tenant Twyla Rendel. Even if you did, those hassles couldn't dim my profitable prospects. World-class properties like Cassina's cottage and Druin don't come up for sale very often, let alone with the same realty in the space of one week. Assuming that Cassina's cottage was worth three mil, Vivika's mini-hotel should fetch more than four. She had bought it for two-point-eight mil and replaced or upgraded everything, including the roof, garage, docks, boathouse, guesthouse, patio, and pool.

Of course, nothing sells till you find the right buyer. That was where Odette came in. She had uncanny connections and schmoozed as naturally as she breathed. She also worked harder than anybody else in the biz. I sometimes suspected that Odette lived to do real estate. Her clients got more of her time than her physician husband did. But he was usually busy, too. Maybe it was the perfect marriage.

"More good news," Odette announced, sliding into the passenger seat. "Vivika's place is just up the road from Cassina's."

"How convenient," I murmured, glancing at the Druin folder that Tina had passed through my window.

"*Convenient,* my ass," Odette said. "This is destiny, Whiskey! We're fated to get a nice thick slice of the fat money pie."

For an instant I could have sworn Odette's pupils were the shape of dollar signs. Not that I was complaining.

———

En route up the coast to Druin, I used Odette's cell to phone Vivika Major. The call was answered by her receptionist, who transferred it to her personal assistant, who transferred it to her personal secretary, who transferred it—finally—to Vivika herself. Although I hadn't talked with the Internet guru in almost four years, I immediately recognized her voice. The word "authoritarian" best describes it. Vivika speaks with a low intensity that oozes power and privilege. After hearing but a few syllables, the listener knows that the speaker will call the shots. Vivika asked for my ETA at Druin, then consulted with several attending associates, and announced that she could give me three to five minutes' "face time." After that, her assistant would conclude the business with Mattimoe Realty. I assured Vivika that we would handle everything to her complete satisfaction.

"Of course you will," she remarked. "If you don't, I'll take my business elsewhere."

About twenty miles north of Magnet Springs, I pulled off Coastal Highway and made a series of sharp turns onto narrower and rougher roads. Finally Odette spotted the landmark we were searching for—a waist-high sign almost hidden by greenery identifying Internet Way, Vivika's private driveway. Moments later, I had braked at the gatehouse and was explaining our business to a solemn security guard whose name tag identified him as Mr. García. After phoning two or three members of Vivika's personal staff, Mr. García ascertained that we were legit; without smiling, he pressed the magic button. *Voilà*. The metal gate before us swung open, and I guided my Lexus RX-330 down the lane. I had been here only twice before. Once to schmooze the people who agreed to sell. And once to show the property to Vivika. The gatehouse was a subsequent addition. As was the heavy overgrowth along the property's perimeter. Clearly, Vivika craved privacy.

"You'd think she was as famous as Cassina," Odette observed.

"She's richer," I said, "and she's probably made more enemies."

The driveway, paved in beige brick veneer, curved again and then widened before us, fanning out to its elegant conclusion. A chateau in Lanagan County might be as misplaced as an A-frame in Manhattan. But Druin was made of such classic and harmonious proportions that it seemed to rise naturally from the bluff overlooking Lake Michigan. The stately mansion—built as a home in 1927, converted to a mini-hotel in 1974, and recently redone as a twenty-first-century estate—struck me as the essence of "grand." The limestone portal that framed the double front doors seemed built for visiting royalty.

An athletic-looking woman with short, prematurely silver-white hair responded to our door chime. Wearing an expensive navy-blue suit and good flat shoes, she introduced herself as Felicia Gould, the chatelaine of Druin. Then she excused herself to notify Ms. Major of our arrival.

"*Chatelaine*? Do we believe in putting on airs?" I whispered to Odette.

"She's more than a housekeeper," Odette replied. "I hear she has a Stanford law degree and rigorously trains Ms. Major's personal staff."

While waiting for Ms. Gould to return, I looked around as best I could without actually snooping. The central hall, where we stood, seemed to demand a processional. Its French doors opened theatrically into a luminous living room decorated entirely in one pale shade of amber. Peering through the glass partition, I felt like a naughty exiled child. But no child I knew, save possibly Chester, could have identified the matching gilt-leg sofas as nineteenth-century Russian. I owed my late husband Leo for that part of my education. In addition to real estate acumen, he'd accumulated a wealth of wisdom about furniture design, and he'd enjoyed sharing it. If I'd known how prematurely I was going to lose Leo, I would have paid closer attention.

Odette busied herself taking notes on the architectural details within our view, features of the house that would stay when Vivika moved on. Neither of us heard the chatelaine re-approach. Her flat shoes must have had silent heels.

"Ms. Major has requested that I give you a quick tour before she meets with you." Her voice befitted a chatelaine—or a head mistress. It was precise, calm, and instructive. "Follow me, please. We'll see the upstairs first."

I knew that would delight Odette. Her notebook at the ready, she simultaneously looked, listened, and jotted down phrases destined to appear in our Druin listing. Felicia Gould was a more than capable tour guide, covering exactly what we'd need to know in order to get the best price for this world-class residence.

"Ms. Major has a deep respect for historic architecture and design. In renovating the home, she has preserved its integrity by using only those materials that were originally specified: the same wood, the same stone, even the same fabrics. During the years when Druin served as a hotel, those elements were regularly disregarded. One might even say, violated."

Despite the strong word choice, Felicia's smooth face remained impassive. She opened doors into two of the six large bedroom suites on the second floor. Both were spacious and airy, featuring pastel monotone color schemes—much like the living room below—as well as cove ceilings and intricate wood trim. We glimpsed one attached bathroom, a small but state-of-the art facility with a glass-enclosed Roman shower, a double-sink marble-top vanity, and an ivory toilet with matching marble pediment. As we moved through the house, Felicia described upgrades in plumbing, wiring, heating, and air-conditioning, as well as the remodeling choices made in the kitchen and wine cellar. The cellar was still being renovated, so we bypassed it. But she did lead us through the kitchen—an expansive wheat-colored room with matching granite countertops, diagonally laid oak floors, painted cabinetry, and professional-grade appliances. The ranges, ovens, refrigerator, freezer, and dishwasher were all tinted to match the room's subtle single-hue palette.

Following our brief perusal of the kitchen, Felicia led us back out to the marble-floored central hallway, past the closed glass doors that sealed off the living room. I was already thinking of that impressive, though isolated, pale amber room as the Salon in a Bubble. Although Druin was theoretically Vivika Major's weekend home, nobody really seemed to "live" here. I doubted that the mogul ever stopped working. Felicia explained that the entire north side of the chateau, where we were headed next, was devoted to business.

She wordlessly led us through three outer offices—probably past the three people whose gauntlets I had to run before reaching Vivika by phone. After swiping her coded cardkey, the chatelaine pushed open a grandly carved oak door to reveal the original library. Built-in shelves on two walls now held banks of televisions and computer monitors instead of books. Two sofas—*demi-lune*, late nineteenth-century, and rare, if I remembered Leo's lessons—formed a modified V (for Vivika?) facing the wide leaded-glass window that overlooked Lake Michigan. Behind the sofas was an ornate burr elm desk, at which sat the Internet entrepreneur. Although two notebook computers were open and running on her desk, Vivika Major busily jotted notes *by hand*, using an old-fashioned lead pencil.

"Whiskey Mattimoe and Odette Mutombo. From Mattimoe Realty," Felicia announced. At that moment I knew how it felt to be presented to the Queen. I refrained from curtsying. We all waited for what seemed like a full minute while Vivika finished writing. Finally she glanced up.

"Hey," she said.

A "hey back at ya" wasn't on my lips. But I managed not to be caught completely off guard. At least I didn't spray spit or trip over my own feet as I stepped forward to shake her hand. Her very large hand.

I had forgotten about Vivika Major's unusual proportions. When she stood, she was almost as tall as me, though "bigger-boned," as my mother would say. In my family we never used that phrase as a euphemism for fat. Mom always meant what I mean here: that the person had large limbs—broad shoulders, huge hands, enormous feet. Although Vivika Major moved with reasonable grace, her physique had the rough shape of a linebacker's. Her face had big bones, too. It was broad and long with prominent cheek-bones, an aquiline nose, and a Jay Leno chin.

"I trust Felicia gave you a quick tour and an overview of the renovations we've done at Druin," Vivika said.

"Very helpful," Odette chimed in. "I've already compiled a list of potential buyers—qualified clients interested in magnificent older properties that have maintained their architectural integrity. Druin combines that element with a panoramic lake view. I'm confident, Ms. Major, that we'll get you the price you want."

Damn, she was good. Odette hadn't had time to compile anything yet. But schmoozing was always Job One. As a business icon, Vivika surely spoke the same language. Our about-to-be-official client nodded once and then glanced at Felicia, who produced a three-ring binder.

"That's a detailed overview of the property," Vivika said. "Everything you'll need to begin doing your job—except, of course, the papers requiring my signature. You'll find those in Felicia's office. I'm asking five-point-five million, and I need to close by Labor Day. We're opening a new office in Auckland, New Zealand, so I'm usually there. Between business and travel demands, I can no longer make use of this coast."

An odd way to put it, I thought. And five-point-five million by Labor Day was an extremely tall order. I was about to launch into my respectful though sobering "Reality Check" spiel when Odette interjected, "I think you're right on the money with that number. And the time frame shouldn't be a problem."

———

I waited until we had concluded our business and were on the other side of the double front doors before I turned to Odette.

"Are you nuts? Five-point-five million with a closing before Labor Day? In this economy?!"

My agent didn't blink. "I've done more amazing deals."

"Name one."

She proceeded to name two. "O ye of little faith," she sighed. "Stand back and let me do what I do best."

I fully intended to. Although Mattimoe Realty bore my name, I wasn't its best representative. Leo, who had started the company while married to his first wife, Avery's mother, was a natural at sales. A real meet-and-greet kind of guy. Everybody loved him. Everybody wanted to buy from him. My specialty, if I had one, was follow-through. I could usually see where we needed to go and how to pave the path so we'd get there. But I was keenly aware that I couldn't do it alone. Hence I prided myself on hiring the right people. At work and at home—which reminded me, happily, that Deely was due back from Amsterdam tonight. If Vestige had a chatelaine, Deely was it.

Climbing into my car, we heard a far-off chorus of barks. I estimated at least a half-dozen dogs, maybe more.

"Do you suppose Vivika employs a kennel master?" I asked Odette. At my house, Deely performed that job, too.

As we drove out, the security gate was open and unattended. "So much for Fort Druin," I said.

Odette speculated that García may have been needed elsewhere.

"Right. For a mine sweep along the southern perimeter," I joked.

"Or a security breach," Odette said. "Maybe that's why we heard the hounds."

Odette had been right about the proximity of Cassina's cottage to Druin. Within minutes of leaving Vivika's vast compound, we were pulling into a narrow dirt driveway that led to a cedar-sided home. I parked between a pair of very tall cottonwoods.

"This would have looked grander if we'd come here first," I said. "Funny how a chateau can diminish almost anything."

Cassina's hideaway was far from shabby. Wedged into the bluff and framed by white pines, it rose like an arrow from the sand. On the side facing the lake, all three stories featured floor-to-ceiling glass opening onto spacious cantilevered balconies. I paused by the side door, next to a waist-high granite sculpture of an unusually voluptuous wood nymph.

"That's got to be the statue MacArthur meant. He said I'd find the key and alarm code under it."

I had already told Odette about Cassina's driver and his real estate aspirations. She had showed zero interest. But then Odette rarely reacted unless a commission was involved. Now she watched me try to lift the sculpture.

"You don't have the right health insurance to do that," she said and reached under the nymph's stone-cut billowing skirt. Her hand came back holding a tiny clear plastic envelope.

"I believe this is what your Scotsman meant."

"He's not *my* Scotsman," I said.

"Not yet. But you're wishing for it."

"Am not!"

I hate it when I blush while trying to deny something. To distract Odette, I snatched the mini-container from her hand and proceeded to do battle with it. If the door proved as hard to open as the envelope, we were in big trouble.

"Here," she said. In one smooth motion, she inverted the envelope and released a tagged key. "Shall I open the door, too?"

I gave Odette the honor; I can be generous that way. Plus, it kept the focus off my face until the redness had a chance to fade.

She expertly inserted the key in the lock, opened the door, and then entered the alarm code.

We were in. But we were not alone.

FIVE

ALTHOUGH NEITHER OF US could see anyone, Odette and I immediately knew what we'd interrupted. We were grown-ups, after all. And we had cars.

Having entered Cassina's cottage through the side door, we found ourselves standing at the foot of a spiral staircase that appeared to wind all the way to the third floor. Floating down from an upper story—probably the top one—were the unmistakable sounds of male-female ecstasy. And I'm not talking about the pleasures of a really good meal.

Since Cassina was supposed to be in Tuscany, I deduced with some relief that those moans couldn't belong to her and Rupert. Overhearing the lovemaking of people you know is far more embarrassing than walking in on complete strangers going at it. My hope was that this was just a simple sordid liaison between two of Cassina's band members, groupies, or servants. Two people I didn't care a fig about who knew Cassina well enough to have access to her retreat.

I hadn't noticed any cars. Then again, there were woods at one end of the property, which would make it possible to conceal a vehicle. Or the party might have arrived by boat. Odette and I had remarked on the Bayline cruiser moored at Cassina's dock; we'd assumed it was one of the singer's toys.

Hearing the sexual soundtrack emanating from upstairs, I automatically turned to leave. Odette, however, was unfazed by our discovery. Not only did she fail to follow me out—to my horror, she kept right on walking toward the kitchen, her notepad and pen at the ready.

Catching up to her in three silent strides, I firmly tapped her shoulder. She dismissed me with a gesture universally considered quite rude. At that point, I appropriated her pen and notepad in order to print my message: LET'S GO.

Odette smiled patronizingly and took back her pen. In a flourish she amended my note to read: LET'S GO MAKE MONEY.

And off she went to the kitchen. Meanwhile the couple upstairs continued to make love—and a whole lot of noise. More noise than I'd ever made with anyone, which left me wondering if I was bad in bed. I dismissed that doubt, for the moment, and tiptoed into the kitchen after Odette. When I caught up with her, she said, "Nobody's going to hear *us*. As long as we're inside, we might as well take some notes." She ran her palm along the countertop. "Soapstone. And note the Asko dishwasher. Top of the line."

I appreciated them, too, but not enough to risk getting shot. Who could predict the mental state of two trespassers in heat?

Odette had moved on to the Electrolux Icon wall oven. Like me, she tended to avoid kitchens, except those she planned to sell. Those she could get quite excited about, as the present moment proved.

"See how the glass-fronted cabinets echo the Big Window theme!" Odette said, writing furiously. "Cassina made fabulous choices."

Not in her personal life, maybe, but Odette was right about the kitchen. It was a designer showcase with the very best appliances. Odette snapped a measuring tape out of her jacket pocket to check the dimensions of the glass-fronted double-door refrigerator. Suddenly we both heard it: absolute silence—followed by footfalls plinking on the metal steps of the spiral staircase.

We bolted for the side door. And opened it smack in the face of the former estate agent from Glasgow.

"What do you think!" MacArthur asked calmly. "Worth more than three-point-three million?"

"I think there's somebody upstairs … on their way downstairs …" I hissed, trying to squeeze past him. No way I wanted to deal with a person who'd just had noisy sex. Unless, of course, that person had just had noisy sex with me.

As Odette suspected, I did find the Scot attractive, especially at this proximity in his present wardrobe. Unlike last night, when he'd worn a charcoal-colored suit, today MacArthur was in khakis and a short-sleeved blue cotton shirt that emphasized both the color of his eyes and the tone of his upper body. Plus, he was standing very close to me, presumably to block my exit.

"They're coming!" I said and instantly regretted my word choice. "Down the steps! You want us to meet naked people?!"

"You've already met this person. And he won't be naked."

"Good to see you again," I heard Odette say to whomever had paused on the staircase.

I recognized the voice that replied. And, fortunately, the speaker was wearing a bathrobe. It was Rupert.

"So Cassina didn't go to Tuscany?" I asked. Presumably, Cassina was upstairs, which was why Rupert was having sex, and Mac-Arthur was standing guard.

Nobody touched my query. It hung in the air like one of Abra's farts. I attempted to fill the void by introducing MacArthur and Odette and reintroducing myself to Rupert. The Scot and the Zimbabwean nodded curtly to each other; Cassina's partner ignored me. His shoulder-length black hair was tangled, and his pale sharp-boned face needed a shave. Even at close range, I failed to detect a single solitary chromosome that he had passed on to Chester.

As Rupert shuffled off to the kitchen, MacArthur called out, "You have ten minutes to get your arse out of here!"

I'd watched enough BBC to know that was not standard servant-to-master talk.

"So Cassina didn't go to Tuscany?" Aimed at MacArthur, I tried the question again.

"She did," he said.

"Then, who's—? *Arrggh*!"

Odette's elbow, which should be registered as a lethal weapon, embedded itself between my ribs.

"If we're going to be on time for our next appointment," she said, "we need to leave now."

"When can we discuss my joining your agency?" MacArthur had not yet moved from the doorway.

"Call me at four," I said.

MacArthur leaned toward my right ear. "Any problems with the wee dog?"

I shook my head. An accurate response since I had delegated the wee dog.

"Since when is Abra small?" Odette said when we stepped outside.

I explained that we weren't talking about Abra. My top sales agent was appalled to learn I'd admitted another canine to my household, even if I'd done it to get this listing. I reminded her that she had made personal sacrifices for business.

"Yes," she said, "but none of my sacrifices required feeding."

Odette didn't want to discuss what we'd interrupted at the cottage. I theorized that Rupert's "squeeze" had to be someone who worked for Cassina. Dozens of exotic young women hung around the Castle. They all had strange-colored hair and Asian-inspired body art.

"How can you not be curious?" I demanded. "You love gossip!"

"I love gossip when it's about interesting people. Or when it helps me make a sale. Rupert is irrelevant."

I didn't care about Rupert, either, beyond the fact that Chester claimed to be his son. As for Cassina, she held my attention like a slow-motion train wreck. Still, I considered it my civic duty to keep current on local gossip. Or try. I tended to fall woefully behind despite regular "news infusions" at the Goh Cup, which is where we were headed next.

Conveniently located right across the street from Mattimoe Realty, the coffee bar was a buzzing hive. If you wanted to know who did what to whom, or who was planning to do what to whom—how, where, when, and why—the fastest way to find out was over a steaming mug. Proprietor and acting mayor Peg Goh brewed the best beans while remaining neutral or at least helpful in most matters. Lucky for Main Street merchants and tourists alike, Peg also made the best *spanakopitas* (spinach pies) this side of the Greek isles. By the time Odette and I got back to town, I was hungry enough to inhale two, along with my usual double-mocha-super-latte.

Odette had planned to join me, but *her* cell phone was working; it delivered a call that changed her plans. We parted after making a pact to celebrate our new super-listings tonight with an appropriately extravagant dinner.

I went straight to the Goh Cup without stopping at my office. Nothing was going to disrupt either my healthy appetite or my good mood. I needed spinach pie, coffee, and gossip. The only problem with eating at the Goh Cup was that some of my least favorite people ate there, too. One of them was sitting right by the front door.

"Well, look who the riptide didn't drag in," announced Rico Anuncio.

Magnet Springs' most flamboyant merchant had a Latin name and Scandinavian good looks, easily explained by the fact that his real name was Richard Anderson. I was under strict orders never to reveal that, however. It was a condition of his not suing me over a frivolous real estate issue from our recent past. Rico ran the West Shore Gallery, a classy joint. But his personal life verged on icky.

Rico's in-your-face sexuality made even our most liberal residents rethink their politics. This being a very small town, I suspected he knew that he was widely referred to as Mr. OGP, short for "Obnoxious Gay Pride." Rico favored large nipple rings that showed through his cropped, scoop-necked silk shirts. Even though he wasn't trying to attract my type, I found it hard to ignore the bulge in his low-riding skintight pants. Clarification: I found him hard to ignore.

"I assume the riptide dragged *you* in," I said. "That's how your clothes shrunk."

Not a classy comeback, but a quick one. I couldn't believe I'd actually said it. A few folks laughed. Although I hoped that was the end of our center-stage moment, Rico had more lines.

"Here's a question, Whiskey: Why do people still let you watch their kids? You keep losing them. And now you don't care if they drown. Lucky for Chester he got reeled in by a fisherman."

I started to defend myself, unwise with someone as glib as Rico. Fortunately, Peg Goh cut me off. Putting a heavy arm around my waist, she steered me determinedly toward the counter, where my lunch was waiting.

"Pay no attention to the man behind the attitude," she advised.

I couldn't decide if that line was a Peg Goh original or something she'd learned from her Seven Suns of Solace counseling with Noonan Starr. I could have asked Noonan herself since she was sitting right next to me. But I didn't feel like hearing more New Age-isms. I just wanted to get my good mood back.

"I hear Jeb's moving to town," Noonan said, her pale eyes wide with enthusiasm. "Have you pondered how his choice might affect your karmic flow?"

I liked Noonan, and she was an excellent tenant. But the only sensible response to that question was a monosyllable.

"No." And I proceeded to chew my spinach pie.

As I listened to the conversations around me, I gleaned that riptides were on everyone's mind. This being a tourist town, a high threat of drowning put a real damper on beach business. Apparently, Chester had been right about riptides churning up debris. Peg was in the process of organizing volunteers to clean the beach.

Rico's confident voice came again. "Maybe the riptide will finally wash up Gil Gruen."

Amid a medley of moans, someone said, "Not while we're eating!"

Rico replied, "The man's still alive. I saw him last week in Chicago."

All chatter stopped. You could have heard a plastic straw drop.

"What are you talking about?" Peg said.

"I saw him leaving a restaurant on Michigan Avenue. Sure looked like Gil—Stetson and boots included."

"Gil's dead," Peg reminded him.

Rico locked eyes with me. "So Whiskey says. Nobody else saw what she saw. Ever wonder about that?"

My face was hot, and not from Peg's steaming coffee. Rico was referring to one of the creepiest moments of my life—when I'd slid into wintry Lake Michigan alongside our blood-covered mayor. Also known as the Cowboy Realtor, Gil Gruen was my major competitor ... before his corpse vanished under the ice. The citizens of Magnet Springs expected his remains to turn up in the spring thaw, but that hadn't happened. Respectfully, Peg insisted on remaining "acting" mayor until the next election. One man had died for his involvement in the attack on Gil Gruen, and another was in jail doing hard time. Although his body was still unaccounted for, nobody believed Gil was alive.

"They say everybody has a double," Peg told Rico. "You must have seen Gil's."

"Maybe," Rico said, still staring at me. He tucked his highlighted hair behind a diamond-studded ear. "Or maybe our former mayor outsmarted us all."

"Why would Gil pretend to be dead?" Peg demanded.

"Maybe he had troubles we don't know about. Maybe he stashed a whole lot of cash. And maybe he had help." Rico winked at me.

A new voice said, "Get real! Near as we can tell, Gil lost more than a liter of blood. He was stabbed. No way he survived!"

We all turned toward the open door. Our feisty police chief Judy "Jenx" Jenkins stood with her hands on her gun belt.

"Why, if it isn't the butchest lezzy with a badge!" exclaimed Rico.

"Talking to the bitchiest sissy with a bulge," Jenx rejoined.

The crowd "oohed" over that.

Rico made a show of appraising Jenx's stocky five-foot-five-inch frame. "Love the steel-toed boots, darling. They're so 'you.'"

"Thanks," Jenx said. "I think of them as a fashion accent that kicks ass."

She focused on me. "Heads-up, Whiskey! Tina Breen's coming this way, and she's hyperventilating."

"She usually is," I sighed.

"Yeah, but she's got her phone. I'm guessing there's a crisis on the line."

I barely had time to shudder before Tina hustled through the door.

"Hold on, please. Her cell phone's not working, but I'm tracking her down!"

Tina leaned against Peg's coffee counter to catch her breath.

"You'd think I'd be in better shape after chasing Winston and Neville around for two years."

She wasn't referring to past prime ministers. Winston and Neville were her tiring toddlers, now in the care of her unemployed husband.

"What's going on?" I asked, lowering my voice in the hope that Tina would, too. Peg's customers were watching us with interest.

"Lots of stuff! I sure wish your cell phone was working. First, you need to talk to Yolanda Brewster." Tina handed me her cell phone. "There's a problem in the house across the street. Yolanda says you need to know about it now."

That wasn't Yolanda's style. She was vigilant but not alarmist and never annoying. I'd just seen her two hours ago. What could have changed?

I turned my back on the dining room and said a cautious hello into the phone.

"Miz Mattimoe, I sure enough hate to bother you, but you want to hear this from me first."

"What is it, Mrs. B?"

"That li'l gal across the street? She got *seven* kids now. I just counted 'em."

"Maybe her kids have friends. Or visitors," I suggested.

"Not from this neighborhood. And Twyla don't got no family, remember? There's something else you should know. She got men in and out of there at all hours of the night."

My heart sank. Yolanda's observations were generally reliable. Which meant I had things to sort out with Twyla Rendel. Unsavory things.

But what distressed me most was the probability that I'd grossly misjudged a rental applicant. I considered myself an excellent judge of character. Although lacking Odette's "telephone telepathy," I could recognize the scent of B.S. Yet not a single mental alarm had gone off when I interviewed Twyla. I'd felt sorry for her and her kids, and admired her pluckiness in the face of adversity. If Yolanda was right, Twyla wasn't who I thought she was.

Then again, Yolanda might be the one who'd got it wrong this time. Despite the neighborhood watcher's report, Twyla might have a perfectly reasonable explanation ... for having seven kids when she'd claimed to have two and for having a twenty-four-hour revolving front door.

I thanked Yolanda for the tip and promised I'd look into the matter after lunch. When I tried to return the phone to Tina, she wouldn't take it.

"There's a lot more than that going on." She checked the palm of her hand, where she'd inked some notes. "What order do you want it in: most recent, most complicated, or most costly?"

"I have a costly problem?" I asked.

"As far as I can tell, you have two." When she saw my stricken face, she added, "But those also count as your complicated problems, so don't panic."

That made me feel so much better. I watched Tina mentally debate how best to break the bad news. Finally she said, "You might as well read it yourself." She held up her palm, and pointed with the index finger of her other hand to two items:

Velcro injured.
Abra gone.

"Are you trying to tell me that Abra attacked Velcro and fled?"

"No!" Tina checked her own palm for the answer. "Abra's gone because—"

When she found what she was looking for, she turned her palm back to me and tapped a third item:

Norman

Neither prospect, client, nor employee, Norman was Abra's true love—a hunky golden retriever and the father of Prince Harry. Abra had run off with Norman at least twice before; hence, Prince Harry. Since Abra was now spayed, I couldn't see why Norman's name spelled catastrophe.

"He's back! He came with his owner—I mean, his human." Tina bit her lip. "I know we're not supposed to think of people as 'owning' their pets. That would be ... oh, what's the word for it? That word Dr. David and Deely always use?"

"*Speciesist*," I supplied. This was not the time to invoke Fleggers doctrine. "Fenton Flagg's in town? Since when is that a bad thing?"

Noonan glanced our way. Of course, the name Fenton Flagg would snag her interest. He was not only the founder of Seven Suns of Solace; he was also her long-estranged husband. Although they'd never bothered to get divorced, Noonan had assured me that the romance was long over. That meant I had a get-out-of-guilt card for feeling mildly attracted to the man. We'd met in the spring while Fenton was doing research for a new book—and Abra and Norman were enjoying their second fling.

"It's not a bad thing," Noonan volunteered from her seat at the counter. "Nothing is intrinsically either good or bad. We live in a world where we make our own values."

"Are we making this good or bad?" I asked Tina.

"Well, it's *good* because Fenton Flagg wants to buy real estate. And it's *bad* because Abra's on the loose. She got away from Chester this morning."

"Maybe she caught a whiff of Norman and went to be with him," Peg suggested as she poured me more coffee.

"If that's true, all we have to do is find Fenton," I said.

"Not quite," Tina said. "Fenton's with Odette. He's the client she went to meet."

"Then this is all good!" I exclaimed, thinking I could use a break from my dog.

"But it could be costly," Tina whined. "Whenever Abra runs away, things go wrong!"

She was right about that. And she was tapping Velcro's name on her palm.

61

"You said he was hurt?" I said. "What happened?"

"When Abra ran off, Velcro got excited. He started jumping around, and then he was yelping in pain, and he wouldn't stop. Your cell phone wasn't working, remember? So Chester called his driver. They took Velcro to the airport so Dr. David could examine him as soon as his plane came in."

SIX

I ASKED PEG TO wrap the remains of my spinach pie to go, and I went.

My plan was to follow, more or less, Tina's triage of messages. Twyla first, Abra (and Norman) second, Velcro third. The little dog was in capable hands, and the big dog was just doing what she always did. But the tenant issue could be critical. Tina had received complaining calls from three other North Side residents. Like Yolanda, they had seen the kids and the late-night traffic. One neighbor suspected that Twyla was selling either drugs or herself. It was a credit to my reputation as a responsible landlord that neighbors complained to me before calling the police. I fixed problems fast.

Arriving at the house on Amity Avenue, I counted six children playing in Twyla's driveway. The oldest looked about four. Twyla was nowhere in sight. I waved to Yolanda sitting on her porch across the street. She nodded.

Before I stepped out of my vehicle, I glimpsed Twyla in the kitchen window wearing the same terrified expression she'd had that morning. When she saw it was me, her face relaxed.

"I come without canine," I announced to Twyla at her back door.

"Pardon?"

"I thought that was why you looked so alarmed to see me. You expected Abra again."

"Oh. Right." She was still on the other side of the screen. When she didn't invite me in, I decided to be blunt.

"Are these your kids?"

Her eyes were already on the mini-daycare class in the driveway.

"No. Well, two are mine. The rest are my sister's. She's real sick. So I'm helping her out."

A baby bawled inside. Twyla glanced over her shoulder. "That one's hers, too."

"Your sister? I thought you didn't have family."

"Well, my parents are dead. And my sister and I ... we aren't close." Color rose in her pale cheeks. "But when family has problems, you gotta help."

I nodded, watching the driveway kids. "But the way I understood it, your family didn't help you."

She swallowed. "Well, I guess they did what they could. You know how it is. I hear you're helping out your stepdaughter and her babies."

She had me there. Except I didn't believe these were her sister's babies. The cute kids before me were of at least three different races and very close in age.

"Level with me, Twyla. You wouldn't be running a daycare here, would you?"

Her hazel eyes widened. "No! That would be illegal."

"So, this is short-term? This baby-sitting arrangement?"

"Yes! Just till my sister gets well."

I wished she'd stop lying to me. It made me feel used. "I've had complaints that there are cars in and out of this driveway late at night. You have noisy visitors."

Her blush deepened and her focus skittered away. "Sorry. Those were my cousins. Bringing the babies over."

"You have cousins? Why can't they take some of your sister's kids? I'm sure they have more room than you do."

"Uh, no, they really don't. They've got kids of their own and ..." Her voice trailed off. Inside the house, the baby's cries intensified. "I gotta go. Sorry." She walked away.

I stared after her, my blood pressure spiking. I didn't know which was upsetting me more—the unsupervised tykes or Twyla's obtuseness. Sure, she needed to attend to the crying baby. But what about the rest of the kids? Why did she have so many? Where did they sleep? And what did she do with them when she worked her shift at Food Duck? Part of me wanted to yank open the door and confront her. Another part of me wanted to get as far away from this mess as I could.

Time to remind her of the terms of her lease—in the form of an official written warning. Stepping around the children to return to my car, I took another head count. No way I was going to risk backing over anybody. Six little heads in a circle. All watching me. I'd been told I had a nice smile, so I offered it now. Nobody in this group responded. I tried harder, pointing to the pink plastic ball they'd been bouncing around.

"Don't chase that out into the street," I said cheerfully. Six tiny children stared blankly at me. "There are cars out there," I continued. "Fast, dangerous cars. You don't want to go near the street. No, you sure don't. Keep the ball here. Right here. Or better yet, put the ball away, and play a different game. Something entirely non-lethal."

No reaction. I sighed, waved, and climbed into my car. I had just started the engine and slid the gearshift lever into reverse when something went *thunk* against my windshield. It wasn't the ball. One of Twyla's little darlings had heaved what appeared to be a rock. It lay on my hood.

My windshield was intact, but my nerves weren't. I shifted into park, turned off the engine, and got out. The "rock" was actually a chunk of concrete, left over from the old driveway that had been broken up before the new one was poured. If it had been heaved with more strength, the projectile would have cracked my windshield.

I held it up for the kids to see, my eyebrows arched in a "What do you know about this?" expression. Too young to run, they simply continued to stare. The oldest one, who I silently fingered as the vandal-wannabe, showed no sign of remorse.

"Hey," I said. "We don't throw things at cars. Especially not my car. Got it?"

They gave no sign that they did. In frustration, I exclaimed, "Hello! Somebody say something! Do you speak English?!"

The alleged rock heaver offered a sly smile.

"Don't do this again," I said, shaking the concrete clod at him. Without thinking, I tossed it into the backyard of the duplex next door, my new soon-to-be "FOR RENT" property. The one I would have a hell of a time finding tenants for if Twyla was the kind of neighbor she now appeared to be.

———

When you don't have a working cell phone, life delivers more in-your-face surprises. You tend to walk right into them.

Exciting news was waiting for me in the lobby of Mattimoe Realty. Fenton Flagg, PhD., was there with Odette, and she was wearing that brilliant smile she saves for Big Money Days. It brings out the dollar signs in her eyes. Fenton had just signed all the forms necessary to make Mattimoe Realty his official buyer's agent. Best news of all, he wanted to buy something really expensive.

"Fenton would like to build a retreat and training center in Lanagan County," Odette announced. "He needs a scenic and somewhat remote location—preferably an existing school or hotel that he could renovate to suit his purpose."

I didn't need telepathy to read Odette's mind. She was already connecting Fenton Flagg and the Seven Suns of Solace with Vivika Major and Druin.

"Or I can buy some land and work with an architect to build from the ground up," Fenton added in his Texas drawl. I liked that drawl, and the rest of the man. Despite being a New Age guru, he seemed like a regular rich guy from the Lone Star State. Fifty-some-years old with thick graying hair and flashing green eyes, Fenton was ruggedly handsome in his denim shirt, jeans, and snakeskin boots. He looked ruggedly healthy, too, which he probably was, in general. But I knew he was an insulin-dependent diabetic. And that brought us to the news that wasn't so good. Fenton was without his canine sidekick, Norman—a certified companion dog whose job was to keep the busy psychotherapist, motivational speaker, and author current on his meds.

"I made a mistake this morning," Fenton confessed. "I drove past your place with my windows rolled down. My boy smelled your girl. And vice versa. Before I could hit the brakes, Norman sailed out the window, and Abra broke away from the kid."

"You mean Chester," I said.

"Right. The dogs took off together into your woods. Chester and I chased 'em till we wised up. No way those hounds are going to let anybody catch 'em till they're good and ready to be caught."

Having been through this before, I was sure he was right. We agreed to keep our eyes peeled as we traversed the county. Those two canine athletes could cover a lot of ground. Abra had been known to make the five-mile trek from my house to downtown in less than half an hour. Or she could choose to wander for days. The only question was "What is she up to?" In this case, we knew. She and Norman just wanted to frolic. When they got hungry enough, they'd trot home.

"Frankly, I can use a break from my dog," I told Fenton. "But yours actually works for a living. Will you be all right without him?"

"I'll miss him, but I need him most when my schedule is hectic. That's when I tend to forget my meds. I was planning to relax here in Magnet Springs for a couple days, so I should be okay without Norman."

He gave me such a dazzling smile I wondered if that was my cue to invite him to dinner.

"Are you staying at Noonan's?" I asked casually.

"No, I've imposed on her hospitality more than I should. She put me up last spring. This trip I decided to get a room at Red Hen's House."

He was referring to the classiest inn in town, a beautifully restored Arts and Crafts-style mansion overlooking the lake. Its proprietor was red-haired Henrietta Roca, partner of our police chief Jenx.

"Odette's going to drive me around to see a few properties," Fenton continued. "After that, I've got no plans at all. Any chance you could join me for dinner? We could compare notes about what we think our canines are up to."

That was as risqué a proposition as I'd had in months. Very tempting. Except that Odette and I had plans for a celebration dinner. I was about to say so, when she caught my eye. Standing off to the side, beyond Fenton's sightline, she was vigorously nodding. No doubt Odette had calculated that a little schmoozing on my part might help our seven-figure deal.

"I'd love to," I told Fenton. "Do you have a restaurant in mind?"

"The locals seem to favor Mother Tucker's," he said. I agreed. We settled on seven o'clock. It made sense for me to meet him there, since he was staying in town.

Odette ushered Fenton out the door. I knew the drill. She would show him the less exciting possibilities first, building up to the grand finale. Whether they would have time to see Druin today, I wasn't sure. Most likely, Odette would give him just a taste of Vivika Major's estate, something to whet his appetite, before scheduling a second visit, which would include the full tour. That would give him time to get excited about the place. To build up expectations and desire. Lots and lots of desire.

My mind was also moving in that direction. Fenton Flagg turned me on. I was easily turned on these days, not having gotten my groove back since Leo died. Oh, I'd had a brief fling with the local jurist—a nice man who made a point of going easy on Abra whenever she broke the law. The judge and I were strictly "friends with benefits." Although he would have preferred more, I didn't feel drawn to him.

But Fenton Flagg … Now there was a sexy man. Tall, too, which mattered to me. And he had to be rich—Texas rich—based on the sales of his popular self-help books and New Age seminars. Therein lay the rub: could a gal who thrived on denial and repression be a match for a man who built an empire on feelings? Oddly, Fenton seemed more like a good old boy with a "Grade A" vocabulary than a spiritual guru. The few times I'd been around him, we'd discussed dogs, diabetes, and real estate. The man drove a pickup truck.

In my office, I kicked off my shoes, closed my eyes, and imagined a world without cell phones. There had been one, once. Now everybody's business depended on keeping continuously in touch. So a day without a cell phone was as close to a vacation day as I was likely to get for a long while. I savored the moment. I gave myself over to it and was just slipping into the sweet bliss of sleep when I became aware of Tina shaking me awake.

"You have a call from a man! He has an accent! He says it's about a listing, a little boy, and a little dog. And he's on line two."

I pushed the appropriate button. "We can talk about the listing and the little boy, but let's leave the little dog out of it. Correction: let's leave all dogs out of it. Including Rupert."

MacArthur said, "He apologizes for any inconvenience he may have caused you today."

"Bullshit! The man couldn't care less."

"True enough. So I apologize. On his behalf."

"Your apology is accepted," I said. "What were you doing there? Besides—I'm going to assume—driving the boat."

"I'm not just the driver, Ms. Mattimoe; I'm also the cleaner."

I'd seen enough mafia movies to know the term. MacArthur's duties had little to do with housekeeping except in a large and ominous sense. Actor Harvey Keitel once played a mysterious amoral man who described his job the same way. His job had involved completing botched assassinations.

"In addition to getting Cassina, Rupert, and Chester where they need to go, I help solve their personal problems," MacArthur said. "I supply the discipline the adults sorely lack. Chester has sufficient self-restraint."

I agreed about the eight-year-old, adding, "Rupert needs a time-out."

"That one's complicated," MacArthur said. "As for Chester, I can give you an update, but not without mentioning the little dog."

"Right. You drove Chester and Velcro to the airport to meet Dr. David!"

"And Deely," MacArthur added. He explained that Dr. David had taken one look at Velcro and asked MacArthur to drive them straight to his veterinary clinic, where the shitzapoo was admitted for treatment. From there, MacArthur drove Deely to Vestige, and Chester and Prince Harry back to the Castle.

"You mean, I have a nanny again? And no dogs?!"

MacArthur vouched for the fact that my house was currently canine-free.

"What happened to Velcro?" It seemed the humane thing to ask.

"Dr. David will give you a full report. I gather that the wee dog strained himself somehow after Abra escaped."

"You're sure Abra didn't do it?"

"Chester swears Abra didn't touch him."

That didn't mean it wasn't her fault. Abra had instantly disliked Velcro as much as I did; I'd seen her snarl at him. Prince Harry was enough of an indignation. Since he'd sprung from her own golden loins, however, she couldn't outright loathe him. But the whiny teacup dog was an outrage.

I was sure Abra had tried to do him in. Nobody knew her deviousness better than I. She was fleet of foot and highly skilled at sleight of paw. The bitch knew how to distract and deflect human attention for her own canine gain.

I considered my own self-interest. "How long could they—I mean, will they—keep Velcro at the clinic?"

"Dr. David will let you know. Could be they'll need to do surgery."

MacArthur shifted the subject to himself and his desire to do real estate with me. He made it sound sexy. I assured him that Mattimoe Realty would be happy to have him as soon as he had his Michigan license. I could say that without hesitation because (a) we needed a man on board, having at present an all-female staff, and (b) he had experience, albeit "across the pond" in Glasgow. Selling real estate was the same basic business wherever you did it. Laws varied, but land was land, and people were more or less the same everywhere.

He was also welcome at Mattimoe Realty because (c) he was easy on the eyes. And ears. I'm a sucker for sexy accents, and I loved that Scottish *brrrrrogue.*

No sooner had I concluded my conversation with MacArthur than Tina buzzed to say that Jenx was calling, as a professional courtesy, en route to investigate complaints at 254 Amity Avenue— Twyla's house. Our police chief knew all my rental properties.

"I've had two calls in the past twenty minutes about little kids playing unsupervised in the street. One caller said she almost ran 'em over."

"Did you hear from Yolanda?" I asked.

"Nope," Jenx said. "I figured she'd call you."

"She did. I checked it out. The kids were in the driveway at that point."

I related my frustrating encounter with a distracted Twyla and her excessive number of kids. Omitting the part about the concrete projectile, I mentioned their disturbing blank stares when I warned them to stay out of the street.

"Maybe they've been taught not to speak to strangers," Jenx said. "FYI, I got an unofficial APB out on Abra and Norman. The sheriff's department's got two pools going: one for when they'll show up, the other for how much damage Abra will do. I'm in on all the action."

My recidivist dog. Also, the bitch had a libido that didn't quit. While I believed that Norman the Golden was her one true love, Abra had been known to hump the nearest hunky hound. "Love the One You're With." If she had a theme song, that was it.

My love life should be so active. God help me, that's what I was thinking when I happened to glimpse the rent application in my inbox, further proof that Odette was very, very good at what she did. Nash Grant had barely walked away from his lease before she'd lined up my ex-husband to sub-let the place. Jeb Halloran had paper-clipped a folded note to his rent application. *Damn.* Just seeing my name in his handwriting still thrilled me, a little. I looked away. I looked back. I looked away again. Then I gave up and unclipped the note.

> *How about catching*
> *the new act at the*
> *Holiday Inn tomorrow night?*
> *Drinks are on the singer.*
> *He misses you.*

The truth was I missed him, too. Jeb and I knew how to have fun together. We also knew how to fight. While we were married, we'd done more of the latter than the former, which is why we weren't married anymore. But he'd been a good bud since Leo died, letting me know I could count on him. The last time we talked, he'd claimed he still enjoyed life on the road—the thrill of singing and selling his tunes wherever he could find an audience. It was un-Jeb-like for him to rent a house and settle down, if only for the duration of Nash Grant's lease. Was the open-ended gig at the Holiday Inn up the highway a coincidence? Or was Jeb growing tired of the gypsy life? Did he want to be part of my life?

I signed my name as landlord on his app, put the form in my outbox, and slipped his note in my purse. Who knew what tomorrow night might bring? Maybe I'd be in the mood for Oldies but Goodies...

SEVEN

In the meantime I had another tenant to think about. I opened Twyla Rendel's file. As good landlords know, a well-written, enforceable lease agreement is the key to successful—i.e., profitable—property management. And peace of mind. Leo had taught me what to stipulate, including how many people can occupy the unit—the exact number of adults and kids. Twyla's lease stipulated a maximum of four occupants, no more than two adults and two children. It also made clear that no one on the premises could violate city codes, including overcrowding. Since Twyla wasn't the first tenant to claim she had "visitors," I had included a provision limiting houseguests, as well. Maximum number: two—one adult and one child. The lease also stated that anyone in violation of the stipulated rules and regulations could be banned from the premises. This savvy landlord had spelled out how to give notice: I need only tape a message to the door.

Of course, errant tenants rarely reform overnight. In the worst cases, eviction becomes necessary. Thus landlords must document the violation(s) in preparation for filing the proper papers in court. I shuddered at the prospect of stepping into that sticky, time-consuming arena. Never mind that I had recently slept with the local judge. Eviction was a messy business. Emotional, too. And I, for one, believed in stuffing as many strong feelings as possible. No way I wanted to evict fragile-looking Twyla Rendel and her kids, however many were actually hers.

I had just typed up an official warning to post on Twyla's door when Jenx called on the line that rings straight through to my desk.

"Nine," Jenx said.

"I beg your pardon?"

"I just got nine kids out of the street in front of Twyla's house, and none of 'em looked older than four. They didn't want to talk to me, either."

"*Nine* kids? Please tell me most of them belong to the neighbors."

"Wish I could," Jenx said. "Nobody around here has ever seen 'em before. Plus, she's got two infants in the house. Family emergency, Twyla says."

"No way her sister could have that many kids under five!"

"Twyla told me she has *three* sisters, and they were all seriously hurt yesterday in a car crash," Jenx said. "They got nobody to take care of their kids, so she's stepping up to the plate."

"Last week she had no family at all!" I exclaimed. "Suddenly she's related to the Brady Bunch? Why did she tell me a different story?"

"Dunno. I explained that the children were not adequately supervised, and the rental unit isn't zoned for high occupancy. Then I gave her a warning, told her she had forty-eight hours to make other arrangements or I'd call Social Services. I also reminded her she was in violation of her lease and could be evicted."

"How'd she react?" I said.

"Contrite—and flustered. She had trouble making eye contact. My take? Something else is going on over there."

"You think she's running a daycare? Or selling something, like her body … or drugs?"

Jenx didn't know.

"What about her job at Food Duck?" I asked. "I verified her employment before I rented to her. But she can't be going to work as a cashier and leaving a dozen kids at her house!"

"Well, she could," Jenx said. "I've seen it happen. Twyla claims she took a leave from Food Duck for the duration of her family crisis. You want to check it out?"

That's how the Magnet Springs Police Department usually conducted investigations: by commissioning volunteer "deputies" like me. Jenx's official staff consisted of one full-time canine officer and one part-time human officer. The canine was better trained, although the human was in grad school. Officer Roscoe, a purebred German shepherd, had been rigorously educated by the Michigan State Police. Officer Swancott, a charming twenty-some-year-old, was earning his master's degree in art history—mostly online from home where he babysat his son while his wife made real money.

I agreed to call Food Duck and find out Twyla's employment status. Jenx said my tenant had been vague about the location of her sister's car accident. The chief was going to run a check on that. She would also talk to Yolanda and at least one other neighbor about what they'd seen on Amity Avenue.

"In the meantime, I'd advise you to do what smart landlords do: give her official notice that she's in violation of her lease."

If I was a smart landlord, I probably wouldn't have rented to Twyla Rendel; I almost never let my heart get in the way of my brain. I'd taken her for a sweet single mom who needed a break, a good kid with two kids trying to play by the rules. Maybe that was her story, but it now seemed unlikely.

Leo wouldn't have let me kick myself for long. He used to say, "The world will smack you upside the head when you need a correction. Your job is to dust yourself off and do better next time."

With that in mind, I called the manager at Food Duck. He said Twyla had failed to show up for her last two shifts and no longer worked there.

Maybe I'd been a fool. Maybe I'd encountered a girl who was damn good at her job, which didn't include operating a cash register. By now I was wondering if Twyla's best talent was play-acting.

By five o'clock, I had pushed around a few papers, reviewed my calendar, and decided I'd have just enough time to post Twyla's notice on my way home to Vestige. I planned to change clothes before dinner with Fenton. My briefcase was full, and my heart was hopeful.

Before I could leave my office, in walked David Newquist, DVM. If I hadn't known him on sight, I would have needed only to read his shirt. Bright yellow, like his Animal Ambulance, it proclaimed more or less the same thing:

MAGNET SPRINGS VET CLINIC
YOUR PET'S A PERSON, TOO

His name was stitched in tasteful cursive on his right sleeve.

"Hewwo, Whiskey," he said. Dr. David was a balding, slightly paunchy man with sparkling turquoise eyes and a noticeable speech impediment. Noticeable to humans, that is. His animal patients paid it no mind at all. They adored him unconditionally, as he did them. Dr. David saved his smiles for his animals—and, presumably, for his girlfriend, Deely Smarr. Around the rest of us humans, the good vet had no sense of humor. Also, very limited social skills.

For example, when I asked—for the sake of politeness only—if he'd enjoyed the Fleggers conference in Amsterdam, Dr. David assumed I actually cared. He went on and on about *anti-speciesist* legislation in the Netherlands and other enlightened nations. I finally had to interrupt and ask if he had a reason for coming to my office.

"Yes! It's about your dog," he said. "Your second dog."

"I'm still having trouble accepting that I have a first dog," I said.

Over the past year, I had mightily resisted the notion that I was legally responsible for Abra. "My dog" was not a phrase that would ever roll trippingly off my tongue. The plural form of the noun was unthinkable. And yet here was Dr. David, making an office call expressly to discuss my second dog.

"What's wrong with him?" I asked.

"Patellar luxation," Dr. David replied. Only it sounded like "patewwahr wucksation."

"What's that?"

"The dog has dislocated knees."

"All four of them?"

"Two," Dr. David said. "Very painful. I feel for the little guy. I got bad knees myself."

"What causes it?"

"I'm afraid it's genetic. Some toy breeds have very weak joints, especially knees and elbows."

"Knees and elbows?" I tried to picture the difference in a dog.

"Layman's terms," Dr. David said.

"Is patellar luxation expensive?"

"Depends on how well he responds to treatment. Surgery is always the last resort."

Last night the tiny dog had seemed a small price to pay for the privilege of selling Cassina's cottage—and insuring myself against a lawsuit in case Chester's mom got nasty about my having almost let him drown. Tonight the shitzapoo looked like less of a bargain. And I wasn't thinking in terms of medical costs alone. Velcro's nerve-grating whine permeated my office. Dr. David had parked him in the hallway, where he was producing unearthly sounds.

"He has amazing lung power," I said, speaking loudly enough to make myself heard. "And he hits such high notes!"

"You don't own fine crystal, do you?" Dr. David asked. "Some of these small dogs have voices that can shatter glass."

Forget glass. Velcro was shattering my peace of mind. "Is he crying because he's in pain?"

"Probably not," the vet replied. "I've treated the pain. I assume he's crying because he's anxious. Another chronic issue in some toy breeds."

"But he's not a purebred," I pointed out. "Aren't mixed breeds supposed to be stronger and more stable?"

"Sometimes. And sometimes they take on the worst of both breeds."

Lucky me. I had taken on a dog who shat a lot, yapped a lot, and had bad joints as well as an anxiety disorder.

Shouting over Velcro's nonstop yips, Dr. David instructed me to keep the dog quiet.

I had only one question: "How? Please?"

He assured me that Deely would know what to do. Ah, yes. Deely! Thankfully the Coast Guard nanny was back on duty at Vestige. I could trust this creature—along with Abra, Avery, and the twins—to her capable care. The woman worked miracles with species I didn't care to contemplate. Including my own.

———

I don't recommend cranking a car radio up to maximum volume, but that was the only way I could drown out Velcro's howl. My ears ached, my sinuses hummed, my jaw throbbed. Music could not soothe the savage beast in my back seat. Or could it?

Although I didn't own a copy of his new Fleggers-produced *Animal Lullabies* CD, I did have several Jeb Halloran albums handy. The first one I grabbed was from his short, doomed stint as a blues singer. CD title: *A Humble White Man from Michigan Sings Songs from the Delta*. That one had gone straight to remainder bins. But I was desperate enough to play it now. Seconds after inserting the disk, Velcro's cries were joined by my ex-husband's cover of John Shines' classic "Cool Driver."

The song didn't suit Jeb at all. But damned if his voice didn't lower Velcro's volume. Dramatically. By the second chorus, the shitzapoo's wail had faded to a whimper. By the song's final bars, Velcro was snoring. And I was silently vowing to buy copies of Jeb's new lullaby CD for every dog owner I knew.

EIGHT

When I pulled into the driveway at 254 Amity Avenue, what I noticed first wasn't Twyla's house. It was the duplex next door. My newly acquired and renovated property, which shared a driveway with Twyla's rental, now boasted a broken window. On the driveway side of the house.

Twyla's car wasn't in the driveway, but it could have been in her closed garage. I left my car running so that Jeb's frankly awful blues would keep soothing Velcro.

The broken window was in the side door. To enter, I had only to reach through the jagged pane and turn the knob. That wasn't the main issue. On the floor inside I found shattered glass—and a chunk of broken concrete. It appeared to be the very one that Twyla's charmless houseguest had hefted at my car. I picked it up and walked around to her front door, where I rang the bell. There was no sign, visual or aural, of any occupants.

As usual, Yolanda was in place on her porch across the street. While I waited for Twyla to respond to the door chime, Yolanda and I exchanged waves. After a minute I realized that she was waving for me to come over. First, I taped copies of the official Notice of Lease Violation to Twyla's front and back doors.

"She in there," Yolanda said. "But somebody come about a half-hour ago. He took a few kids."

"Was it one of the men you've seen before?"

"Those men come at night. I couldn't see 'em too good. This man, he look Hispanic to me."

At least four of the kids I'd seen that afternoon could have been Hispanic. What was the connection? Or was there one? Part of me still wanted to give Twyla the benefit of the doubt.

"Maybe she called one of her brothers-in-law."

Yolanda gave me a look that implied my brain was made of cheese.

"Okay," I conceded. "If the guy you saw isn't the father of some of those kids, then who could he be?"

Yolanda wouldn't play my guessing game. But I kept trying. "Maybe he's Twyla's boyfriend. Or cousin. And he's helping out."

"Or her pimp. That be more likely," Yolanda said. "That girl got troubles, for sure. I saw you taping up the notice. You gonna evict her?"

"Only if I have to," I said.

Then I realized that Yolanda would have witnessed the window-breaking. So I asked what she'd seen. It was just what I'd suspected—and almost certainly the same kid who'd gotten my attention earlier.

"They was playing," Yolanda said. "Biggest kid run over to the yard next door. Pick something up and throw it. You know boys and rocks. He bust that window, and all the kids run." She shook her head, laughing. "Boys will be boys, Miz Mattimoe. My own boys busted a few windows, too, while they was growing up."

Suddenly I felt more responsible than victimized. After all, I had supplied Twyla's kids with the "rock." Excusing myself, I phoned Roy Vickers about the window damage. He promised to nail up a temporary cover tonight and replace the pane tomorrow. I'd once had serious misgivings about Roy; maybe I shouldn't prejudge Twyla, either. Yes, she had violated the terms of her lease. And, yes, her situation looked fishy. But she could be as earnest and innocent as my handyman.

I thanked Yolanda for her help, declined a glass of her famous sweet tea, and re-crossed the street to my car. By now I had little more than an hour to get home, get dressed for dinner, and get back to town to meet Fenton. I held my breath and cautiously opened the driver's side door. Jeb's voice was singing Furry Lewis' hit "I Will Turn Your Money Green." And Velcro's voice was silent. Hallelujah.

I was about to shift into reverse when someone tapped on the passenger-side window. Fortunately, the knock was light enough not to disturb Velcro. Twyla peered in at me.

I eased my way out of the car again. Joining Twyla on her side of the vehicle, I waited for her to speak first. Her eyes were red, and her face was blotchy. She wiped her leaky nose with the back of a chapped hand.

"Mrs. Mattimoe, I…just want to tell you I'm sorry. I'm doing my best to get things back the way they were. Please don't evict us."

She sniffed loudly but still didn't meet my gaze. I looked where she was looking, at her feet. Her toenails had once been painted bright red. Now the enamel was mostly chipped away. She wore cheap pink rubber flip-flops that couldn't have much tread left. Her jean shorts were frayed, and her yellow halter top had baby spit-up on it. Twyla's skinny white legs and arms reminded me of un-cooked chicken. If this girl was a whore, she wasn't selling one bit of glamour.

"Twyla, I'm sorry for your problems, and I hope you can get things under control." Against my better judgment, I added, "I wish you hadn't lied to me. I wish you'd told me straight out what was going on."

Brimming with tears, her eyes met mine. Her thin lips parted as if she was about to speak. Then she must have thought better of it. She turned toward the house. I was getting back in my car when she called out, "I didn't lie, Mrs. Mattimoe! I just couldn't tell you everything."

There were lies of commission and lies of omission. In either case, Twyla's excuse didn't compute; I felt compelled to say so. "First you told me you had no family. Then you said your sister was sick, and you were taking care of her kids. Later you told Police Chief Jenkins that your *three* sisters were in a car accident, and you had to take care of all their kids. That sounds like at least one lie, Twyla. Possibly a whole lot more."

My voice was harsher than intended, and I regretted that. But dammit, I wasn't about to be misled again.

"Good luck getting things straightened out," I said as I opened my car door. What lousy timing. I managed to shout my last comment during the dead air between tracks. In his carrier in the back of my Lexus, Velcro awoke with a start. And a piercing howl.

"What's that?" cried Twyla, jumping in alarm. Her eyes darted about as if she expected a pack of wild dogs to appear.

"Sorry," I said. "It's just a shitzapoo with bad joints. He won't hurt anything—except your ears."

Jeb's ill-chosen arrangement of Big Joe Williams' "Baby, Please Don't Go" was starting. Within seconds, Velcro had dialed down his yowl.

"Wow," Twyla said. "It's like that song turned the dog right off."

"It's the voice, not the song," I said. "Puts dogs straight to sleep. The singer's Jeb Halloran." Then another thought struck me. "Hey, if his voice works on a dog as uptight as this one, it ought to put kids to sleep, too. You should try it. On your own two." I stressed the last word.

Twyla's glance shifted back to her chipped toenails. Without comment, she slunk into the house.

———

My good luck with Velcro lasted all the way to Vestige, where Deely Smarr was on duty. I entered the kitchen with Velcro, and without a Jeb Halloran soundtrack. But the Coast Guard nanny was standing by. She had her official Jeb Halloran *Animal Lullabies* CD cued up in a boom box, her finger poised on the play button. As soon as she saw us, she hit it. To my extreme delight, strains of "Lullaby and Good Night" filled the kitchen. Velcro went right back to sleep.

I heartily welcomed Deely back home and asked how she knew I'd need the CD.

"David told me about the shitzapoo, ma'am. This was the obvious solution." She explained that a consultant had recommended conducting market research before Fleggers signed Jeb to record *Animal Lullabies*. "I'd seen Jeb's music put Abra and Prince Harry to sleep. If it worked on them, I knew we had a mega-hit on our hands."

A snoozing Velcro was the ultimate proof. Before Deely could exit with the boom box and shitzapoo, I whispered, "Is Avery around?"

"No, ma'am. I haven't seen her. She left a note that she was taking the twins with her for the day."

How unlike Avery to be fully responsible for herself *and* her children.

Deely informed me that Chester and Prince Harry had gone back to the Castle. And of course she knew that Abra had run off with Norman.

"We've been through this before," I sighed.

"Technically, this time is different, ma'am. As far as we know, Abra hasn't stolen anything."

"Yet," I said. "Unless you count Norman. Fenton needs that dog."

Deely nodded thoughtfully. "I suppose seduction equals abduction in this case."

In other words, my dog had committed another felony.

"When she comes back, we need to get Abra her own boom box," I said.

"I'll see to it, ma'am."

Upstairs I couldn't find anything exciting to wear. Maybe that was because my wardrobe was almost entirely beige. I buy high-quality clothing; I'm just not into color. The way I see it, clothes are body cover. Plain and simple. So what I need are good fabrics that fit. Since I'm just not a "pastels" or "jewel tones" or "artsy-black" kind o' gal—and unlike 99.9 percent of all females, I hate matching colors—what I need are neutral tones. How wrong can you go wearing mushroom, camel, or ecru? With my dark hair and rosy skin, I look okay in beige. But I will admit to having learned one fashion lesson: adding a black camisole under it all can work wonders for your self-image … as well as your sex life.

For my dinner with Fenton, I was careful not to overdress. I'd never seen the man when he wasn't wearing denim and snakeskin. Since those don't usually come in beige, I defaulted to my wardrobe's casual equivalent: khaki. And I added a plain black silk camisole, for kicks.

One benefit of being in a hurry to leave was a reduced risk of running into Avery. With a small thrill I realized that I might get through an entire day without making contact.

No such luck—although I came close. I had made it all the way to the breezeway that connects my kitchen to my garage when Avery opened the door. She was pushing the double stroller that held Leah and Leo. And, miracle of miracles, she didn't look pissed off. At least her face wasn't twisted into its usual grimace.

"Hey," I said cautiously and bent down to make affectionate noises for the twins.

"Hey yourself," Avery replied, her voice uncharacteristically neutral. Usually she greets me with a complaint. Or an expletive. "What's with the camisole? Got a date?"

"Just business," I mumbled, keeping my head down. I fought an urge to stay hunched over like that so I could scoot right past her. But that would be weird. So I straightened to my full height, which exceeded Avery's by only about an inch, and gave her my best poker face. "See you later."

"Not so fast," Avery said, angling the stroller to block my path. She cocked her head. "Is that Jeb's voice I hear? Why the hell is he singing?"

"Actually, that's the recorded version of Jeb. And he's singing because he was handsomely paid to do so."

"Why the hell is the recorded version of Jeb playing in our house?"

I felt my blood pressure spike the way it always did when Avery presumed shared ownership of Vestige. Her father had left the house to me, free and clear. It was only through my misplaced sense of duty that she had a room here. Make that free room, board, and baby care.

"Consider it my gift to you and the twins," I said brightly. "That's Jeb's new lullaby CD, guaranteed to relax anybody. And I mean *anybody*."

Avery looked startled, as if she had no reply to that one in her vast, nasty repertoire. I seized the moment and side-stepped the stroller, waving good-bye to the twins.

Avery and her brood were Deely's problem now. I had a date.

NINE

On my drive over to Mother Tucker's Bar and Grill, I tried not to think about how long it had been since I'd had a date. But, being in real estate, I tend to do math automatically, so the answer popped right up: nine and a half weeks. Wasn't that also the name of a very bad sexy movie from the mid-1980s? Just a coincidence, I was sure.

Mother Tucker's had a well-earned reputation as a lively, classy place. Local merchants and tourists alike favored its rustic bar and upscale menu. Owned and operated by two of my favorite people, Walter and Jonny St. Mary, Mother Tucker's was one of those rare restaurants that appeared to run itself. In truth, Walter brilliantly managed the front of the house while Jonny made sure that the kitchen promptly produced one gourmet meal after another. A charming gay couple from Chicago, Walter and Jonny, had kept me fed and reasonably sane during the dark months following Leo's sudden death.

Now that it was almost summer—high season on the shore of Lake Michigan—Mother Tucker's was enjoying the return of its warm-weather regulars, those affluent folks who owned or rented beach houses in the area. I waved to a dozen familiar returnees. Several inquired as to how I was faring after a full year of widowhood. I smiled and told them that things were looking up. And how. I was moments away from a date with a handsome multimillionaire.

Fenton was already seated at the bar, sipping a frosty cola. He rose when he saw me, like the true Western gentleman he was. Walter St. Mary had poured a goblet of my favorite Pinot Noir. I hesitated, however, when I saw that Fenton was abstaining.

"Diet soda—on account of my blood sugar," he explained. "With Norman away, I don't want to risk getting myself in trouble. You drink, though, Whiskey. I hear you can handle it."

I wasn't sure what that meant, but I decided to accept it as a friendly, maybe even flirtatious, compliment. Had Fenton heard about one of my rare post-Leo nights of excess? On two or three occasions, I had consumed a little more than I should. For at least one of those blunders, I blamed my scotch-drinking ex-husband; Jeb liked to order the "cool burn" for both of us, but one of us didn't handle it so well.

I asked Fenton if he had any updates on the whereabouts of our wayward canines.

"One," he said. "Jenx kindly called to say that an old woman on Uphill Road reported seeing a furry yellow-gold creature the size of a Shetland pony in her yard. It appeared to be having convulsions."

"Huh?"

"The woman has notoriously bad eyesight. Jenx thinks she saw Abra and Norman. Humping."

I slugged down half my wine. No doubt he'd got the order of their names right. My dog was known to prefer being on top.

"Uphill Road is part of their usual territory," I said. "Shouldn't be too long before they wear themselves out and come home."

Even that remark felt vaguely embarrassing; I took another gulp of my wine.

"In the meantime, Fenton, are you sure you can get by without Norman?"

"I'll be fine, as long as I have good friends in town."

He smiled and leaned closer, giving me a whiff of his head-spinning aftershave, a manly mix of leather and old leaves. My momentary high was probably less the effect of inhaling Fenton's aftershave than imbibing vino on an empty stomach. I had parked my lunchtime spinach pie in the glove compartment of the Lexus so that Velcro wouldn't smell it and have one more reason to cry. As a result, I'd forgotten to eat it.

"Care for another?" Walter St. Mary asked, the bottle of Lynmar Pinot Noir already poised above my glass.

"Why not?" I said, admiring my own cavalier spirit. Life can be good when you're in real estate, sitting next to a fine, fragrant, almost-single man who's also a prospective client. After a few sips from my second glass, I felt emboldened to ask Fenton about his marital status. "What's up with you and Noonan? Separated but still married after—how long?—almost eighteen years? Why didn't you ever get divorced? If you don't mind my asking…" Fenton said they'd "just never got around to it," mainly because neither had a desire to remarry.

"And we like each other," he added. "We have many mutual friends and common interests—including, of course, the Seven Suns of Solace."

"Of course!" I said.

"So we don't mind still being married, in the eyes of the law."

I couldn't imagine still being married to Jeb. Without a break, I mean. As unpleasant as our divorce had been, it had made marrying Leo possible. And that had been very nice, indeed. Then, after Leo died, there was Jeb again. Among other men … including, quite possibly, this one.

"Options," I said, realizing what divorce had done for me.

"Pardon?"

"Divorce gives you options you don't have if you stay married! Does that make sense?" With the wine in me, I wasn't sure.

Fenton said, "Noonan and I have a pact: if either of us ever feels we need the options that divorce would give us, then we will grant the other party their legal freedom. We want only the best for each other."

Not the usual motivation for divorce. But in this case it made sense. Fenton and Noonan were hardly your typical couple. I found that comforting since I genuinely liked her and was beginning to lust after him. In their version of marriage, my feelings would pose no problem at all.

"Are you two ready for dinner?" Walter St. Mary asked. "I've saved Whiskey's favorite table by the window."

When I stood up, the room tilted slightly and then corrected itself. Probably a sign that I needed food. Fast. No breakfast and no lunch does not a wise wine-sipper make. As attractive as Fenton was, I needed to remember that this was essentially a business dinner. I was there to represent Mattimoe Realty, not fawn all over the man because he looked and smelled good.

Ever the faithful friend and excellent restaurant manager, Walter immediately dispatched a waiter bearing bread to our table. The waiter also suggested that I might like coffee.

"Why not?" I said more loudly than necessary. Fenton requested some, too. The waiter returned with decaf for him, espresso for me. I couldn't remember ordering espresso, but that may have been a management decision. Between the caffeine and the carbs, I was sober by salad time.

"Did you go for a drive with Odette?" I asked Fenton.

He said they'd looked at three properties, the last of which was "intriguing." Assuming that Odette had shown him Druin last, I tried to draw Fenton out, to get a reading on his interest level. I quickly realized that he hadn't made his millions by channeling positive energies alone. The man was a player; he kept his cards close to his chest.

"I can afford to look till I find exactly what I want," he said. "The west coast of Michigan feels right for what I have in mind. I listen to the land, Whiskey."

I nodded respectfully. "It's a spiritual thing."

"It's a financial thing," he said. "I'll have to convince my board of directors that our collateralized debt obligations can provide a versatile means of financing commercial real estate development."

A sudden commotion at the bar claimed my attention. Fenton's too. In fact, everyone in the dining room had turned toward Officer Brady Swancott.

"Good evening, everybody. I apologize for interrupting your dinners, but Walter St. Mary has consented to let me make this announcement." The young part-time policeman smoothed back his black hair and cleared his throat. "A couple hours ago, two swimmers were caught in another riptide. Fortunately, they realized what was happening and managed to ride safely in to shore."

Mother Tucker's patrons gasped and murmured. One called out, "Why don't you put up some signs out there before people drown?"

"Chief Jenkins and I are working with the DNR, and with Lanagan County sheriff's deputies, to post riptide warnings along the shore," Brady said. "But there's no way to close the beach. If somebody's determined to swim in the lake, we can't stop them. That's why I'm going from business to business tonight, to make sure everybody understands how dangerous conditions are."

"Is this alarmist approach really necessary?" That question came from one of my fellow Main Street merchants. "You make it sound like the tourists should cancel their vacations and go home."

"I'm not saying that at all," Brady insisted. He focused on the out-of-towners among us. "The Lanagan County coast has a lot to offer besides water sports. The beaches are still open. You can sunbathe, hike, or play volleyball. And here in town we have world-class restaurants—you're eating at one—as well as fine shops and other guest services. If you need suggestions for things to do, I invite you to stop by the Visitors' Center at Main and First. Thank you for your attention. On behalf of the Magnet Springs Police Department, I wish you a safe and entertaining vacation."

I expected Brady to head out the door; instead he walked straight to our table and asked if he could join us.

"Don't you have more merchants to visit?" I said. It wasn't that I disliked Brady; it was that I liked Fenton more. I also liked the notion of doing business with Fenton. Brady's doom-and-gloom announcement, tempered though it had been by a promotional message, wasn't helping my case.

"I have two more stops," Brady conceded, "but I thought you'd want to hear my other news."

"Is it better than the news you just gave us?"

Brady reflected on that. "Well ... it's weirder."

"In what way?" said Fenton.

"It's one of those things that sounds too strange to be true. And yet the reports are coming in."

"What reports?" I said, willing him to speak fast and be gone.

Brady leaned his lanky frame across the table and whispered, "Gil Gruen's back from the dead."

"Oh please!" I exclaimed. "Have you been listening to Rico?"

"I've been listening to the dispatcher. We've had two Gil Gruen sightings tonight."

"That's because Rico started a rumor!" I said. "Today he told everyone at the Goh Cup he saw a Gil look-alike in Chicago. Now he's got people spooked."

When Fenton asked who Gil Gruen was, I let Brady explain. To my dismay, Fenton responded that he'd once had a similar experience.

"My senior year of high school, the music teacher died in a fiery car crash. Her body was completely incinerated. Months later, students reported seeing her in the auditorium, spying on rehearsals of the spring musical."

"Why would she do that?" I said.

"Don't you mean how could she do that?" Brady asked.

"I know she couldn't do that! What I'm saying is why would anyone think she'd want to? Oh, wait." I looked at Fenton. "You're talking about high school kids, right? Case closed."

Fenton gave me a slow, thoughtful smile. "Are you saying you don't believe in anything you can't explain?"

"I don't believe in *ghosts*, if that's what you're talking about. Gil Gruen is dead! I saw his bloody body. There's no way he's back."

Fenton asked Brady where Gil had been sighted. Brady said one caller had seen him near his now-closed real estate office. The other had spotted him walking along the street where he used to live.

"It's like the high school kids seeing the dead music teacher back in the school auditorium," I said. "Sure, people think they saw Gil where they used to see him. It wouldn't make sense to see him anywhere else!"

"Rico saw him in Chicago," Brady reminded me.

"Rico made the whole thing up! He's the troublemaker here, not the ghost of Gil Gruen."

"You're the only one calling him a ghost," Brady said. "The general consensus is that he's probably still alive."

I turned to Fenton. "Did you see your dead music teacher in the school auditorium?"

Fenton gave me that smile again. If the topic of conversation had been less annoying, I would have considered his grin sexy.

"I never saw her myself," he said. "But years later, she was discovered to be alive and well, and living in Dallas. Her visiting spinster cousin had died in the car crash that night. Our teacher found it convenient to be presumed dead. It was her ticket out. A free pass to a brand new life."

TEN

"Nice story," I told Fenton in response to his account of the high school music teacher who was falsely presumed dead. "Sounds like a movie of the week. Gil's really gone, though. End of story.

"Jenx is checking out the sightings," Officer Brady Swancott said. To my chagrin, he signaled our waiter to bring him coffee.

"I thought you had two more Riptide Alerts to deliver tonight." Translation: Please leave.

Brady seemed blissfully oblivious to the fact that he was no longer welcome. If he went on much longer about either riptides or our mysteriously reappearing mayor, he would completely derail my evening with Fenton. Until the young officer had arrived with his dark news, I was on the cusp of wooing Fenton—as a client and possibly more.

"Yeah, two more stops to make, and my energy's flagging," Brady yawned. "I'd better order a couple of Jonny's Choco-Gonzo cookies."

"To go," I said.

Finally, one of my subtle hints caught his attention. For the first time since settling at our table, Brady seemed to sense that he'd interrupted something.

"Right," he said, standing. "Got to keep moving. Lots of laws to enforce out there..."

"Magnet Springs isn't as dangerous as it seems," I told Fenton after Brady left.

"I don't think it's any more dangerous than anywhere else I've been," Fenton said. "Where there are people and forces of nature, things happen."

Undoubtedly true. Still, I wanted Fenton to understand that riptides were rare. And reappearing dead mayors were completely unprecedented.

He insisted on picking up the check for our dinner—my curried chicken and his lobster tails, plus strawberry shortcake for me and a sugar-free lemon-crème tart for him. Then Fenton walked me to my car. Under a starry early-summer sky, he did the most charming thing: he asked if he could kiss me good night. It was all I could do not to swoon.

I wasn't as moonstruck by Fenton as I had been by, say, Nash Grant... or a couple other handsome clients who'd come along since Leo's death. By now I had recovered from the initial shock of widowhood. I felt less vulnerable and lonely. Losing Leo had briefly unhinged me, making me doubt my ability to carry on, let alone hook up with another human being. Gradually I'd noticed that new people continued to enter my life. And about half of those people were men. Some were even eligible—or semi-eligible, like Fenton Flagg.

Back to the good-night kiss: it was almost chaste. But that was all right. That was proof, in my mind, that Fenton was a gentleman as well as a guru. The notion of dating a client who was married to another client who also happened to be a friend didn't daunt me. Much. Nothing in Noonan and Fenton's world quite fit the usual rules of morality. Ergo, I didn't foresee a big problem. Either Fenton and I would see each other again, or we wouldn't. I knew that Noonan had had relationships with other men. Moreover, she'd assured me that she and Fenton were no longer "in love." As for Fenton, he was far too successful and charming to ever be lonely for long.

To be frank, I was more concerned about the potential mess of adding sexual sparks to a business deal than of dating a man who was still technically married ... to a friend. Hell, Noonan was cool. Too cool, most of the time, for my brain to compute. I didn't anticipate trouble on that front.

Trouble on the homefront, however, was something I anticipated day and night. Even with Deely in place, I still had to face the reality of living in the same house as Avery. Fortunately, Fenton's sweet good-night kiss, plus Mattimoe Realty's lucrative new listings, put me in a deliciously upbeat mood. Without Velcro in the car, I was able to drive home playing CDs I wanted to hear.

My relaxation was short-lived. Upon entering my kitchen, I found Avery waiting for me. She had positioned herself at my Vermont farmhouse table squarely facing the door. And she had brewed herself a pot of very strong coffee, nearly half of which she'd already consumed. Avery on caffeine, especially at night, was as combustible as gun powder.

I had to make a split-second decision: try to talk her down or make a break for my bedroom. Summoning Deely was not an option since she was off duty—and off site—till six AM.

My mental calculations went like this: With an after-dinner brandy and a full meal in my stomach, following a long hard day doing real estate, my reflexes weren't at their sharpest. I wasn't fast enough to compete with cranked-up Avery. Or to escape her. Ergo, my best approach was deflection.

"Gee, that coffee smells delicious. If it weren't bedtime, I'd be tempted to have some," I yawned, edging toward the hallway that led to the rest of the house and my freedom. "But it's late, so good night!"

"What the hell is this about?" Avery said, whereupon she flung something at me. Something white. I flinched as it struck my face.

Happily for me, the projectile was made of cloth. Unhappily, I realized it was the guest towel Odette had given me to give to Avery. Only I hadn't given it to Avery. So how had she gotten it to throw back at me?

"'*Do not mistake endurance for hospitality*'?" Avery roared. "These are my father's grandchildren! The heirs he never knew he had! How dare you!"

My strategy shifted from deflection to ignorance. I genuinely didn't know how Avery had found the towel. I couldn't even remember bringing it home.

And then, cringing, I did remember. Before leaving the office with Velcro, I'd stuffed most of the folders and loose papers on my desk into my already overfilled briefcase. Odette's package had been among the clutter. Later, when I removed my belongings from the car, my briefcase contents spilled on the garage floor.

I scooped up what I could and laid it on top of Velcro's carrier, which I handed off to Deely. No doubt the nanny found Odette's gift—including her note which said, "Hang in Avery's bathroom. Immediately!" Being the obedient helper she was, Deely must have followed directions. Fortunately for me, she had left them pinned to the towel.

"Check out the note," I told Avery. "Is that my handwriting?"

Very carefully, so as not to strike *her* in the face, I tossed the towel back.

Avery studied the note. "It's the kind of thing you'd write, all right."

"Except I didn't. You know my handwriting. And that's not it."

She flicked her tongue. "So? You got somebody to write it for you. Big deal."

I calmly removed the wall phone receiver from its cradle and handed it to Avery. "Odette gave me the note and the towel. You can call and ask her."

More tongue flicking. "You put her up to it! But she'll back up your story cuz she has to. You're her boss."

That made me laugh. "Odette may work at Mattimoe Realty, but she doesn't take orders from me. She's there for the money. If you don't believe it, ask her!"

Avery stared at the phone, which she gripped so tightly that her hand quivered. Then her lips quivered. Then she burst into tears.

"Why do you hate us? We're part of my dad, and you used to love him!"

There was no winning or even coping with Avery. I didn't let myself look at her as she sobbed and moaned. The girl was more melodramatic than Fox News.

Quietly I said, "You know I don't hate you and the twins. I won't be baited into an argument, either. What's the point? Let's talk another time, preferably when I'm less tired and you have less caffeine in your bloodstream."

With that I scooped the towel from the table, pushed the foot pedal on the trash can, and deposited Odette's offending gift. I had almost reached the staircase when Avery called out, "I can take care of myself and my kids, ya know! I don't need your help!"

I stopped but did not turn around. There would be more. I would wait for it.

"Guess where I went today, Whiskey? Come on, take a wild guess!"

I glanced over my shoulder. She was wiping her snotty nose on the back of her hand. Too bad I'd discarded the guest towel.

"I'm clueless, Avery."

Her bloodshot eyes brightened. "Yes, you are clueless! I won't tell you, and you can't guess! Men love me—they do!—and that's why I won't need your help. Before you know it, I'm going to leave here with the twins and never look back."

"Is that a promise?" I shouldn't have, but it was just too tempting.

"Absolutely! I'm way more woman than you'll ever be! That's why I won't end up alone. Like you!"

Here we go again, I thought. That was her refrain when Nash Grant invited her and the twins to stay with him … before he discovered that the twins weren't his. For about a month, Avery had flaunted the fact that she was having sex, and I wasn't. Specifically, that she was having sex with someone she knew I found attractive.

"You've got another lover?" I said without inflection.

"Yes I do!"

"Well, that didn't take long."

"No it didn't!" She glared at me triumphantly.

"Nash barely threw you out, and you've already landed in some other guy's bed! Wow. Congratulations." I started up the stairs.

"Congratulations for sure!" she shouted after me. "He's not only hot, he's rich!"

"How nice for you, Avery. Good night!"

Safely locked in my bedroom, I changed into a cotton nightshirt and then washed my face and brushed my teeth. I should have felt pleased at the way I'd handled Avery. Mostly, I'd stayed cool. I checked my reflection; the veins in my forehead weren't even pulsing. But I couldn't stop thinking about her announcement. Odds were she'd made up the new boyfriend just to mess with my head. Then again, she might really have one. Her twins were proof that even a big klutzy girl with a sour attitude and a nasty mouth could get laid. If the boyfriend was real, who was he? Between full-time residents, part-time residents, and tourists, there were a few thousand men around Magnet Springs, most of them fairly affluent. Even if Avery had exaggerated when she said he was rich, chances are he was at least solvent. If he was real…

Why did I care? Why was I even thinking about Avery's sex life when mine appeared to be heating up? Even if Fenton didn't make another move, Jeb was back on the scene. And if I decided not to rekindle those flames, I might want to get to know MacArthur. Granted, a carnal relationship would be inadvisable if he worked for me. But if Cassina and Rupert's cleaner wanted to rekindle his real estate career, I could surely enjoy the scenery.

———

I knew Deely was back on duty the next morning because strains of Jeb singing "Day is Done" greeted me as I stumbled down the stairs for my morning coffee. Although listening to lullabies ran counter to my efforts to jump-start my day, the alternative—whining, howling, whimpering—was unbearable. So far the Fleggers CD was working. My home was blissfully free of doggie sounds. I peered into Velcro's carrier, where the teacup pup was unconscious.

"Is he alive?" I asked Deely.

"He's doing fine, ma'am. I've already had him out for gentle stretching exercises, as prescribed by Dr. David. And now he's settled back down for his morning nap."

I yawned. Jeb's rendition of "Twinkle, Twinkle, Little Star" was making me sleepy. I was tempted to turn around and go straight back to bed. But I had real estate to manage and sell, plus a social if not legal obligation to find my missing canine. As Jenx had pointed out last night, Abra wreaked havoc when she was on the loose. At the very least, her current sexual exploits were depriving Fenton of his medical companion dog. Last spring, when Norman fled with Abra, Fenton fell into a diabetic coma. No way I could let that happen again. Maybe I could make up for the current inconvenience by offering to stand in for Norman. Surely, I could remind Fenton when to take his medication. I mentioned my brainstorm to Deely.

"Admirable, ma'am, but inadvisable."

I asked why.

"Because you can't keep track of the details in your own life. That's why you hire Tina Breen and me. And Chester."

She was right, of course, but I secretly believed I would have no problem keeping track of someone else's details. Especially if I was hot for that person.

I was surprised to find Tina Breen in her office before eight, and I told her so. "You don't usually come in till nine. Do you?"

"Sometimes I don't come in till noon. I work flex-time, re-member?"

Deely was right; I didn't pay attention to the details I delegated. But I delegated well, dammit. At my desk, I buried myself in the never-ending stream of paperwork that is part of being a real estate broker and landlord. Before long, Tina buzzed me.

"There's a Felicia Gould here to see you."

It took a few seconds for my brain to register the name—probably because I'd wrongly assumed that a chatelaine's duties were limited to the chateau. What had brought her my way? And so early, without an appointment?

I welcomed Felicia to my office, which she quickly and dismissively perused. My furniture was apparently unfit for human use—or at least use by the kinds of humans accustomed to a historically intact chateau; when I offered her my leather guest chair, she glanced about for an alternative. Not finding one, she sat in the original—but not happily. She also declined coffee, which was unfortunate. I could fault Tina for the way she did or, more often, didn't do lots of office management tasks, but there was no question that she made excellent French roast coffee. And Felicia looked as if she might benefit—and in turn I might, too—by the mood lift afforded by Tina's brew.

"What can I do for you, Felicia?" I began, relying on my smile to relax the woman. It didn't work.

"I'm afraid, Ms. Mattimoe, that I'm here to lodge a complaint."

"Really? Please call me Whiskey."

She didn't. "It concerns showing the property."

I asked her to tell me what was on her mind. Felicia Gould explained that Odette had brought someone around late the previous afternoon for a brief look at "the grounds"—the lawns, the gardens, the bluff, the beach.

I said, "It was my understanding that she phoned you ahead of time, never entered any buildings, and was on the property for a total of twenty minutes or less."

"That is correct," Felicia replied. "And completely unacceptable."

"I can assure you that the client is eminently qualified and extremely interested—"

"That's not the issue," Felicia said, shaking her head for emphasis.

"Then please tell me what is." I willed myself to be very, very good when in fact I was becoming extremely annoyed.

"Ms. Major has gone to great lengths to ensure the security of her person and her business at Druin. No doubt you noticed the gatehouse."

I nodded.

"That is the obvious security," Felicia said, "the tip of the iceberg, so to speak. It may surprise you to learn that Ms. Major has at least three security officers on duty at all times."

So the woman was paranoid. So what? Wearing a neutral expression, I waited for Felicia to continue.

"Therefore, you must understand, Ms. Mattimoe, that short-notice visits are beyond the pale."

Clearly she was not ready for a first-name relationship. Or to facilitate the rapid sale her boss had commissioned us to accomplish.

Next step: a little Deely-inspired damage control. "I apologize, Ms. Gould, for any conflict caused by our attempt to execute Ms. Major's instructions. From now on, I'm sure Odette will work closely with the security staff to prevent such complications."

I sorely wanted to point out, but didn't, that Mr. García had abandoned his post by the time we left Druin yesterday. So much for Ms. Major's stellar security force.

ELEVEN

"I REALIZE I COULD have telephoned, but I like to conduct important business face to face," Felicia Gould said, rising.

"I'm glad to know the chatelaine occasionally gets to leave the chateau."

My attempt at a light-hearted conclusion failed. Felicia slid her shoulder briefcase back into place and extended a chilly hand. When I offered to show her out, she replied that she remembered the way. Of course she did. It was a short walk, a mere fraction of the distance she no doubt covered every day at Druin. This morning Felicia had chosen sturdy flat black shoes as perfectly silent as the navy pair she'd worn yesterday. Apparently stealth footwear was *de rigueur* for chatelaines.

Tina buzzed immediately to inform me that a Mr. MacArthur had stopped by while Ms. Gould was in my office.

"He had an accent!" Tina said. "The same accent I heard on the phone yesterday. He sounds like Sean Connery!"

"That would be because he's the same man who called yesterday, and, like Sean Connery, he's from Scotland," I said.

Although MacArthur had told Tina he could wait to see me, he stayed only a few minutes.

"Yolanda Brewster called. Again," Tina whined. "I was talking to her when Mr. MacArthur got up and left. She said she saw Twyla this morning, and something's not right over there. Twyla was loading trash bags into the back of her Ford Taurus—so many she couldn't even close the trunk! And get this: Mrs. Brewster said there was no sign of kids. Not a single one! She said she hoped Twyla hadn't damaged the property..."

Groaning, I leaned back in my desk chair, which tilts far enough for me to count my ceiling tiles, a calming distraction when the going gets rough. "Did Twyla leave? Or was she still there when Mrs. Brewster phoned?"

"Mrs. Brewster said Twyla went back in the house."

I told Tina to call Roy and have him meet me at the property ASAP. So much for getting to the office early. It wasn't yet nine, and I'd already received two complaints and missed the sexiest visitor I was likely to have all day.

———

En route to Twyla's house, I spotted an oncoming green Ford Taurus that looked like my tenant's car. One block ahead of me it made a screeching turn down the road toward the shore. I was briefly tempted to follow; if in fact it was Twyla, I wondered where the hell she was going with a trunk full of trash bags. However, I had told Roy I would meet him at the property *pronto*. I wasn't near enough to identify the Taurus's driver, or to tell whether the trunk was latched.

As I expected, Roy was already on site, his pickup truck parked in the double driveway between my two properties. Twyla's car was gone.

"You just missed her." Looking grim, Roy held open the back door. "She was all worked up. Insisted I come in and take a look around so I could see for myself that all the kids were gone."

"Where did she go?"

"I don't know. She said she had an appointment. She insisted I come in and see that she did what you asked and 'got rid of the kids.'"

A sick feeling twisted my stomach. "Did you go in?"

Roy nodded. "Looks fine to me. Her stuff's all over the place, but there's no sign children ever lived here."

When I told him that Yolanda had seen Twyla loading trash bags in her car, Roy said he'd noticed that her trunk was lashed with a bungee cord.

"Probably stuff for the kids," he concluded. "I suppose she's taking it to them, wherever they are."

I wanted to agree but felt compelled to utter the worst thought on my mind: "You don't think she … did anything to them, do you? The kids, I mean?"

Roy stared at the empty house. "One thing I learned during my nine years inside was how to read a person. Twyla Rendel's not capable of hurting kids."

"But is she capable of telling a whopping lie?"

Roy said simply, "We all are."

My peripheral vision picked up Yolanda waving broadly from her porch. I'd been so single-minded when I arrived that I hadn't noticed her. Roy joined me as I jogged across the street to hear her latest report.

"I missed your coming and her going," she confessed, referring to Roy and Twyla. "Even I have to go to the bathroom once in a while. I thought the action was over after that other guy left."

"What other guy?" I asked.

Yolanda described a tall, dark-haired white man in his early to mid-thirties who drove a black sedan. She didn't remember having seen either the man or the car before.

"He say something to Twyla got her all upset. I couldn't hear him, but she was plenty loud, yelling how it wasn't fair to send goons to threaten her. I know you don't hire goons, Miz Mattimoe! You don't have to, with that crazy dog o' yours."

I turned to Roy. "Why would Twyla think I sent the guy?"

"Maybe this has something to do with Tina Breen," offered Roy. "She was agitated when she called me this morning."

"Tina's always agitated," I reminded him.

"This morning she said she'd had a guy in the office who reminded her of James Bond."

"Sean Connery," I revised. "MacArthur reminds her of—"

Roy and I stared at each other.

"You go first," I said.

"I have two questions," he said. "One: does Tina use speakerphone? And two: is there any chance that this MacArthur fellow fits Mrs. Brewster's description?"

I knew the answers. One: Tina liked to use speakerphone even though I urged her not to. I considered it poor form to broadcast the other half of phone conversations except during conference calls. Two: tall, dark-haired, white, thirty-something, and driving a black sedan…like Cassina's Maserati, maybe? The description fit MacArthur, except that Yolanda hadn't said he was handsome.

I turned to my tenant. "Would you say the man you saw talking to Twyla was good-looking?"

Yolanda cocked her head thoughtfully. "He wasn't bad. For a white man."

"Excuse me." Flipping open my cell phone, I enjoyed a rush of personal pride; I had remembered not only to charge it last night but also to slip it into my briefcase this morning.

My speed-dialed call to Tina was brief but emotional, on her side. Yes, she had been using her speakerphone, and she was very, very sorry. Was I mad? No. Had she screwed up big time? I didn't think so.

"I know an office manager is supposed to be discreet, but it's so much easier to talk on the phone when I don't have to use my hands!" she said.

I reminded her that a headphone provided the same benefit, plus privacy.

"I know, I know," Tina sniffled, "but I like the comfort of another voice filling the room. It's like being home again, with the twins."

I hung up before I said something I might regret.

Roy was still studying me. "I have a third question. Maybe you can answer it. Is there any reason MacArthur would take it upon himself to set Twyla Rendel straight?"

You mean because he's the cleaner? And he wants to impress me so that he can get back in the real estate game? I didn't announce

116

those thoughts, but they were front and center in my head. And they started me speculating in disturbing new directions. For example, did MacArthur already know Twyla? Could she have been the woman with Rupert yesterday? I wouldn't have imagined that a man who traveled in Rupert's orbit would meet a woman like Twyla, let alone ... *ahem* ... desire her. Wait. Twyla couldn't have been with Rupert yesterday; she was tending all those kids. Was there another way the cleaner might know my tenant? Say, from her very brief stint at Food Duck? Or from her past life in Flint? Neither seemed likely.

Stumped, I thanked Yolanda and told Roy it was time to move on. Roy planned to spend the day tidying up the new duplex next door to Twyla's, so he was where he needed to be. He promised to phone me if he saw Twyla, the kids, a certain dog, or anything else worth mentioning.

Although Twyla no longer appeared to be in violation of her lease, I felt deeply curious, a little worried, and, truth be told, *guilty*. Where were all the kids, including her own two? How had she managed to make them disappear so fast? Yolanda had to sleep occasionally, as well as use the bathroom, so I couldn't rely entirely on her observations, as accurate as they tended to be.

What was in the trash bags Twyla had hauled from the house? And where had she taken them? The wildly imaginative part of my brain played with the notion that she might have smuggled the children, disguised as trash, to another location. If so, where—and why?

Mercenary though it might seem, I had another concern, too. As her landlord, I couldn't help but wonder how Twyla intended to pay the rent now that she'd lost her job at Food Duck.

Despite Roy's assurance and my own intuition that Twyla wasn't the type to inflict bodily harm, things didn't add up. Twyla had seemed way better suited to watching other people's kids than I was, yet the ones in her charge had vaporized. Granted, the ones entrusted to me sometimes vanished, but at least they left a trail.

———

On my way back to the office, I left urgent voice mail messages for two real estate professionals. The first was for Odette, informing her that an issue had come up regarding Druin, and we needed to review the way we were showing that property. The second message was for MacArthur; that one was harder to word. I didn't want to drag him into matters best kept confidential unless I was reasonably sure he was the man Yolanda had seen talking with Twyla. Leo had taught me to be very cautious about making assumptions. Even if MacArthur had gone to Twyla's house and said something that upset her, I had no way of knowing what was up. And I'd seen enough mafia movies to know I didn't want to anger the cleaner.

One hazard of a career in resort real estate is getting buried in business hassles and losing sight of that most basic truth: location, location, location! I was blessed to live and work in a simply gorgeous locale, a place where many people chose to vacation, and others—like Twyla—dreamed of starting a better life. As I drove the few miles back to Mattimoe Realty, I pondered the charms of my hometown, with its picturesque location on the shore of what is arguably the Greatest Great Lake. Although the North Side neighborhood where Yolanda lived was "in transition," most of Magnet Springs measured up to its travelogue reputation. A quaint harbor village with nineteenth-century architecture and pristine beaches, it was a more or less authentic version of the simpler, sweeter world Walt Disney had spent billions trying to simulate in his Magic Kingdom. Sure, the people who lived and visited Magnet Springs were capable of behavior as petty and appalling as the rest of the human race. But whatever our sins of omission or commission, we made them against a backdrop of scenic tranquility.

That being said, I had barely set foot inside Mattimoe Realty before our new part-time receptionist informed me—without so much as a bracing "Hey, Whiskey"—that Odette was in my office, and there seemed to be "something wrong with her." Considering the receptionist's age (no more than eighteen), race (even whiter than I am), and length of time on the job (less than two weeks), I doubted she'd be able to tell when something was wrong with Odette. My superstar sales agent had a mysterious habit of occasionally retreating into what I assumed was a traditional Zimbabwean meditative state. Although it never lasted long, it could be alarming to the uninitiated since it affected Odette like this: she narrowed her eyes, pursed her luscious lips, and refused to respond in any way whatsoever. The only sound she made during these episodes was a vibrating "mmmmmmm" on every third or fourth exhalation.

I was both relieved and, admittedly, a little annoyed to find her in exactly that mode in my office. In my desk chair, to be precise; that was the annoying part.

"Do you realize you just freaked out our new receptionist?" I said.

"Mmmmmmm," Odette replied.

As far as I could tell, her nearly closed eyes were fixed on a point in the middle of the room. I tried to line up my body with her stare, thinking it might help the communication process.

"Hello!" I exclaimed, bending down to match her eye level.

"Mmmmmmmm."

"Is that a hello or just another exhalation?"

When she didn't respond, I decided it was a breathing thing. Waving my arms got no result, either. If only I could remember a convenient Tonga language phrase. Trouble was I'd never learned any. Or had I? Something I'd often heard Odette mutter popped into my brain.

"*Mubike ... tasiki ... bana,*" I offered. The syllables came out haltingly, but I was pretty sure I'd got them right.

"And yet you do not," Odette sighed.

"Huh?"

Emerging rather quickly, I thought, from the trance that had rattled our receptionist, Odette said, "Do you have any idea what you just said?"

"Nope. But it seems to have done the trick. Now do you mind getting your butt out of my chair?"

"Keep away from children," Odette intoned.

"Excuse me?"

"That's what you said to me in Tonga."

"It is?" I gaped at her. "I was trying to shock you awake using a phrase from your native language. Guess I got it wrong."

She shook her glossy head. "You got it right. That's exactly what I say every time you take care of someone else's kid. It always turns out badly, and it always distracts you from running your business."

Keep away from children? That was too close for comfort, given the events of the past twelve hours and my prickly twinges of remorse. In my zeal to be an efficient landlord, was I to blame for whatever had happened to the kids left in Twyla's care?

I forced myself to focus on Odette. "Why the 'mmmmmmm'? What's up?"

"I just drove past Best West Realty," she said, "and I saw someone I shouldn't have seen."

"Who?"

"The owner."

"Of what?"

"Best West." She spat the two syllables at me.

Our eyes locked. Gil Gruen's office was closed, and had been since shortly after his death. His very certain death.

"Damn that Rico!" I said. "Ever since he made his announcement at the Goh Cup yesterday, everybody's on the lookout for the ghost of Gil!"

Odette gave me her signature shrug, an indignant rise and fall of her narrow shoulders. "I don't know what you're talking about. Gil was the last thing I expected to see this morning. I took my usual shortcut back from the bank. When I turned down the alley, there he was—peering into his office window. I nearly lost control of my car!"

"You're saying you didn't know about Rico seeing Gil in Chicago?"

"Not a clue! Last night Reginald and I went to bed early. I've heard no local gossip."

Until that moment, I'd been able to explain away every rumor of our dead mayor's return. Now my head hurt.

"But if you were driving down the alley, and he was peering in his own window, you couldn't have seen his face," I said. "So how can you know it was Gil?"

"I know that body, Whiskey. And the back of that head. Who else around here dresses like a cowboy?" The memory made her shudder. "I am positive I saw Gil Gruen."

"That's impossible!" I said, slamming my desk so hard that day-old coffee sloshed out of my mug. "Even if he was alive, which I'm sure he's not, why the hell would he poke around town in broad daylight?"

Odette reminded me that she had seen him in the alley, where there was virtually never any traffic.

"*You* were there! *You* saw him! I mean, you saw someone! There's no way you saw Gil!"

I continued to rant, pointing out that the former mayor wouldn't need to peek into his office; he could surely come up with a key.

Odette disagreed, reminding me that Gil's attorney had ordered the locks changed when he'd estimated how many disgruntled former Best West employees—and their key copies—were still around town. Until decisions could be made about Gil's estate, including the disposition of the building that housed his now closed realty, the attorney wanted to keep the office contents intact. If he could have gotten away with it, the lawyer would have nailed plywood over the windows and doors. But the Main Street Merchants Association vetoed that notion. Boarded-up downtown buildings had a negative effect on the tourist trade.

My desk phone buzzed, interrupting our argument about Gil. The caller had dialed the direct line that bypassed both Tina and the new receptionist. Frankly glad for the distraction, I grabbed the receiver on the second ring.

"Whiskey, it's Jenx. You're at your desk, right?"

"Right. Why?"

"I want to make sure you're sitting down. You're not going to like a single thing about this call."

I steeled myself for what was coming next.

"Brady apprehended Abra at the beach by Thornton Pointe." Jenx's voice was flat.

"That's good news, right?" I said.

"Yeah, most people would think that part's good, but most people don't have as much trouble with their dog as you do."

When Jenx paused, I wondered if the second part was that Abra—or Norman—was hurt.

"No sign of Norman," she said, "but Abra's fine. She had a kid's tennis shoe in her mouth. Brady thought she wanted him to follow her. So he did. You're sitting down, right?"

"I said I was," I snapped.

"Abra led Brady to a god-awful mess. A quarter-mile-long spew of black plastic trash bags. Debris everywhere."

"From the riptide?" I pictured the beach location Jenx meant, less than two miles north of downtown.

"Maybe," the chief said. "Kids' clothes and toys scattered all along the shore. And something else."

"Not the kids," I moaned. "Please don't let it be the kids."

Jenx was silent for so long that I took her wordlessness as confirmation. Tears were already coursing down my cheeks when she said, "Not the kids, Whiskey. Twyla. She's dead."

TWELVE

EITHER BEFORE OR DURING my crying jag, I dropped the phone. I'm confused about the sequence because I never cry. Well, almost never. And Odette almost never hugs anybody. But she held me and rubbed my back and whispered soothing phrases in my ear. Mostly in English, I think, but a few were in Tonga.

I didn't have Jenx's call on speakerphone; Odette had used her telephone telepathy to pick up the police chief's highly charged message about my tenant's drowning and the scattered evidence of lost kids.

I wasn't crying for myself, although I felt plenty awful. A twenty-three-year-old woman was dead. A young mother trying to make it alone in the world. Moreover, the fate of her two small children— and possibly nine or ten other children—was unknown.

Whatever had gone wrong, it seemed obvious that I, as tight-assed landlord, had played at least a small role. I didn't need the Seven Suns of Solace to remind me of my karmic obligation to make amends; the way to begin was to figure out what had gone wrong. Only then could I do my part to help those I had directly or indirectly hurt. Of course, there was no bringing Twyla back. Assuming the missing children were still alive, I had a cosmic imperative to help find them.

The chief had said that Brady spotted Abra near Thornton Pointe with a kid's shoe in her mouth. I wondered if she'd found it among the debris at the shore. If so, had I seen that very shoe on someone's tiny foot only the day before?

I found temporary comfort where I needed it most. Not in Odette's back rub, nice as that was. No, I found reassurance in the knowledge that she was too cool to ever reveal my momentary emotional lapse. For Odette, all actions flowed from the answer to one simple question: "Will this help me sell real estate?" There was no way in hell that stories of Whiskey Mattimoe's self-loathing would contribute to Odette's commission-based income.

As proof of her professionalism, she interrupted my noisy nose-blowing with a reminder that I'd left her a voice mail message regarding "an issue at Druin." That brought me back to earth. I quickly recapped Felicia Gould's early-morning visit.

Odette's nostrils flared. "I called the chatelaine at least thirty minutes before we arrived!"

"What did she say?"

"That she would notify the guard to expect our arrival."

When I asked Odette about Felicia's mood yesterday, she replied, "Neither happy nor unhappy. Like somebody doing her job."

I suspected that Felicia had a bad day; perhaps Vivika criticized her performance, and Felicia lashed out at Odette. If there was one thing I'd learned from dealing with people, it was that most problems were personal.

Although Fenton hadn't wanted to discuss Druin with me last night, Odette was confident that his first reaction to the property was positive.

"He said I could call him today, and of course I will," she said. "I expect him to request a complete tour."

"I wonder how much notice Felicia will need for that," I said.

My direct line rang again, and I froze. What if that was Jenx calling to report more bodies along the shore? Spotting my hesitation, Odette scooped the receiver for me.

"Whiskey Mattimoe's office."

I watched her listening to a voice I couldn't hear. A voice belonging to someone who had called to talk specifically to me. It was an odd sensation, like watching a movie about your life with the volume dialed down.

Her face expressionless, Odette grunted a few times, then said, "All right," and hung up.

"Well?" I asked. "Was that Jenx?"

She nodded.

I said, "How bad is it?"

"Bad. But not horrific."

When the implied subject is unnatural death, how much difference is there between "bad" and "not horrific"?

I demanded details.

"I don't have any," Odette replied. "Jenx said to meet her at the police station. And bring a leash for your dog."

Abra's leash, the last time I'd seen it, had been hanging from a peg in the kitchen at Vestige. But I wasn't sure when that was, or if

I even still owned a leash. Abra had a maddening tendency to run off, whether tethered or not. Although she always turned up again, sometimes the leash didn't.

I called Deely. If we still had a leash, she could grab it, meet me at the MSPD, and haul Abra home. If we didn't, she could buy one en route. I needed the Coast Guard nanny by my side when I faced that demon dog. There was strength in numbers as well as restraining devices. Ever efficient, Deely located a leash while we were still on the phone.

"Excellent!" I felt stronger already. "Put the twins in their stroller and come on downtown!"

"I won't need to bring the twins, ma'am. Avery took them with her again today. It's just Velcro and me here at Vestige."

"Don't bring him," I said quickly.

Deely assured me that she would put *Animal Lullabies* on repeat-play and head straight out the door.

Two days in a row of independent Avery? Where was she off to with the twins? Maybe she really had found herself a new boy-friend, and he liked her kids, too. Of course, he would like the kids. It was the Avery attraction that mystified me.

Like the rest of downtown Magnet Springs, our local police station could have been lifted directly from the set of a TV se-ries about a quaint bayside village. It was a small white clapboard building sandwiched between two gift shops. In fact, the police station could have been mistaken for a gift shop, too, if not for the vertical bars on one window. The window belonged to one of two holding cells.

Officer Brady Swancott was manning the reception desk; I didn't immediately spot the other officer on site because he was under the desk. Who could blame Canine Officer Roscoe for hiding from Abra? Although she had been locked in the rear holding cell, the one deemed more secure, Roscoe wasn't taking any chances. Deely and leash had not yet arrived.

When I arrived, Brady was busily typing on his computer.

"Are you writing up your report on the crime scene?" I said.

"I'm forwarding a joke I just found in my email," Brady said. "Wait till you read it!"

"About the crime scene…" I reminded him.

"Technically, it's not a crime scene. Twyla's death looks like a drowning. Unless the coroner rules otherwise."

"But what about the missing kids?" I demanded. "Their stuff was all over the beach!"

"As far as we know, that's just debris that washed up with the riptide. We haven't yet linked it to Twyla."

Brady explained that Jenx was at Thornton Pointe now, combing the beach with a sheriff's deputy and a couple DNR officers. I told him he needed to talk with Yolanda and Roy.

"It's like Twyla wanted to remove all evidence of children from that house!" I said. "Something was very wrong."

I added that I was pretty sure I'd spotted her turning off Amity Avenue toward the lake, her tires squealing.

"What time was that?" Brady asked, finally picking up a pen to take notes.

"A little after eight thirty. What else do you need to know?"

"Are you ready to accept custody of Abra? Jenx wants me to get her out of here."

The mere mention of my dog's name elicited a whimper from under Brady's desk.

"Easy, boy," the human officer said. "She can't hurt you anymore."

"What did she do?" I said.

Brady lowered his voice. "She was probably still in a heightened state of arousal from being with Norman—whom we haven't found yet. The minute Abra saw Roscoe, she dropped the shoe she was carrying and started humping him. I think she threw his back out."

The unseen canine officer moaned again.

"Sorry, Roscoe," I said.

"If he's still crying after you get her out of here, I'll call Dr. David," Brady assured me.

Deely arrived then with the very necessary leash, as well as grooming equipment.

"I'm going to transition her back to Vestige," she explained. "After a traumatic capture, re-entry should be accomplished in stages."

That made sense, except that the only traumatized creature in this scenario seemed to be Roscoe. When I accompanied Brady and Deely back to the holding cell, we found Abra fast asleep on the cot. Her blonde coat was matted and littered with evidence of a wild night spent under the stars.

Deely whispered, "I expect her to wake up hyperactive, ma'am. First, we'll go to Vanderzee Park, where I'll help her run off some energy. Then I'll remove the debris from her coat."

"Better bag it," Brady said, producing a plastic evidence holder. "In case we find a crime."

Abra woke when Brady jangled the key in her cell lock. She lazily blinked and yawned as if expecting room service rather than parole. My presence barely warranted a tail wag. That was typical. Never mind that I was her legal guardian and also the sole financial provider for the myriad pricey services she required. I asked Brady if I should hire a lawyer.

"Not unless she's committed a crime we don't know about. In that case, *you'd* need the lawyer."

I failed to see the fairness of my being charged with crimes committed by a creature I could not control. Call me *speciesist*.

Brady suggested that Deely take Abra out the back way to spare Roscoe the trauma of seeing her again so soon after the sexual assault. Deely agreed, although Abra fiercely resisted. Her refined nose told her that a male dog was in the building, and she wanted another piece of him. I was glad Deely regularly worked out; she needed all the upper body strength she could muster to drag my horny fifty-pound hound out into the alley.

"She ran off with Norman! Shouldn't she have gotten this out of her system?" I asked the Coast Guard nanny.

"I hate to say, ma'am. They may have suffered *coitus interruptus*. Perhaps they witnessed something shocking out there."

"Maybe something involving Twyla—or her kids. Too bad we have no way of knowing what happened."

Except that wasn't necessarily true, and the other humans in the room knew it. Sometimes Chester could communicate with Abra in ways that confounded logic. It wasn't pretty, but I'd seen those two share pre-chewed food and bark at each other like littermates. Following my thoughts, Deely said she would invite Chester to come by and "have a chat with Abra." Brady liked that idea. It seemed our best option in the circumstances. After all, a young woman had died, children were missing, and a valuable dog was still AWOL. Abra might know exactly what had happened to all those creatures.

Still, asking an eight-year-old boy to interrogate a dog famous for her sexual escapades didn't feel quite acceptable. Should Cassina happen to hear about it on a day when she felt like suing, I would be well-advised to have Velcro as insurance.

Deely had just dragged Abra out the back door when Jenx marched in the front door. Officer Roscoe slunk to her side, apparently seeking the protection of her steel-toed boots. It was sad to see the stately German shepherd reduced to quaking. Jenx herself seemed uncharacteristically weary for eleven in the morning. She frowned at her only full-time employee.

"He looks pussy-whipped. What the hell happened to him?"

When she glared at me, I did my best impression of "hear no evil, see no evil, speak no evil." After all, I hadn't been there. That left Brady to explain.

"Actually, Chief, Abra's libido might be the key to our whole case," Brady said. He outlined Deely's *coitus interruptus* theory, concluding with the hopeful notion that Chester, the canine translator, would soon be on duty to relay Abra's story.

"I don't know," Jenx sighed. Her super-short light brown hair, which usually looked GI neat, didn't. I noticed that her nails were dirty, her shirt was rumpled, and even her steel-toed boots were scuffed. The chief was overworked.

"Damn riptides," she muttered. "Damn Gil Gruen. I've had a dozen calls about him this morning. One of them from your office manager. She's now on her way to Coastal Med with a severe case of heebie-jeebies."

"*Heebie-jeebies?*" I repeated. "Is that a medical term?"

"All I know is Tina's messed up. She saw Gil put the whammy on Twyla."

Okay, now I needed to sit down. In a world-weary voice, Jenx told me what had happened: Tina took her morning coffee break at the beach near Vanderzee Park. She said Noonan, her guru, had urged her to get more fresh air. While at the park, Tina saw a man and woman arguing. Although they were a ways down the beach, the man looked disturbingly familiar. Tina was so distressed by her vague sense of recognition that she went straight to Noonan's studio to request an emergency session. Noonan facilitated a "healing meditative trance," during which Tina realized that the man she'd seen was none other than Gil Gruen.

"Then Tina called the cops," Jenx said. "When Brady told her we'd just found Twyla's body, she realized that Twyla was the woman she'd seen with Gil."

Brady picked up the story. "Tina screamed. Noonan got on the phone to say that Tina had just spilled scalding hot herbal tea all over herself."

"So the medical crisis wasn't heebie-jeebies," I said. "It was second-degree burns."

"Tina's lucky Noonan was there," Brady said, and Jenx nodded.

I thought Tina's problems were Noonan's fault, but I kept my mouth shut. When you're in as much trouble as I seemed to be, the less said, the better.

The door to the police station swung open, admitting someone destined never to be a member of the Whiskey Mattimoe Fan Club. Mr. Gamby, the fisherman who'd scooped Chester and Prince Harry out of the surf, stopped in his tracks when he spotted me.

"You again!" To Brady and Jenx, he said, "What's she in for? Don't tell me she let those babies die!"

"What babies?" the human officers asked. The canine officer scooted back under Brady's desk.

This being a small town, Jenx and Brady already knew about my negligence with Chester, Prince Harry, and the riptide. The fisherman was concerned about my fitness to care for Avery's twins.

"It's okay," Jenx told him. "Whiskey hires people to do the hard stuff."

The fisherman signaled that he wanted a private word with her. She said she was too tired to walk all the way back to her office, and if he wanted to say something confidential, he could whisper it in her ear. Gamby leaned over and hissed loudly, "Keep that woman away from children."

Jenx promised she'd do her best. Brady asked what had brought Mr. Gamby into the station.

"It's about the drowning this morning," he said.

"I had nothing to do with that!" I declared and hoped it was true.

"While I was fishing, I think I saw that girl," Gamby said. "She was arguing with a man on the beach by Vanderzee Park."

Jenx flipped open her notepad and clicked her pen. "What time was that?"

"I don't wear a watch when I fish. That's the point of fishing, to enjoy time instead of keeping track of it!"

Jenx asked why Gamby thought the woman he saw was the woman who drowned.

"I was listening to the police scanner when I brought my boat in. I heard a description of the body: Caucasian female, early twenties, dark blonde hair. Wearing jean shorts and a yellow top. The girl I saw looked like that. And she was right by the water."

Jenx nodded as she wrote everything down. Then she asked Gamby to describe the man he'd seen. That gave him pause.

"Hmmm. Well. Now." After a few moments' concentration during which Gamby squeezed his eyes shut as if trying to summon back the scene, he shook his head. "Sorry. I don't look at men like I look at girls. Why would I? Not being a fruit, I mean." As soon as he'd said that, he glanced at Brady and muttered, "Sorry."

"No offense taken here," the junior officer said with a smile.

"No? I hear you like art."

"I do," Brady said. "I'm doing my master's in art history, but I'm as straight as you are."

Gamby flinched.

"Maybe straighter," I said. "Brady's wife's pregnant. Is yours?"

Jenx said, "Since when does liking art mean you're gay? I don't know a thing about art, and I'm gay."

Then the police department door opened again, and in walked the gayest person in town.

"I haven't seen this much action at the local PD since I can't remember when!" exclaimed Rico Anuncio, fluttering his bejeweled hands. "Somebody threw a party and forgot to invite me!"

"And yet here you are," I said.

Rico was wearing one of his signature cropped, scoop-necked silk shirts, but instead of skintight low-riding pants, he was wearing skintight low-riding shorts; they were extremely, if not obscenely, short. I, for one, thought I saw something I shouldn't have. Quickly turning back to Gamby, I said, "*He* likes art. Maybe you should tell him your theory."

Rico appraised the stunned fisherman, raking his long-lashed eyes up and down the man's stocky body. "What theory is that?"

Speechless and rapidly reddening, Gamby looked to Jenx for support. Then he must have recalled that she was gay, too, and felt surrounded.

To Brady he said, "I … uh … didn't notice much about the guy with the girl. If something comes to mind later, I'll call ya." Deliberately avoiding eye contact with Rico, he lurched toward the door.

"One more question, Mr. Gamby," Jenx called out. "Assuming the girl was five-foot-six—would you say the guy you saw her with was *more* or *less* than six feet tall?"

I can't speak for Rico, and would never want to, but I could feel Brady and Jenx holding their breaths right along with me. We were all thinking that Gil Gruen had been well under six feet tall.

"That's easy," the fisherman said, sounding relieved. I noticed he had cocked his head at an odd angle, no doubt to exclude Rico from his field of vision. The gallery owner was sitting on the corner of the reception desk, his long hairless legs crossed like a glamour queen's.

"The guy and girl were standing close to each other," Gamby said. "I could see he was taller than she was."

Jenx said, "Like a couple inches taller … or more than that?"

"More than that. The guy was tall. Over six feet, for sure. With dark hair. Like yours."

Gamby nodded at Brady, whose well-groomed hair was black. Gil Gruen's hair had been the color of sand, the last time we saw it. Our late mayor wore a Stetson most of the time.

Then Gamby was gone, and I sighed. "Well, that wasn't Gil Gruen. So we can forget about him!"

"Not so fast, Whiskey," Rico said. "You know Odette saw him this morning. I did too! I was putting out my trash in the alley, and she nearly ran me down. Good thing I saw what she saw, or I'd have thought Mattimoe Realty was trying to kill me!"

THIRTEEN

"THAT'S WHY I'M HERE," Rico told Jenx. "To file a report about seeing Gil. Or whatever it is you have people do when things like this happen."

"Things like this don't happen!" I exclaimed. "Dead men don't crawl out of Lake Michigan and walk around town five months later!"

"And yet it's happening." Rico looked smug, sitting on the desk in his little summer sex ensemble, swinging his legs, which were shapelier than mine.

Brady mused, "Which form would that be, Chief? We can't use a Missing Person Report because the point is... Gil's no longer missing."

"Yes he is!" I shouted. Then I corrected myself. "No he's not! He was never *missing*. He was always dead. Gil was dead, and he is still dead!"

Jenx suggested I join her in the kitchenette for a cup of coffee.

"Do I look like someone who needs caffeine?" I said.

"You look like someone who needs a smack in the face. Shut up and come along."

When I hesitated, Jenx broke out her handcuffs. I assumed she wasn't serious, but I'd already been wrong a couple times today, and it didn't feel like my luck was changing. So I followed her to the kitchenette.

She closed the door and motioned for me to sit at the stained pink Formica table that couldn't have been any police department's notion of "standard issue."

"What the hell is wrong with you?" she demanded.

"Well, for starters, this chair wobbles." To prove my point, I rocked it back and forth. Jenx manually stopped the wobbling by locking an iron grip on my shoulder.

"I'm going to ask you one more time," she said in a monotone. "What the hell's your problem today? Don't make me call you Whitney."

I cringed. One common bond that endured from our days together at Magnet Springs Middle School was a deep dislike of our own first names. I was no more a Whitney than she was a Judith.

How had this day gone so wrong? Yesterday I'd landed the two most lucrative listings of my whole career. Plus, I'd had a date with someone not only attractive but almost eligible. Then tragedy had struck one of my tenants—and possibly all of her kids—and now I felt guilty.

I decided to tell Jenx what was bothering me, and ended up blathering on about not only Twyla, but also MacArthur, the cleaner, and Velcro, the nightmare.

"Sorry about your luck with the shitzapoo," Jenx said. "We get twenty calls a month from people complaining about their neighbor's little yipper. Welcome to Small Dog Hell."

I reminded Jenx that I already lived in Big Dog Hell.

"Yeah, and your big dog likes to spread her hell around. That's one of the things we gotta talk about. Thanks to Abra, I got an injured canine officer and a tourist with a missing companion dog. Remember what happened the last time Norman got away from Fenton?"

"He ended up in the hospital," I said.

Jenx cocked an eyebrow at me. "And I understand you care more about him now than you did then."

"Odette told you about the commission we could make if Fenton buys Druin?"

"I'm not talking about real estate. I'm talking about romance! Everybody who was at Mother Tucker's last night saw you two ogling each other."

"You mean I wasn't ogling alone?"

Between my wine buzz and my lack of dating practice, I hadn't been sure whether or not my "chemistry" with Fenton was based mostly on wishful thinking. In any case, I didn't want Abra's fling with Norman to cause Fenton another health crisis.

"You seem to be feeling guilty enough," Jenx concluded with satisfaction. "So here's the deal. I need you as a volunteer deputy. Starting now. Don't give me any crap about this being your busiest season. It's my busiest season, too, and at least half of my problems are related to you or your dog!"

"But—"

Jenx rattled her handcuffs. "I got sufficient cause to lock you up, just for violating local leash laws. So work with me, Whitney."

Through gritted teeth, I said, "Okay, Judith."

"About MacArthur the cleaner," she began. "He fits the description of the guy Yolanda saw scaring Twyla this morning. And he sounds like the guy Gamby saw with Twyla at the shore."

I told Jenx what I knew about him, including his job as Rupert and Cassina's mobile conscience.

"And now he wants to sell real estate?" Jenx asked.

"Yeah, but he still wants to be a driver and cleaner. He's into making big money."

"So are most crooks I know." Jenx told me to interview MacArthur, find out everything I could about him, including his relationship with Twyla.

"I don't think they had a relationship," I said. "Unless—"

"Unless what?"

Reluctantly, I told the chief about the tryst Odette and I had interrupted at Cassina's cottage.

"That couldn't have been Twyla," I added quickly, "unless she was in two places at the same time. But if Twyla sold her 'favors,' so to speak—well, maybe she knew Rupert. And MacArthur."

"I thought you said MacArthur was Rupert's conscience—not his pimp."

"He says he is. But Rupert's not a nice guy."

Jenx said, "MacArthur might not be either."

We heard voices on the other side of the kitchenette door. Voices that were ordinarily never loud. One belonged to Brady, who was almost always calm. The other belonged to a person frequently hired for her calming effect. Noonan Starr burst into the room, shouting. At me.

"Whiskey, we need to talk!"

"Not now, Noonan. Jenx is interviewing her," Brady said.

"Why? Did she bust up someone else's marriage, too?"

Uh-oh. Maybe Fenton wasn't quite as eligible as I had thought.

Jenx glared at me. "You didn't say you were serious about Fenton."

Brady added, "I assumed you were just flirting last night. You were a little drunk."

"You two got drunk together?" Noonan demanded. "Do you have any idea what that could do to his diabetes?"

"Fenton drank Diet Coke," I said. "And nothing inappropriate happened! Fenton is a client. I often have dinner with clients."

"And how often do your clients go home to their wives and tell them they want a divorce?" Noonan demanded.

Then she burst into tears à la Avery. I had never seen anything like it. Except, of course, with Avery.

"Fenton told you that?" I asked. "I swear, I had no idea! Better check the guest list at Red Hen's Inn. There's probably somebody hot staying there."

"No. He wants to get to know *you*. Incredible, isn't it?"

Tears were coursing down Noonan's pale cheeks. Jenx got up from the table to comfort her. Brady had already wrapped an arm around the New Age healer, who now seemed in need of a healer herself, which reminded me ...

"Noonan, I thought you were driving Tina to Coastal Med. For her herbal tea burns ...?"

That was also the wrong thing to say. Noonan emitted a fresh batch of wet, wrenching sobs. Jenx gave me the closest thing to an evil eye anyone completely lacking in Italian blood could muster.

"That was the turning point," Noonan said. "We were on our way when Tina shouted for me to stop. She said her burns weren't bad. Nothing a little aloe applied in her own kitchen couldn't fix. Suddenly I realized that I was doing no one in this town any good!"

"Now just a minute," I began, but Noonan wouldn't stop.

"I made Tina's problems worse, not better! When she came to me after her sighting at the beach, I made her more agitated, not less. If I hadn't gotten her so worked up, she wouldn't have spilled the tea. And then, if I hadn't made such a fuss over the spill, I would have realized that she wasn't really burned. She kept trying to tell me, but I just wouldn't listen!"

I tried again to soothe Noonan, but she wouldn't let me.

"Don't you see? I'm making everything *worse*. And that's the opposite of what I'm supposed to do. Of what Fenton trained me to do. I'm supposed to be a healer!"

"You are a healer!" I said emphatically.

"Not today. Not since Fenton told me about his interest in you."

"Oh, come on," I said. "That thing with Tina was a fluke. Don't tell me you've never made a mistake until today!"

"I've never made *three* mistakes in a row until today," she declared. "Before Tina came in, I was on the phone with a woman I telecounseled to sell candles from home. While we were talking, her house burned down! Because she followed *my* advice. Then I convinced a German tourist that he needed a deep-tissue massage. I reactivated his old groin injury, and he left my studio on a stretcher!"

"Shit happens," Jenx said. "You're just jealous of Whiskey. As weird as that sounds."

Noonan turned her wide pale eyes on me. "What I can't handle is that my soulmate and guru would leave me for someone as un-evolved as you."

I was speechless, but Jenx and Brady made sympathetic noises. Rico Anuncio, who had been listening from the lobby, entered the kitchenette to cast his vote.

"Who'd have thunk it? The founder of the Seven Suns of Solace woos Whiskey Mattimoe, Queen of Denial!"

"That's why I have to leave town. Immediately," Noonan said. "Until further notice my massage studio is closed. Also, my tele-counseling practice. I can't help others until I help myself."

A stunned silence filled the tiny kitchen. Then the mini-fridge clicked on, which alarmed me. Based on prior experience, I feared that Noonan's announcement had triggered Jenx's magnetic energy. Whenever that happens, electrical appliances—and humans—can go haywire. But the mini-fridge was just in the midst of a self-defrosting cycle, and so was Jenx. We all started talking at once, trying to convince Noonan not to leave. But she tearfully insisted that she had to find a new spiritual guru.

I must admit it was distressing to see the calmest person in town completely lose it, especially since she was blaming me. Never mind that, while married to Fenton, she had personally admitted having at least one messy affair herself. The petty part of me wanted to point that out. Except that the practical part of me knew it would only make me look petty. Pettier.

Finally Jenx said, "We all feel for ya, Noonan, we really do, but this is a police station. Unless you plan to press charges, let's move it along."

The chief glanced meaningfully at Brady, who steered Noonan and Rico out of the kitchenette.

"Is there anybody you haven't pissed off today?" Jenx asked me.

"It's still early."

The chief reminded me that my first job as volunteer deputy would be to find out more about MacArthur, the cleaner—where he'd been and who he knew besides Rupert and Cassina.

I agreed, relieved to be off the topic of me as marriage buster. "I already know he's from Glasgow."

When Jenx didn't respond, I added, "That's in Scotland. He's Scottish. You can tell by the way he talks."

Jenx snorted. "Like nobody fakes an accent? Rule One for being a deputy: Bring some healthy skepticism to the job. For all you know, MacArthur the cleaner is an unemployed actor! Assume nothing. That's where your work begins."

Like I needed one more reprimand before lunch. With all the self-righteousness I could manage, I said, "And where does your work begin?"

"I'm gonna try to figure out what happened to the kids who lived in your rental house."

FOURTEEN

Ordinarily I enjoy eating lunch away from my office. But not today. After the ordeal at the police station, I didn't think I could bear one more accusatory or even curious glance. So I hunkered down at my desk and dispatched my part-time receptionist to bring me back my usual from the Goh Cup.

When I heard a knock, I was deep into a spreadsheet and didn't bother to lift my eyes from the computer screen.

"Just set it on my desk," I said.

It wasn't my receptionist at the door, after all. And what was set on my desk turned out not to be lunch but a tush. A very nice tush belonging to the man I had just been drafted to investigate.

"Could I buy you lunch?" MacArthur said. "While we eat, we can talk about real estate. And how I'm going to sell lots of it."

I had been planning to put off doing him—I mean interviewing him—until after I ate, but sometimes Fate hands you other plans. Besides, he was offering to buy. So I closed down the spreadsheet, grabbed my purse, and informed the just-returning receptionist to put my lunch in my mini-fridge.

MacArthur suggested we go to Mother Tucker's. Only the best for the cleaner and his friends. I liked that idea, not only because I knew we'd have a splendid meal with a fine view of the water, but also because people would see me there. Some of the same people, no doubt, who had seen me last night with Fenton. Given how gossip works in Magnet Springs, two contradictory sightings within twenty-four hours would cancel each other out. Ergo, my dinner with Fenton followed by my lunch with MacArthur would yield me a big fat zero on the local social radar. Two men at two more or less consecutive meals meant I had friends and/or clients but no lover. In everybody's busy little mind, I would be still be Whiskey, the lonely widow.

Things didn't go quite according to plan.

First, as we passed through the bar on our way to my favorite table by the window, Walter St. Mary intercepted us.

"Fenton was just here looking for you, Whiskey. I sent him to the Goh Cup because that's where you usually have lunch. Unless you're going to start dining twice a day with us again? Wouldn't that be nice."

Walter was referring to my basket-case days just after Leo had died, when he and Jonny kept me fed and calmed with the best local meals and vino. Back then, I'd even eaten the occasional breakfast at Mother Tucker's, and they're not open for breakfast.

Second, and this was worse, Rico was at the bar.

"Hello, hello!" he called. "Out to break some more hearts? Who knew you could! You go, girl."

Rico made an elaborate show of checking out MacArthur and then punctuated his response with a low whistle. Fortunately, my lunch companion seemed oblivious. Maybe we were a good match. MacArthur seemed as into denial as I was.

"I'm taking my licensing exam Friday," he said when we were seated. "Any last-minute tips?"

"Cram till you think your head will explode, and then do your best."

I smiled at his incredibly blue eyes, wondering if they were the color of the North Sea and then wondering if the North Sea bordered Scotland. Did I know enough about anything to know if he was lying?

Time to play volunteer deputy. As MacArthur's prospective boss, I had a legitimate excuse for quizzing him.

"So. You say you're from Glasgow. And you were an estate agent. Tell me about it."

"What would you like to know?"

"Everything. Start with your childhood—parents, friends, hobbies, sports, grades in school, girlfriends—and then go into how you became an estate agent, how you got licensed, and all the properties you sold. You know, the usual job-interview stuff."

I beamed at him, wishing really hard that he was a good guy and, more important, a stellar realtor. I could use another stellar realtor.

"You always ask about girlfriends?" MacArthur's eyes twinkled.

"Always. I've found they make wonderful character references."

"If it's character references you need, why not call Rupert? He and I go way back—to when we were wee lads."

"Yes, well, I could do that. But I'd like the names of people who don't pay you to be their conscience. By the way, what does Rupert think about your plan to sell real estate?"

"He likes the idea. It fits well with his own plans."

"And what are those?" I said.

"Rupert's on a learning curve. He's almost ready to take responsibility for his own actions."

"How mature of him. So—no more need for a cleaner?"

MacArthur leaned forward confidentially. "Rupert's coming to terms with his identity as a father figure."

"Don't you mean as a father, period? I mean, he is a father. He's Chester's father."

MacArthur nodded. "There are other factors, too. Other children who may require Rupert's attention."

"How about his own child?" I demanded. "Chester gets almost no attention from Rupert!"

"That you know of," MacArthur said. "To you, the inner workings of the Castle probably appear labyrinthine."

"*Labyrinthine*? You learned that word from Chester, didn't you?"

"Actually, I had an excellent public school education."

"All I know is Chester spends way more time at my house than at his own house, even when his dad's in town. What's that about? Not to mention Rupert's unseemly extracurricular. The man makes time to make whoopee—and cheat on his partner, I might add—but can't spend quality time with his son!"

MacArthur gave me an amused, almost affectionate, look. It sucked the hot air right out of my lungs.

"If I weren't interviewing for a job right now, I'd tell you that you look damn cute when you're angry," he said.

I felt my face getting rosy. "I want to know about your real estate career in Scotland," I said, when in fact I would have loved to hear him go on about how "damn cute" I was.

"Commercial or residential?" He proceeded to give me plenty of details about both. MacArthur was either a superb actor who had spent many hours researching his role, or he was as Scottish as Sean Connery and as much into real estate as I was.

I was inclined to believe the latter. But I found my brain repeatedly looping back to his earlier remark about Rupert working on himself as a "father figure" because there were children other than Chester who might need his attention. Children that MacArthur had removed from Twyla's care, perhaps? As temporary volunteer deputy, I doubted I had either the skills or the authority to pursue that line of questioning. So I made a mental note to pass it on to Jenx, along with my impression that the guy was legitimately Scottish and licensed to sell property in the UK. He also seemed to know enough about Michigan real estate law to convince me he'd handily pass his exam. As long as his personal ethics checked out, I wanted him on my sales team.

We managed to get most of the way through the interview and all the way through our meals—gazpacho with shrimp and rice salad for me, a pressed pesto and havarti cheese sandwich for him—before my cell phone rang. When I saw my own home number on caller ID, I knew it couldn't be good news. But when I discovered that the caller was Chester, I felt better. He had been recruited to translate for Abra.

"Is there a break in the case?" I asked.

"Sorry, no," Chester said. "Not yet, anyway. Things got crazy here when Abra saw Velcro. That's why I'm calling. Deely thinks you should come home. Now."

When I asked to speak to Deely, Chester told me she had her hands full trying to calm two dogs and two crying babies.

I said, "I thought Avery took the twins with her ... wherever she went."

"She brought them back," Chester said. "And then she went to bed. Frankly, Whiskey, everybody who lives at your house is upset."

"Why isn't Deely playing *Animal Lullabies*?" I said. "It worked before."

"Velcro ate the CD," Chester said. "Avery got sick of hearing lullabies, so she put in her own CD and left Jeb's on the floor."

More like she threw Jeb's CD on the floor and stomped on it. Not that I really blamed her. Nonstop lullabies could make a person crazy.

"How many dogs am I listening to right now?" I asked Chester.

"Three. Prince Harry's here, too. I got him under control, mostly."

After I hung up, MacArthur asked, "Problems at your house?"

"Labyrinthine," I sighed.

As Fenton had done the night before, MacArthur insisted on picking up the tab. I wouldn't have minded if, like Fenton, he had also walked me to my car and kissed me. But that wasn't going to happen—for three reasons. First, it was broad daylight. Second, MacArthur was on the cusp of coming to work for me. And third, Fenton was heading straight toward our table. I'd almost forgotten that Walter had said he was looking for me.

"Hello, Whiskey," Fenton said.

The guru and the cleaner exchanged nods. MacArthur thanked me for my time and told me he'd let me know the results of his exam as soon as he got them. I wished him luck and turned to Fenton.

"Is everything all right?"

I hoped he wasn't going to make a big deal about the fact that he'd left his wife for me. Sure, that sounds like the kind of story every girl wants to hear. In reality, though, it creates a lot of pressure. I didn't think I was up to it. This was my busiest real estate season. And everybody at my house was unhappy.

"Never better," Fenton said. I liked the way his tanned face creased when he grinned. But why was he grinning?

"Did you find Norman?" I asked.

"No. But I left Noonan. And you made it possible."

"No I didn't—"

"Yes you did. You inspired me. With your brilliant insights into how divorce frees us to follow our destinies."

"I said that?" I couldn't believe I'd said that. "It must have been the Pinot talking—"

"No, Dear, it was you. May I call you Dear? Just until I come up with another nickname that we both like better."

"Actually, I already have a nickname that I like better. Whiskey?"

"Of course you have a nickname!" he exclaimed. "Let me make myself clear. As I grow close to another human being, I like to choose a term of endearment that becomes mine alone to use. In the meantime, I call the other person Dear."

Oh, dear.

"Fenton," I began.

"You can call me Dear, too," he said. "Until we find the name that you will use to show your tenderness for me."

"Fenton," I said again, more firmly. "Aren't we moving a little fast? I mean, we're in a business relationship, and we're friends, but I never asked you to leave Noonan for me."

"I didn't leave Noonan for you! I left her for my future. And for her future, too! She and I were stuck in legally-married-limbo, but neither of us could see that until *you* opened our eyes! No matter what happens between you and me, Noonan and I will always be grateful that you liberated us. I'm sure she plans to thank you, Dear."

By filing charges, I thought.

Fenton went on, "I believe in seeking karmic balance. So I'd like to take you to dinner and a show. And I suggest that we include your ex in our celebration."

"Jeb!"

"That's right, Dear. How about we take in his performance at the Holiday Inn?"

The fact that Jeb had already invited me didn't seem like evidence of karmic balance. More like a hideous coincidence.

My cell phone rang. Once again, the calls were coming from inside my house. I asked Fenton's pardon and flipped open the phone to find Avery on the other end.

"You've got to do something!" she shouted. "This place is a zoo! Deely can't handle it alone!"

"You're there," I pointed out.

"Yes, and I have a massive headache! How the hell I'll get one minute of rest I have no idea—with the dogs howling and the babies wailing! Do something, Whiskey! Or I'm going to lose my mind!"

I started to remind her that she'd ejected the *Animal Lullabies* CD, but she hung up.

"Trouble, Dear?" Fenton asked.

"Not a lot more than usual," I said. "I'm going to have to run home."

"Would you like me to accompany you? Maybe we'll spot Norman along the highway. He's got to be out there somewhere looking for Abra. He may even be making his way to Vestige right now."

I sincerely hoped not. There were already three dogs at my house.

Odette was due to take Fenton back to Druin for part two of the tour. He said she had called to say she was trying to work out the arrangements. I wondered what that meant. Had Felicia created more complications? Did Vivika Major want to sell fast or not?

Fenton promised to pick me up at Vestige around seven, and together we would go hear Jeb sing at the Holiday Inn. I expected an evening of oldies but not necessarily goodies...

Even though I was facing an emergency at home, I found myself driving more slowly than normal. In fact, I took a detour. I told myself that I was hoping to find Norman along one of the back roads. But of course I was really hoping to stall long enough so that the emergency at Vestige would be over by the time I got there.

And it almost was. Dr. David was closing the rear doors of the Animal Ambulance when I pulled into my driveway.

"What did Abra do to him?" I said, leaping out of my car.

"Do to whom?" the vet asked.

"You mean there's more than one victim?"

"There are no victims, Whiskey. Only casualties," Dr. David said.

That did not reassure me. When I pressed him for details, he said that Abra had not physically attacked Velcro. However, she had chased him through the house, howling and snarling. And, as he ran, the shitzapoo had lived up to his name.

I winced. "You mean, he had *accidents* all over Vestige?"

"Only indoors," Dr. David said. "The chaos was confined to the first and second floors. But there was other damage."

Of course there was. Even though he was her boyfriend, Deely would not have called the vet and his ambulance just to help her clean up.

"While he was running, Velcro suffered severe patella luxation. I've had to immobilize him."

Dr. David's speech impediment failed to soften his bad news. I don't care how you pronounce it. Patella luxation is no laughing matter.

"You mean, he's in doggie traction?" I asked.

"Not exactly. I splinted his legs and gave him a tranquilizer. Deely's going to keep him secluded and medicated for twenty-four hours, at which point, I'll decide whether he needs surgery."

I was tempted to ask whether the good doctor had left any tranquilizers for me. Then I realized that if Velcro was medicated, he was probably quiet. No need for lullabies when you've got good drugs.

"Avery is another issue altogether," Dr. David sighed. "Technically, of course, she's human, and that's beyond my expertise. But I would say she needs a therapist."

"She has a therapist! She sees Noonan twice a week—"

Then I saw the problem. The new problem. I stopped Dr. David before he could tell me what I already knew about Noonan leaving town. I did let him talk a little, though. He told me that Avery got hysterical about the dogs. But he knew it couldn't really have been about the dogs because she kept on screaming long after they were caged.

"In layman's terms, I believe she had a quasi-psychotic break—probably caused by Nash Grant's rejection, her sense of maternal inadequacy, and, of course, her resentment of you."

"For a veterinarian, you know a lot about psychology," I observed.

He shrugged. "Behind every mad dog is a crazy human."

FIFTEEN

When I opened the front door of Vestige, I was greeted by Jeb's *a cappella* version of "Golden Slumbers." Apparently Dr. David had supplied a new *Animal Lullabies* CD.

"Deely!" I called out. "Are the lullabies necessary now that we have drugs?"

Deely did not appear, and, oddly, the music grew louder.

"Hello?" I tried again. "Can't you turn that off?"

"Sure, but I'd rather turn you on." The singer was right there in front of me, live and in person.

"How did you get here?" I said. "I didn't see your Van Wagon."

"It's on the guest parking pad. Dr. David's Animal Ambulance must have blocked your view."

I had a clear view of Jeb, however, and it was surprisingly pleasant. He looked good. Really good. Way better than I felt comfortable with. When he moved in for the kiss, I bolted for the window; Jeb's decrepit vehicle was where he'd said it was.

"You're still driving that thing?" I was determined to stay negative till my pulse rate settled. Jeb's sudden presence was tingling parts of my anatomy he hadn't been allowed near for years.

"I won't be driving the Van Wagon much longer," he said. "Thanks to *Animal Lullabies*, I've got a Beamer on order."

"Congratulations. You've finally found your musical style, and it's crooning for canines."

"It's crooning for rich people who feel guilty about ignoring their canines. My voice works for kids, too. I was just singing Leah and Leo to sleep. Wanna see what my voice does for you?"

Jeb had come up close behind me—so close I could feel his breath on my neck. Exes never forget which buttons to push. I knew what Jeb wanted. What bothered me was that I wanted it, too. At least my body was telling me I did. Even though I'd just inspired another man to leave his wife.

"Fenton Flagg and I will be in your audience tonight," I blurted. "We're coming for the karma."

"I'll play all your old favorites," Jeb said.

I wheeled on him. "Don't you dare try that!"

Jeb knew exactly what he was doing. The last time he'd played all my old favorites was in the middle of our divorce. I'd ended up crawling back into bed with him for a week and almost canceling the whole break-up. Fortunately, I'd come to my senses and moved far away. We got the divorce, and eventually I married Leo.

"I think tonight I'll start with 'It's All Been Done,'" Jeb said, his eyes twinkling, "and then play 'The Old Apartment.' As I recall, my Barenaked Ladies covers always made you hot...."

"You cannot sing 'Barenaked Ladies'! I absolutely forbid it!"

"Why? Remember what used to happen when you'd hear my cover of 'Call and Answer'? That was our cue for make-up sex."

And then he started singing. Damn if I didn't get that tingle again. I stuck my fingers in my ears, squeezed my eyes shut, and trilled, "La-la-la-la" to drown him out. The next thing I knew, someone was tugging on my shirt. I was pretty sure it wasn't Jeb because he would have caressed rather than tugged. So I opened one eye.

Chester was grinning up at me. I could only assume that he found me amusing.

"Do you need something?" I said.

He giggled. There was a slight chance that I appeared ridiculous.

"I don't need anything," Chester said, "but Deely does. She wants to talk to you about Velcro and Abra." He pointed upstairs, which I assumed meant that the nanny was on the second floor in Abra's room. Yes, my felonious hound had her own quarters. It was preferable to letting her share mine.

"Did you have any luck translating Abra?" I asked Chester.

"Not yet. She's still upset that Velcro's here. Maybe later she'll feel like talking about Norman."

Once again I questioned the appropriateness of drafting an eight-year-old as intermediary between adult humans and my wanton dog. I cast a sidelong glance at Jeb.

"Why are you here?"

"Chester called me. Didn't you, bud?"

"Yup," Chester said. "I heard Jeb was in town, and I thought it would be good if he came by and surprised you."

Since when did I need the assistance of a middle-grade matchmaker?

To Jeb, I said, "Well, I am officially surprised. And now you can go."

"Not so fast. We haven't even talked about my taking over that lease for the summer—you know, the one the professor from Florida walked out on. What was his name? I think you kind of liked him, for about five minutes…"

"His name was Nash Grant!" Chester said, unnecessarily. "He liked Avery a lot better than he liked Whiskey."

I was already flying toward the staircase, ready to take it three steps at a time. Better Deely and my dog than this conversation.

"That's right, Chester. I remember now," Jeb said, sounding like a bad actor. "Hey, Whiskey! How about I make a pot of coffee? When you come back down, we can talk. Won't that be fun?"

I found Deely sitting on Abra's queen-size bed, the dozing Affie's head in her lap. She informed me that the twins were asleep in the nursery, Avery was asleep in her room, and Velcro was resting comfortably in the guest room. Apparently my home was a sanctuary for everyone but the homeowner.

"I've made a startling observation about Velcro and Abra," Deely said. "Prince Harry has a calming effect on them both. He's a natural mediator, ma'am. With time, Dr. David and I believe he could foster the tone for a tranquil, dog-filled home."

I shuddered. No way in hell three dogs were better than two, even if one was a mediator. I reminded Deely that Prince Harry was still the Pee Master. He did not yet have his flow under control. As proof, I vividly described him peeing all over my deck two days earlier. My story was stronger when I chose to omit the minor detail that he'd just been rescued from a riptide. Unfortunately, Deely knew the truth and offered it in his defense.

"He really is doing better, ma'am, except when he's allowed to almost drown. Dr. David and I firmly believe that Prince Harry can be the link between Abra and Velcro."

"But why do we have to link them?" I pleaded. "Why can't we keep them apart? What's so bad about letting me pretend I only have one dog at a time?"

Still asleep, Abra farted. The smell was so foul I couldn't believe she didn't wake herself up.

"How can she look so angelic and make a stink like that?" I said, switching on the ceiling fan.

"We don't know what she ate while she was on the road with Norman," Deely said, which reminded me that the man I used to go on the road with was waiting in my kitchen. I needed to wrap up this silliness.

"Anything else I should know?"

"Only that Avery is stressed out, ma'am."

"How can she be stressed out? I pay for everything! Plus she told me last night she has a rich new boyfriend."

"I don't know about that, ma'am. But she is stressed out."

"Yeah, well, that makes two of us."

"Three, if you count Velcro, ma'am."

I took one more look at my snoozing Afghan hound, who twitched erotically. I wondered if she was having a sex dream.

Chester and Jeb were playing checkers at the kitchen table. Prince Harry was under the table, chewing one of my brand new shoes, an expensive loafer made of soft leather. As calmly as possible I pointed that out to Chester.

"Sorry, Whiskey," he said. "Avery gave it to him. She said you didn't need it anymore."

When I tried to pry the shoe from Prince Harry's mouth, he mistook my gesture for play and bit down harder, furiously shaking his shiny head.

"You might as well let him have it now," Chester sighed. "He's already chewed most of the toe off."

So he had. Jeb reached down and pulled me up from the floor, where I was kneeling. And cursing.

"You're out of coffee," Jeb said, "but you did have a couple beers in the fridge. I took the liberty of popping one open for you. And one for me, too."

I blinked at him, seeing red. Literally seeing red because he had handed me a Killian's. I handed it back.

"Some of us have real jobs," I said with ominous calm.

"And some of us play for a living," Jeb said. "I like what I do. How about you, Whiskey? Having fun yet?"

"I am!" Chester interjected. "As soon as I win this game, I'm going to teach Jeb how to play chess."

"Jeb already knows how to play chess," I said. "Don't let him hustle you."

"More likely he'll hustle me," Jeb said. "Chester's going to teach me speed chess. Says he learned it from a street punk in Chicago."

Chester nodded. "During one of Cassina's concerts. I won twenty bucks from the guy! He said I was a natural."

We all had our special talents. Avery, for example, had the gift of pissing me off. And I felt that deserved acknowledgment. So I rummaged through the foyer closet until I found the perfect medium for my message: her favorite Ugg boots. I selected one and carried it to the kitchen, where I generously smeared it with peanut butter, inside and out. Happily, I still had a good supply of that. When I offered it to Prince Harry—who preferred it to my mangled shoe—Jeb disapproved.

"Think about your karma," he said.

"I did. And now I'm thinking about Avery's karma. Believe me, she has it coming."

Before I could scoot out the door, the phone rang. Not my cell phone, which I had conveniently left in my car next to my briefcase. My home phone. Chester seized the receiver and answered it like a paid service.

"Whiskey Mattimoe's residence. Chester Casanova speaking."

It still jarred me to hear his last name; I had learned it only a few months ago. Inspired by Cher and Madonna, Cassina never used a surname, and Chester rarely did. I watched as my small assistant pondered what the caller was telling him. Finally, he said, "Just a moment, please." Then he hit the mute button on the phone base and told me, "Jenx wants to know why you're not answering your cell phone. Did you forget to charge it again?"

"No, I didn't forget to—"

I snatched the receiver from Chester's hand and gruffly explained that I had left it in my car as folks often do when they think they're just running inside for a moment and don't realize that people and animals are waiting to ambush them and eat up half their day, not to mention their new shoe. Suddenly I realized Chester was still pressing MUTE. When I paused, he said, "You might want to talk a little nicer to the chief of police. She's on your side."

I swallowed and smiled. Then he released the button.

"Hey, Jenx. What's up?"

The chief wanted to know if I'd learned anything new about the cleaner.

"I think he's legit," I told her, not wanting to get specific in front of Chester. The kid didn't need to worry about his driver unless we were sure there was something to worry about. "He seems to know what he should know, if you know what I mean."

"Chester's standing right there, isn't he?"

I grunted, and Jenx continued, "Here's the scoop: Brady and I interviewed six people who were in the vicinity of Vanderzee Park this morning. All of 'em saw Twyla down by the water. Three said she was talking to a guy who fits the description Gamby gave us. In other words, MacArthur."

"What about the other three?"

"They saw what Tina saw: the ghost of Gil Gruen."

"Ghosts don't come out in the daytime!" I blurted. Chester and Jeb looked up from their checkers.

"Okay," Jenx said. "They saw live Gil. Is that better?"

"There's got to be an explanation," I whispered, walking the portable handset into the next room. "Rico started a rumor that alarmed a lot of suggestible people. Now when they see someone suspicious, they automatically think it's Gil Gruen!"

"I wouldn't call Odette suggestible," Jenx said. "Besides, MacArthur's six inches taller than Gil. And built. Nobody's going to get them confused! Here's what I think, Whiskey: Before she drowned, Twyla met two different guys."

"On purpose?"

"I don't know. If we find out, it might explain what happened to her and the kids. I still think Abra's our best shot."

I pointed out that Brady had found Abra near Thornton Pointe, where Twyla's body washed up—not the beach near Vanderzee Park, where she was last seen alive.

"That dog of yours can cover a lot of ground in a very short time," Jenx said. She ordered me to put my young neighbor back on the line.

Although he had just set an egg timer for ten-minute speed chess, Chester cheerfully stopped it. After consulting with the chief, he informed Jeb that their game would have to wait until after he "interviewed" Abra.

"She won't like it if you wake her up," I said, picturing the sleeping beauty.

"She doesn't like it when *you* wake her up," he corrected me. "I already told her she and I need to talk."

Chester said Deely could stay, but he didn't want anyone else in Abra's room during the interview. That suited Jeb just fine. He led me out onto my deck and inserted the still-chilled Killian's in my hand.

"Drink up, Whiskey. It's a great day."

"Easy for you to say. You're drinking free beer."

"You know what your trouble is?" Jeb said, squinting into the sun over Lake Michigan. "I can tell you because we're not married anymore, and now you might actually listen."

"Yeah?"

"The trouble with you is you get so wound up with things that don't matter, you end up missing the best part of life. Even when it's right in front of you. Allow me to fix that."

He pulled me into his chest and kissed me on the mouth. I couldn't stop him. The sun was in my eyes, and I had a beer in my hand.

Did I kiss him back? I might have, a little. For just a second or two. But I quickly remembered that we were happily divorced, and I had a date with somebody else.

Jeb grabbed my wrist when I turned to go back inside.

"This is what I mean about you," he said. "You're missing the show. Look around! The sun is shining on the water...no dogs are barking...and your handsome ex-husband has money in his pocket. Better yet, he still cares about you. He's not afraid to show it, either."

I looked straight at him, willing myself to resist the sparkling blue eyes and dimples that used to do me in. Although I could resist them now, I couldn't pretend they had no effect. More important, I found myself wondering if Jeb was right. Did I miss the best parts of life?

When Leo was alive, I'd felt fully alive, too. He and I always had fun together, no matter what we were doing—loving, working, playing, eating. There was an ease between us, a lightness of spirit, that infused everything we did.

It had been different with Jeb. When we were married, we had two modes only: passionate love or passionate anger. If we weren't falling into bed together (which we did several times a day), we were throwing things at each other. Big things, like bottles and vases and lamps. Actually, I was the one who did most of the throwing because Jeb made me mad. Looking at him now—and he looked damn fine—I was glad I'd married him, but gladder still that I'd left him...so I could find Leo.

"How about it?" Jeb said, pulling me close again. "Are you happy to see me?"

There was no question that he was happy; I felt his firm joy. And it made me smile. Between my ex, Noonan's soon-to-be-ex, and the cleaner, my love life was on the rise.

SIXTEEN

CHESTER WAS A PROUD though diminutive graduate of every online course offered by dogstrainyou.com, the world-renowned authority in canine-human communication. Last fall, when I hired Chester as Abra's official keeper, I witnessed a bizarre array of bonding behaviors. By comparison, a human-canine interview seemed almost ordinary. At least the way Deely explained it.

"As you may know, my late father Arthur Smarr was the leading authority on interspecies communication. His most celebrated studies involved graduate students interviewing street dogs in East Los Angeles. By posing simple, non-threatening questions, the students were able to elicit amazing biographical data from the dogs. Of course, such communication provides a dog's-eye-view only. Chester will use his canine-language skills to offer basic questions and then interpret the answers that Abra gives him. The downside is that we humans may be interested in details that have absolutely no relevance to the canine involved. And vice versa."

"She's exhausted, but she was very forthcoming," Chester announced when he emerged from Abra's bedroom with Deely at his side. The nanny hung a DO NOT DISTURB sign on Abra's door.

Chester, Deely, Jeb, and I adjourned to my home office, where we set up a conference call with Jenx. We were gathered in a semi-circle, with Chester in the seat of honor behind my desk.

"Abra told me everything she could," Chester said.

Deely nodded. "I'm not as gifted as Chester in canine narrative, but I can vouch for the fact that he posed brilliant questions. And of course Abra trusts him completely."

"Norman was with Abra when she found Twyla's body," Chester began. "Or what Abra refers to as Dead Twyla."

"Whoa. Let's do this in chronological order." Jenx's voice crackled through the speakerphone. "First of all, did Abra see Twyla go into the water?"

"No, Chester replied. "The last time Abra saw Live Twyla was when she stole Twyla's bangle bracelet in the driveway by Live Twyla's house. That was a lot of fun. For Abra. She said she really enjoyed having Whiskey chase her."

"She always does," I muttered.

"For the record, Chester," Jenx said, "Are you telling me that Abra and Norman were nowhere near Vanderzee Park this morning?"

"Right. Abra said they spent the night at Thornton Pointe. They've made a cool little den there, like a love nest, where they go when they want to cuddle up and—"

"Time out!" I interjected, glancing at Chester. "Jenx—is this line of questioning appropriate for an eight-year-old?"

"We can skip ahead a little," Jenx conceded. We heard her flip a page in her notepad. "So, buddy, what did Abra tell you about finding Twyla?"

"Well, it happened like this. Abra and Norman were running along the beach, sniffing each other's butts, when they came upon a whole lot of good-n-stinky stuff. They knew it had just washed up because it had that musk-of-the-lake smell on top of the stink-of-the-dead smell. Abra found it very stimulating."

Hoping to steer the story onto safer ground, I said, "Was that when they found Twyla?"

"Yes, that was when Abra found Dead Twyla."

"Which registered in her canine brain," Deely added, "as something very different from Live Twyla. More interesting, in sensory terms."

"Abra said Twyla had that 'new-dead' stink," Chester reported. "Not 'old-dead,' like some of the fish on the beach. If you're a dog, you prefer 'old-dead.' But 'new-dead' is better than not dead. When it comes to good stink."

"Back up a little," Jenx said. "To the part where Abra and Norman are sniffing each other's asses."

"Do we have to?" I asked.

Jeb whispered in my ear, "Relax. You're not his mother. You're better."

Was I? Nervously I listened as Chester answered Jenx's question, "They weren't alone on the beach for long. Abra said a human showed up and interrupted their fun."

"You mean Brady?" Jenx said.

"Somebody else came first. Abra and Norman were all set to roll in good-n-stinky 'old-dead' fish when a human female—HF for short—showed up. She was near Dead Twyla. Abra checked her out because HF was wearing a shiny watch that caught the sun real sweet. Abra tried to grab it and run. But HF didn't like that game. She started a new game: she picked up a piece of driftwood and threw it as hard as she could."

"Probably at Abra's head," I said.

"Norman brought it right back," Chester said. "He's a retriever."

Jenx asked Chester to describe the woman.

"All I know is she was HF," he said.

"That means, she didn't smell familiar to Abra," Deely explained. "Or especially interesting. She didn't stink."

Jenx said, "Then what happened?"

"Well, HF threw the stick a few more times," Chester said. "Once Norman caught it in his mouth. Then HF got tired of that game. So she threw the stick in the water, and Norman went in after it. That was the end of Norman."

I sat up straight. "What do you mean?"

"I mean that was the last time Abra mentioned Norman. She said she saw him paddling out after the stick. And then he wasn't in the story anymore."

"Are you saying Norman drowned?"

The Coast Guard nanny cut in. "I don't think we should assume that a dog as athletic and water-oriented as Norman *drowned*—although there is the threat of riptides to consider ..."

"Fenton needs that dog!" I exclaimed. "We have to find him!"

"Not now, Whiskey," Jenx said. "I'm trying to figure out what happened to Twyla."

"HF rolled over Dead Twyla," Chester volunteered.

Collectively we shuddered. We were so caught up in Chester's story of dogs rolling in good-'n-stinky flotsam that we automatically pictured the mystery woman getting down on all fours.

"I mean, HF turned Dead Twyla over. Like she was searching her body," Chester said.

"You mean, looking in her pockets?" Jenx asked.

"Abra didn't say 'pockets,'" Chester said. "I don't think there's a dog word for that. Anyway, that's the end of the story. Oh—there's one more part! Abra found a shoe by the water and started chewing it."

"A little shoe?" I asked.

"Maybe. Abra said she liked the way it fit her mouth, and it was a good chew. When HF tried to take it away from her, Abra took off running. HF was supposed to chase her, but she didn't play the game. She got back in her car and left. She wasn't much fun. Then Brady came."

"Jenx," I said, "that must have been the shoe Abra had when Brady found her! Do you think it belongs to one of the missing kids?"

"Too early to tell," the chief replied. "But maybe Brady saw HF's—I mean, the woman's—car. Chester, did you get the color of the vehicle?"

"Abra didn't say."

"Aren't dogs colorblind?" Jeb asked.

"They have trouble with greens and reds," Deely said. "And they're not too precise about the rest of the spectrum."

I was still stuck on the point in the story where Norman had vanished into the lake.

"Did Abra try to find Norman?" I asked Chester.

He shrugged. "She didn't mention him again."

Some love affair; the guy drowns, and the girl keeps looking for good-'n-stinky.

"This could be an incomplete narrative," Deely cautioned. "We have a language and species barrier."

Jenx thanked Chester for his service to the MSPD and the good citizens of Lanagan County. I heaved a sigh of relief that his report hadn't crossed the line into doggie lewdness. Then Jenx excused Chester and said she'd like a word with the adults in the room. Since Jeb was a musician, I wasn't sure he could stay. But he did. In fact, he laid one arm across the back of my chair.

"I don't know what to make of the woman in Abra's story," Jenx began. "As far as we know, Brady was the first human on the scene, and he was there to post riptide signs."

"You think Abra's lying?" Jeb asked.

"I don't know what to think," Jenx said. "She might be an unreliable witness."

"No, ma'am," Deely said. "I was in the room when Chester questioned her. That dog was sure about what she saw."

"That dog," I reminded everyone, "is an Afghan hound!"

Jenx said, "I'll go over her statement with Brady. See what he can add. Last I heard, the sheriff's department and the State boys still had their crime scene investigation teams at Thornton Pointe. I need to find out what they found out."

"Will they tell you?"

"I'll insist on it."

Jenx had long-standing issues with other law enforcement agencies, who generally regarded her department as a joke. They scoffed at the notion that Jenx and her team could solve a real crime.

The chief said, "Twyla was last seen alive near Vanderzee Park. That's in my jurisdiction."

"But she was found dead at Thornton Pointe. That's a state park," I said.

"Whose side are you on?"

"I'm sure Whiskey's on the side of truth, justice, and the American way," Jeb said smoothly.

I nearly jumped out of my chair. Not because of what he'd said but because of what he'd done. Jeb had chosen that moment to stroke the back of my neck. The sensation was extremely pleasant. However, it was a move forever linked in my brain and heart to Leo. My late husband used to absent-mindedly play with the curls at the base of my skull. And now Jeb was doing it—in Leo's house, or rather, in the house where I used to live with Leo.

"Is she all right?" Jenx asked.

I realized then that I must have yelped.

"She's fine," Jeb said as he resumed stroking. Part of me wanted to lean into him and let it all go. Another part of me wanted to set him straight and send him packing. For now, I decided to let the first part of me win.

"Whiskey, did you have a chance to question the cleaner?" Jenx said.

"Uh-huh," I murmured, relaxing into Jeb's neck massage.

"Well? What did you find out?"

"He's for real, I think. I mean, he's really into real estate. I believe him …" My voice trailed off, and my eyes closed. I didn't want to think about police work when Jeb was touching me like that. I didn't want to think at all.

"Excuse me, ma'am," Deely said. I didn't know whether she was talking to me or Jenx—and I didn't care. "Are you talking about MacArthur the cleaner who's also the driver?"

"Yeah," Jenx said. "What do you know about him?"

"Only what Chester tells me. He says MacArthur always makes everyone wear their seatbelts. And he obeys speed limits and stop signs. No rolling stops, ever. MacArthur is very conscientious. That's why they call him the cleaner."

"That's not the only reason," I said.

"He's a driver," Deely repeated. "But he doesn't only drive Chester and his parents."

"You can say that again," I said.

"Let the nanny talk," Jenx barked. "What are you saying, Deely?"

"This may mean nothing, ma'am, but I thought about it when Ms. Mattimoe mentioned the missing kids. Chester said MacArthur runs a 'shuttle service'—for children. He 'delivers' them where they need to go."

SEVENTEEN

"MAYBE THE DRIVER'S A cleaner even when he's a driver," Jenx mused. Over the speakerphone, we could hear her writing something down.

"You think MacArthur made Twyla's kids disappear?!" I jerked myself away from Jeb's massaging fingers.

"I don't know what to think yet," Jenx said, still writing. "But he might not be the nice guy you wish he was."

"Who is this guy?" Jeb asked.

"Some hunk Whiskey wants to hire," Jenx said.

"He was an estate agent in Glasgow," I told Jeb. "Now he's Rupert and Cassina's conscience. And their driver."

"Or so he told you," Jenx grunted. "Deely—did Chester identify the kids MacArthur 'drives where they need to go'?"

"No, ma'am, he didn't," the Coast Guard nanny replied. "But Chester made it sound like it was something MacArthur just started doing."

My watch reminded me that I still had an entire afternoon of work to squeeze into the next two hours. It was almost three o'clock; I was sure that my cell phone, parked in my car, would have several messages requiring my immediate attention. So I concluded the conference call with Jenx and dispatched Deely to tend the various life forms under my roof. Deliberately not making eye contact with Jeb, I coolly acknowledged that I'd see him later. Sure, that neck rub had been nice. But why, oh why, did Fenton insist on a karma-based date? Things could get complicated.

I had just opened the front door on my way out when something whizzed past my nose. In that split second, I caught the distinct whiff of Jif peanut butter, and I recognized my own name in a long string of expletives. Apparently Avery had gotten her lazy butt out of bed because she needed a snack. She had located the peanut butter, but it was in her favorite boot... in Prince Harry's jaws. I thought it best to keep moving.

When I played my voice mail messages, I found two from Odette about Felicia's lack of cooperation regarding showing Druin, one from Roy requesting that I inspect his final work at the new North Side duplex, and one from my part-time receptionist that made no sense at all. I called her back, but she didn't answer— the Mattimoe Realty number rolled over to my recorded message. Not a good sign on a Thursday afternoon. Since the receptionist's message had sounded hysterical, I made an executive decision to exceed the speed limit. Getting a ticket seemed unlikely, given that riptide alerts were keeping most local law officers busy at the beach.

I was relieved to find Mattimoe Realty open for business and my receptionist at her desk looking calm. In fact, she was doing her nails. Since part-time teenage hires came and went with the frequency of flicks at the nearest Cineplex, I rarely bothered to learn their names. That wasn't a problem as long as they wore their nametags. But this one must have thought the red badge clashed with her naturally red hair. At any rate, she wasn't wearing it.

"Hey," I said, standing in front of her desk.

"Hey," she said, concentrating on her nails.

"I just called the office and got our recorded message."

"Cool!" she said.

"Cool?" I asked.

"Well, I wasn't sure if I, like, knew how to turn it on, but I guess that, like, proves I do!" She was still painting her nails.

"I guess it, like, does," I said. "But you're, like, *here*, so why is it on?"

"It's on because I can't answer the phone *and* do my nails!" She held out her gleaming pearl-tinted digits for me to admire.

"I can see where that might be a problem. Why aren't you wearing your name tag?"

"Please. Everybody in town knows my name! And, anyway, it looks totally lame with this shirt."

"Of course," I said pleasantly. "I understand why you're not wearing the name tag or answering the phone. But I need you to explain the voice mail message you left me."

She frowned.

"The hysterical one?" I prompted.

Her round brown eyes opened surprisingly wide considering the volume of mascara weighting her lashes. "This guy came by from the IRS and left his card!"

After my insides had rolled over, I said, "Where is it?"

"It's in the drawer next to my name tag, but my nails are, like, still wet."

Obligingly she rolled her chair back so I could find it myself. I opened the drawer, which was a jumble of paper clips, rubber bands, and cosmetics. Mostly cosmetics. I did not see a business card from the IRS or any other organization.

"What's your name?" I said.

From the way she blinked those amazing lashes, I knew nobody else had to ask. "Sari Decker."

"Here's the deal, Sari Decker. Find the business card and go home."

"You mean, like, I get to go home early?"

"Not early. Permanently. You're, like, fired. No, not *like* fired. You are fired. But first, find the card!"

At that point, Sari Decker moved so quickly and found the card so efficiently—wet nails or not—I almost wondered if I should keep her. But it didn't seem fair to come between a girl and her beauty regimen.

In one smooth move, she yanked out the drawer, dumped its contents on the desk and plucked the lone business card from the pile. As she swept everything else into her purse, I read: Damon Kincaid, Federal Revenue Agent, Internal Revenue Service.

Then the phone rang. Since I had relieved Sari Decker of her duties, I leaned over to check caller ID. The incoming number matched the cell phone number of Damon Kincaid.

My tax bills were paid. Of this I was sure, because I hired a very good accountant. Ergo, I mastered my natural fear of the IRS and answered the phone. After identifying himself, the nasal-voiced agent politely informed me that he would appreciate my cooperation in a current investigation. I swear, it sounded like he was reading from a script.

"You're investigating *me*?" I asked.

"I have a few questions, Ms. Mattimoe. And I would appreciate the opportunity to ask them in person."

When I offered to call him back after setting up a date and time convenient for both my accountant and my lawyer, Damon Kincaid announced that he was just down the street and would be at my office in five minutes.

"I can't get my accountant here on such short notice—let alone my lawyer!"

"I'm not auditing you, Ms. Mattimoe. At least not yet."

Exactly five minutes later, Damon Kincaid was sitting across from me, his regulation brown vinyl briefcase open on his lap. And I was feeling better. Why? Because he really wasn't auditing me. The IRS agent had a few questions about local real estate because he was auditing my deceased former competitor, Gil Gruen.

Damon Kincaid wasn't bad looking for a government hatchet-man. He was young—under thirty-five for sure—and fairly pleasant. If anything, he reminded me more of a Mormon missionary than an IRS agent—except, as far as I knew, Mormon missionaries always traveled in pairs.

"Of course, I'm not at liberty to discuss Mr. Gruen's case," Damon Kincaid said. "However, there seems to be some discrepancy as to whether his firm or yours managed the following properties. So I was hoping you could clarify the matter."

He presented a photocopy of what looked like an old computer printout made when spooled paper and dot-matrix printers were still widely used. It featured a long column of addresses. I recognized a few; they had belonged to Mattimoe Realty before I became a Mattimoe. Or a realtor. I remembered Leo telling me about those properties when I married him and joined his business. That was six years ago. Leo had sold those properties to Gil Gruen a few years before that—back in the day when Gil was launching his real estate business, and I was lead music groupie for Jeb Halloran.

I relayed that information to Damon Kincaid, who nodded as if he'd already heard the story.

"So, to the best of your knowledge, Mr. Gruen and Best West were still operating those properties at the time of his death?"

"That is correct, sir."

His *death*. I was delighted to hear an official government employee use the correct term for Gil's fate. As Damon Kincaid added a note to his legal pad, I couldn't resist asking one question myself. Technically, it was more of a request.

"I know the IRS isn't in the PR business..." I began.

"Actually, we are. One of our missions in the twenty-first century is to improve our public image."

Damon Kincaid smiled, revealing small, very straight teeth.

"Cool," I said, quoting my former part-time receptionist. "So maybe, before you leave Magnet Springs, you wouldn't mind spreading the word that Gil Gruen really is dead? It would help settle things down around here."

The agent frowned. "You mean there's some doubt that Mr. Gruen is dead?"

"Only among the crazies!" I laughed. As Damon Kincaid continued frowning, I added, "This is a tourist town. There's a lot of New Age nonsense."

With that, he grimly scribbled a few more lines in his legal pad and then slipped it, along with the computer printout, back into his briefcase.

"You're still sure Gil's dead, right?" I said, hoping against hope that my request hadn't bollixed everything.

"I'm not at liberty to say," Damon Kincaid replied. "But if he's not, I'm going to need some back-up."

After the Federal Revenue Agent departed, I sat at my desk, holding my head in my hands. This being our busiest season, the office phone rang and rang. Fortunately, the answering machine was still turned on so I could keep on mentally kicking myself without interruption.

Odette appeared at my door. "You look like you've seen a ghost."

"Just an IRS agent who's investigating a ghost."

Masochistically I confessed my chatty blunder. Odette, as usual, was unfazed. She reminded me that the IRS was auditing Gil, not me, and that we had our own issues.

"Fenton wants to see all of Druin tomorrow, but Felicia, the Castle Nazi, won't cooperate."

The chatelaine had informed Odette that she would be refused entrance at the gate because of "insufficient notice."

"You know what you need to do," my star agent told me.

I sighed. "Call Vivika Major."

Odette handed me my own phone and helpfully dialed the Internet magnate. When I asked if we were calling Vivika's direct line, Odette replied that nobody had that number.

"What if the Castle Nazi answers?" I said.

"She won't. A receptionist will. And you know how to get past receptionists."

I knew how to get rid of receptionists, that much was true. I identified myself and my business to the young man who answered and then requested Ms. Major's personal secretary. Bless the boy, he wanted to follow the organizational chart, box by box, but I impressed upon him that a matter of this magnitude required speed. Then I told Vivika's personal secretary that her boss had insisted that I keep her confidentially informed in the event of a crisis. And we had us a crisis.

Within moments, I had the mogul herself on speakerphone. Odette beamed.

"Whiskey, what's the problem?" Vivika began.

I envisioned the tycoon at her immense antique desk surrounded on three sides by bookcases filled with glowing computer screens.

"Here's the short version: your chatelaine isn't on the same page as the rest of us. Odette Mutombo has a qualified prospect for Druin, but Ms. Gould won't work with us to arrange a showing."

"Won't work with you how?"

"She won't comply with our requests to schedule a visit."

Vivika Major was silent. In the background a phone bleated.

"Hello?" I said.

"I'm here," Vivika replied.

When she didn't continue, I assumed that someone or something had distracted her. Perhaps the chatelaine herself was in the room. I heard papers being shuffled and pictured Vivika's large, masculine hands.

"My point, Ms. Major, is that we at Mattimoe Realty are doing everything possible to get you the offer you want within the time frame you want, but your chatelaine seems to be working against us."

Muffled voices on her end told me she wasn't listening. Odette flashed the universal sign to be more aggressive: she bared her bright white teeth and clenched her neatly manicured hands.

"Ms. Major, can you hear me?" I said.

Through the speakerphone came an indistinct voice, followed by what sounded like a closing door.

"I hear you, Whiskey," Vivika said. "And I'll speak to Felicia about your concerns. Call me back if there's another problem. I'm counting on you to bring me a good offer *soon*." Click.

Odette gave me her signature shrug, that eloquent gesture of detachment. "She'll get it done."

"How do you know?"

"Vivika Major is a deal-aholic. She lives for the orgasmic high of out-negotiating the competition."

I had often thought the same about Odette. The difference was that Vivika Major appeared to work 24/7, no matter where she was. Druin was a fabulous corporate fortress, not a vacation retreat.

Odette checked her diamond-studded watch. "I'll give Vivika twenty minutes to re-set Felicia's attitude, and then I'll call back. Fenton wants to see Druin tomorrow afternoon. That's because he plans to sleep late tomorrow morning. With you."

She timed that announcement to coincide with my swallowing the last of my bottled water.

"He told you that?" I choked.

"He didn't have to," Odette said. "I can read between the lines."

"With your 'telephone telepathy'?"

"Who needs telepathy? Everyone in town knows Fenton asked Noonan for a divorce. And tonight he's taking you on a date to see Jeb. Fenton's First Sun of Solace is to restore karmic balance. Before he has sex."

Resistant though I was to New Age thinking, you couldn't live in this town without learning a little about enlightenment. I knew that the First Sun of Solace was whatever you needed it to be.

I just hoped I had sufficient sexual karma. Recalling Rupert's noisy anonymous lover at Cassina's cottage, I wondered. If size matters—and I think it does—is it also true that volume matters? As in female vocal expressiveness? No one had ever complained about my being too quiet in bed, but then nobody had ever praised my sound level, either. Was I deficient in a potentially vital skill area?

Jeb and Leo were the only two lovers with whom I'd had long-term exclusive relationships. Neither husband had seemed disappointed that I didn't make much noise. Nor had the local judge when he helped me graduate last spring from my post-Leo celibate funk.

I told myself that I was probably okay in the sack. Jeb was back and eager for action, so I must have left a good impression. I shrugged off my pre-coital anxiety. If Fenton felt destined to have sex with me, I was up for it. Especially if he didn't make me call him "Dear."

EIGHTEEN

When sex is in the offing, I need time to get ready. Most days, I simply open my closet and randomly select a couple clean beige separates, plus a comfortable pair of shoes. Then a I run a brush through my hair and dash out the door. Makeup is something I save for weddings, funerals, and dinner dates that might end in the bedroom.

Tonight I wanted to make sure everything I wore looked like it belonged together. Fortunately, I had just purchased a lovely taupe linen pantsuit at Town 'n' Gown, the best clothing store in Magnet Springs. I'd left it there for alterations, which were now complete. I only needed to pick it up on my way home.

I had known Martha Glenn, the senile octogenarian proprietor of Town 'n' Gown, my whole life. Lately she tended to mistake me for other people—mostly people she intensely disliked. Tonight Martha thought I was her long-dead stepmother. Her pale blue eyes gave me a cold once-over.

"You must have put my father under a spell to make him marry you," she snarled. "You're as wicked as Cinderella's stepmother. And twice as ugly."

Then she flicked her pink tongue. I wondered if she'd been coached by Avery.

"I don't care how much money you have," she hissed. "You can't make me wear that to the Country Club dance!"

"I won't make *you* wear it, Martha," I said gently. "*I'm* going to wear it."

She pointed a gnarled finger and told me to hold up the suit so she could see how it looked on me. When I did, she almost fell over laughing.

"What's so funny?"

She cackled, "I just pictured you having sex!"

"I'll take the suit off first," I replied and threw my cash on the counter.

Before I could get out of town, my cell phone rang. Roy Vickers said, "Whiskey, I'm on Mrs. Brewster's front porch. And I think she should speak to you directly."

Yolanda began, "Miz Mattimoe, I seen something this afternoon you need to know about."

"Twyla's kids?" I asked hopefully. "Did somebody bring them back?"

What a pathetic, ridiculous notion. I had chased them away while Twyla was alive and able to care for them. Now she was dead. Guilt washed over me. Again.

"No, nothing about Twyla," Yolanda said. "I seen our former mayor."

I swerved the car. Fortunately, I swerved it toward the curb, where there was an available parking space. So I stopped.

"Don't tell me *you* believe in ghosts," I said.

"Maybe I do, maybe I don't. But this weren't no ghost. I seen Gil Gruen. Our dead mayor's come back."

Fifteen minutes ago Yolanda had seen Gil poking around a property he'd owned on Amity Avenue—two doors down from Twyla's rental. It was one of the addresses on Federal Revenue Agent Damon Kincaid's printout. According to Yolanda, Gil was trying to pry open a basement window.

"When the family that live there come home, I told them what I seen. I called Chief Jenkins, too. She over there now, checking things out."

I thanked Yolanda and asked her to put Roy back on the line.

"What does this have to do with Mattimoe Realty?" I said.

"Nothing, I hope. But it speaks to the general paranoia in town. Too bad you drove Noonan away," Roy sighed.

I started to explain that I'd done nothing of the kind when another call beeped on my line. Recognizing Jenx's number, I told Roy we'd talk later.

"Still think Gil's dead?" Jenx began. "He was trying to break into his rental property on Amity Avenue. When the tenants came home, he ran. Yolanda saw him. So did two kids playing in the alley."

"Yolanda believes in ghosts!" I moaned.

———

I turned off my phone and drove straight home. It was almost five thirty, which wouldn't leave much time for the relaxing bubble bath I'd planned—not to mention a manicure and the application of full-face makeup.

There's nothing like finding an ambulance in your driveway twice in one day. Even if it's Dr. David's Animal Ambulance. I'd turned off my phone just five minutes ago. What could have gone wrong in that time?

The front door opened and out stepped Deely Smarr, dressed like I'd never seen her. The Coast Guard nanny was all dolled up: Instead of her usual Doc Martens, khakis, and starched oxford shirt, she was wearing espadrilles and a dress—a feminine-looking pastel cotton dress that fluttered in the early evening breeze. Moreover, she had curled her usually flat hair and added makeup. Dr. David was right behind her. He was spiffed up, too. For the first time since I'd known him, he had traded his yellow and white Fleggers-wear for a sports jacket.

These two were on a date. Wherever they were headed, they were going there by Animal Ambulance.

"*Hewwo*, Whiskey!" Dr. David called out as Deely waved.

"Hey, have fun tonight, whatever you're up to!" I said. "Seeing your ambulance scared me. Thank god it was a false alarm."

Deely looked somber. "Didn't you get my message, ma'am? I called your cell phone five minutes ago."

She explained that she had been unable to calm Avery following the peanut-butter-boot incident. After I left, my stepdaughter continued to rant and throw things, including my favorite Medici bronze table lamp and Sasaki vase. Avery considered the lamp and vase fair payback for her chewed boot, forgetting that the chewed boot was payback for my chewed loafer.

"You won't want to go in there, ma'am, until you're mentally prepared. I regret to say that my damage control skills were insufficient for the situation. Even Jeb's songs failed to quiet her."

Where was Avery now? I craned my neck to check the guest parking pad, where she usually kept the gecko green VW Bug she'd bought with part of her inheritance from Leo. I stiffened at the sight of it. Unless Avery was locked in the back of the Animal Ambulance, I'd have to deal with her now. That wouldn't leave me enough time and energy to get all dressed up, let alone psyched for sex.

"Avery's gone," Deely said. "She had a date."

"With whom?"

"I'm not sure, ma'am. She got picked up by a driver. And she took the twins with her."

Driver? Kids? Shuttle service?

Breathless, I asked, "Did you see the car?"

"Sorry, no. I was getting dressed for my own date. I only know she had a driver because she told me so before she left. Avery said her new boyfriend is into money. And he likes kids."

"Deely, how many drivers do you know who pick up kids?"

She raised a single finger, making the Chester connection.

"But I don't know if it's the same one, ma'am. Chester was long gone by then. I sent him and Prince Harry home when Avery went out of control. I don't think the young should be exposed to rage like that."

Was it possible that Avery's driver was the cleaner? If so, did that mean my stepdaughter was "dating" Rupert? I flashed back to the moaning and shrieking I'd overheard at Cassina's cottage … and then shook my head to erase the memory.

"Ear mites, ma'am," said Deely.

"What?"

"The way you shook your head reminded me that Prince Harry has ear mites. Dr. David is treating him—and Abra and Velcro, too. Ear mites are highly contagious. And Velcro has so many problems."

"What's the latest?" I sighed.

Deely looked to Dr. David on this one. I couldn't miss her reverential expression. Oh, yes, my nanny was in love.

"When she pitched her fit, Avery woke Velcro, despite his sedation," Dr. David said. "The little guy tried like hell to get out of your guest room. He chewed off his own splints."

"How about my door? Don't tell me he chewed through that?"

Deely shook her head. "By the time I got to him, he had worked himself into a panic. Despite his injured knees, he attempted to run up the stairs. It was pathetic. He yipped nonstop. I knew he was trying to tell me something. But without Chester to translate, I wasn't sure what it was."

Dr. David continued her story. "Deely carried Velcro to the second floor. And inside your room, she witnessed a miracle."

"The moment I laid him on your bed, he fell asleep! Sound asleep!"

"I was able to redo his splints without additional sedation," Dr. David said. "Deely and I have reached a startling conclusion: Velcro needs to be with you, or with your things, 24/7. That dog has bonded with you, Whiskey, and the essence of *you* is what calms him."

"What about Jeb's *Animal Lullabies*?" I said. "I thought they calmed him. I thought they calmed everybody!"

"That's the other lesson we've learned," Dr. David replied. "Avery Mattimoe—*in extremis*—cancels out the calming effects of Jeb's music. We should probably add that to the liner notes."

NINETEEN

I DIDN'T KNOW HOW on earth I would handle Velcro now that he was living up to his name.

"You don't mean I'm supposed to let him stay in my bedroom?" I demanded.

Dr. David nodded. "Tomorrow I'll come by with some assisted-living devices to make Velcro's life easier."

"How about some devices to make *my* life easier? Like an unlimited supply of dog tranquilizers. If they don't work on him, I'll take them."

"We have to go, Whiskey," Dr. David announced. "We're catching your ex-husband's opening night at the Holiday Inn in Grand Rapids."

"So am I!" I said.

"We know," Deely said, "but we're going to get there on time."

Striding through the house, I tried not to notice the empty places where my Mission lamp and Sasaki vase used to be. And I tried not to think about Leah and Leo. Avery was old enough to make her own mistakes, but the twins were just babies. Pure innocents.

Rupert was short, scrawny, and arrogant. Avery was tall, fat, and negative. I couldn't picture those two hooking up, not only with each other but with anyone. They were unpleasant, unattractive, irresponsible people. Maybe they were perfect for each other.

I had more immediate issues, such as the ominously named dog now residing in my bedroom. Cautiously I cracked open the door. Very softly Jeb Halloran was crooning "Itsy Bitsy Spider." Deely must have inserted a replacement *Animal Lullabies* CD in my portable boom box.

Asleep in the center of my bed, the little dog looked so sweet. Barely as big as a baby's Teddy bear, he lay snoring softly. Really, he was pathetic, with that curly black hair, that shiny wet nose, and the splints on those two tiny hind legs. I entered and closed the door behind me.

Suddenly he was awake, yapping nonstop. I knew he was glad to see me because his stubby tail was a wagging blur. But that was small comfort amid the high-pitched din. I tried to remember something helpful from Chester's many informational lectures on canine behavior. The kid had learned a lot; too bad I rarely listened.

I couldn't remember whether the best thing to do in a situation like this was to maintain eye contact or avoid eye contact. I opted for a compromise: no direct stares but lots of furtive glances. My plan was to crank up the volume of Jeb's voice and jump into the shower. But my peripheral vision picked up Velcro trying to jump off my bed. I knew that was a bad idea; in human scale it would be like leaping from my rooftop. And two of the little guy's legs were already wrecked.

I didn't know what to do other than place an emergency call to Deely. Frankly, I didn't expect her to answer since she was off duty and on a date. When she picked up on the first ring, I concluded that Fleggers members take an oath to protect animal rights round the clock.

Very loudly, so as to make myself heard over Velcro's piercing cries, I told her what was happening. She put Dr. David on the line. He suggested that I hold Velcro in my lap and pet him until he fell back to sleep. Or I could put him in a crate and find myself a pair of earplugs.

I needed Deely back on the line; she was the only human in my household who kept track of dog paraphernalia, including crates. She dispatched me to the kitchen. There I found one and also remembered my stock of wine. I paused to pour myself a generous portion of Pinot Noir. Then I followed Dr. David's directions, inserting dog in crate and plugs in ears. I could still hear Velcro, even in the bathroom with the shower running and Jeb's voice at top volume.

Very gradually the wine and warm water worked their magic on me, and Velcro wore himself out. When I stepped from the shower, all I could hear was an absurdly loud version of "Lavender Blue." I tiptoed into my bedroom and spun the dial down. Peering into Velcro's crate I wondered if he was even breathing. Then his round brown eyes popped open, his tail thumped, and I held my breath. But he was okay. Better yet, he was silent.

As long as he kept me in sight, that is. The instant he couldn't see me, he set up a howl. So I rotated the crate as I moved about my quarters. Of course that slowed down the whole date-preparation process, but it had one unexpected benefit: it distracted me from my worries about being intimate with Fenton.

It also distracted me from the fact that I was still wearing ear plugs. As a result, I didn't hear my date ring the doorbell five minutes before seven. When Velcro resumed whining, I naturally thought it was because he didn't like his view. I adjusted his crate a few times before noticing that my cell phone was flashing, indicating a missed call. When I checked for messages and couldn't hear them, I realized I still had plugs in my ears. Fenton was phoning from my front porch.

Knowing that Velcro would resist my departure, I made sure I had everything I might need for the evening before I bolted from the room. I tore down the stairs and paused inside the front door just long enough to recover some semblance of composure before turning the knob.

Fenton greeted me with "What went wrong?"

I hoped he meant Velcro's ear-splitting *yay-yay-yay* chorus and not my appearance. After checking the latter in several lighting conditions, I was reasonably sure I had got it right.

I said I'd prefer to explain after we got underway. We started for the driveway, where I spotted our shiny new ride. Fenton had hired a sleek black Lincoln Town Car. Expectations were running high tonight...

Very high. When we reached the vehicle, the driver's door opened and out stepped a handsome man in a dark suit. We not only had us a Town Car; we had us a driver. But not the driver who was also a cleaner. So maybe my stepgrandbabies' driver wasn't the cleaner, either.

This chauffeur provided champagne, which instantly erased Velcro from my mind. We had music, too—surround-sound Sinatra the whole forty miles to Grand Rapids. Very romantic and not remotely like *animal lullabies*; I completely relaxed without feeling the least bit sleepy. In fact, I felt sexy. For the first time since my guilt-inducing nap in the sun two days earlier, I forgot all about riptides, kids, and dogs.

Fenton Flagg, PhD, was a classy guy. Although he'd made his fortune peddling a New Age step program, he knew how to spoil a woman. In addition to the limo, champagne, and seductive music, Fenton had made arrangements for us to enjoy an intimate candlelit dinner at Rigi, an elite dining establishment partway up the coast. It offered a customized high-end culinary experience that Leo would have loved. Each table—and there were only four—occupied its own dark and cozy little room. Diners selected every detail of their meals in advance by either Internet or phone, including not only food and drink but also the flowers on the table, the music in the air, and the flawlessly trained serving trio waiting to deliver the dinner of one's dreams.

Fenton had somehow learned all my dinner-related favorites, including cut flowers and music. Odette must have been his source. I entered our dark walnut dining nook to find yellow roses on the table and Susan Werner singing in the background. Our "host," as Rigi calls its servers, was exactly as attentive as we wished him to be. He provided a fabulous bottle of Maso Canali Pinot Grigio, fresh Maryland crab cakes, a divine artichoke-heart salad, tender salmon filets served over couscous and roasted red peppers, orgasmic macaroon cheesecake and, finally, strong black Columbian coffee.

Mindful of his diabetes, Fenton skipped the high-carb items. He assured me that there was no need to worry, even though Norman the medical-reminder dog was still on the lam. We lingered over our meal for three hours. Although Jeb never wore a watch and claimed he didn't care about time, I wondered how he'd feel if we arrived to catch only his last set. Maybe Fenton had planned it that way. Maybe that was the karmic order he'd intended.

So it was almost midnight when we arrived at the Holiday Inn. We stepped from the Town Car to find Jeb Halloran, Deely Smarr, and Dr. David just outside the front entrance consulting with a Grand Rapids cop. Fenton asked what was going on.

The policeman, whose badge identified him as Officer Curdy, said, "I'm investigating a report that a man missing since January was in the lounge tonight."

To Jeb I said, "Don't tell me Gil came to hear you play!"

Jeb shrugged. "Surprised me, too. I never knew he was a fan."

"The man is fish food!" I insisted.

Officer Curdy said, "What's that supposed to mean?"

"I slid into Lake Michigan alongside his bloody corpse!"

A real conversation stopper. After an awkward silence, Dr. David asked the officer if he and Deely were free to go. Curdy seemed surprised to notice they were still here. Deely asked me if I would like them to check on Velcro.

"Forget about him," I said. "The splints are in place, and he's secured on my bed. If you wake him, he'll just start howling."

The cop arched an eyebrow. "I'm going to need the exact spelling of your name. And also your address."

After I gave Officer Curdy that information, he asked Jeb to autograph a CD. Jeb's always more than happy to do that, and I'm always curious to see which of Jeb's money-losing CDs someone actually bought. Curdy had Jeb's Celtic CD in his cruiser. The cop promised to come hear Jeb play on his next night off.

"See? Told ya I have a following." Jeb winked at me after Curdy left. "*Animal Lullabies* is going to make me a star."

"Sorry we're late," Fenton announced. "Whiskey and I had so much fun together we lost track of time."

"Whiskey's like that," Jeb replied. "She and I used to lose track of whole weeks together."

I changed the subject. "Who called the cop?"

Jeb said that Dr. David spotted Gil in the lounge and slipped out to the lobby to phone Jenx, who explained they were way outside her jurisdiction.

"She called the Grand Rapids police, and Curdy came. But Gil must have got a whiff something was up. I thought for sure I could keep him in his seat if I sang 'Brian Wilson' or 'One Week'—"

"You played Barenaked Ladies for Gil Gruen?" I said.

"I would have played 'em for you, but you weren't here. Gil slipped out the rear. Dr. David wasn't fast enough to follow him. And the cop got here too late."

Jeb excused himself to prepare for his last set of the evening. Then another cop arrived, in a perfect storm of electromagnetic superconductivity. We were still outside, under the Holiday Inn portico, when the mercury-vapor security lights flickered. Then the headlights of at least fifty parked cars flashed, and their horns and alarms blared. Although it seemed like a scene from the Twilight Zone, it was only Police Chief Jenx.

Her magnetism was the stuff of local lore. Our hometown was reputedly built over a powerful geomagnetic field, which she involuntarily channeled. Either that field was forty miles wider than we had thought or Jenx was potent enough to make it portable. When riled, she could redirect energy to short-circuit a room, a parking lot, or maybe even the south side of Grand Rapids.

Jeb, Fenton, and I jumped back as her cruiser screeched to a halt—siren wailing, flasher pulsing. Wide-eyed, she emerged and lurched toward us. When she drew close, I noticed with a start that horns, lights, siren, and flasher all pulsed in rhythm with an artery in her neck.

"This is way out of your jurisdiction," I reminded her. "And Gil's long gone. I mean the guy who's *not* Gil but looks like him."

"This isn't about Gil," Jenx wheezed. "We got enough Gil sightings of our own. Why would I drive forty miles for one more?"

I had no idea.

"I'm riled about Twyla," Jenx said. "Coroner's report came in. She didn't drown. Somebody strangled her and tried to make us think the riptide did it!"

TWENTY

"TWYLA WAS *MURDERED?*" I said.

Jenx nodded, wheezing hard. "Bruises on her head and neck. Broken blood vessels in her eyes. No water in her lungs."

I couldn't find my voice to ask the next question: *Does that mean her kids were murdered, too?*

Lights flashed. Horns blared. A siren howled. I was about to lose my two-hundred-dollar Rigi dinner.

Placing both hands on her shoulders, Fenton promised Jenx that he could guide her through a series of visualizations to achieve complete serenity. She agreed. The first step in that process was to get rid of me.

"Go inside, Dear," he said. "I'll join you when my work here is done."

I informed him that I was about to puke. "Do you have a visualization to cure that?"

He told me to go to the bar and suck ice. I did; it helped my stomach, if not my head. I couldn't stop thinking about Twyla and her final ordeal. She was last seen talking to two different men near Vanderzee Park. Did one of them do her in? I didn't believe our former mayor existed, and I sure as hell didn't want to believe Chester's driver was a killer. Never mind that Yolanda had seen a man matching his description arguing with Twyla before she left her rented house for the last time.

What was the Twyla-MacArthur connection? Did it involve the shuttle service for children that Chester had mentioned to Deely? What the hell was that?

As for our reappearing dead mayor, one of three things had to be true: Either Gil was alive, Gil was a ghost, or Gil had an identical twin nobody had ever heard of. All three options were impossible. Born and raised in Magnet Springs, Gil had no siblings or cousins; I had personally known him and his family my whole life. He was long-divorced with no children, and his parents were deceased. That's why the whole town wondered about his designated heir. His lawyer sure wasn't talking. And now that the IRS was in town, I wondered what kind of a mess Gil had left.

Before starting his final set, Jeb informed his sparse, bleary-eyed audience that the woman they'd all been waiting for was now in the building.

"I'm pleased to introduce Whitney Houston Halloran Mattimoe, my ex-wife," he said. "Twenty years ago, I gave that woman her nickname, and it stuck. Everybody, say hey to Whiskey!"

There was a slurred chorus of my name, followed by scattered applause. The barkeep looked confused. He probably thought Jeb was buying everybody a round.

Since there was no sign of Fenton, I assumed he was still in the parking lot working on Jenx's serenity. So much for the rest of our date. I ordered a glass of seltzer to go with my chipped ice.

Jeb was in fine form, although his playlist of "Oldies but Goodies" turned out to be more good than old. This set consisted entirely of songs from our touring days—in other words, the 1990s. Ever the chameleon, Jeb executed graceful covers of tunes by Seal, Blues Traveler, and the Dave Matthews Band. Pleasant memories for me, but not too pleasant since he fortunately omitted "Barenaked Ladies."

"And now I'd like to make a request on behalf of that liquor-named lady who's here tonight," Jeb announced. "She was with me on the road when those tunes were new. But now she's with somebody else—"

"No, she's not," shouted a drunk at the bar. "She's all alone! Hey, baby!"

Jeb said, "Whiskey missed my earlier cover of 'Call and Answer,' which used to be our make-up song. So I'd like to play it for her now as I close out the evening. Thank you, everybody, for coming tonight!"

As he strummed the opening chords, Jeb leaned into his microphone and said, "Whiskey, you know it's true. . . ."

That was when Jenx and Fenton joined me. Jenx looked completely relaxed, which was more than I could say for Fenton. He and Jeb locked eyes.

"Fenton's amazing," Jenx whispered to me. "I'm gonna buy all his books."

Jeb was amazing, too. He dazzled his audience with five minutes' worth of closing guitar riffs. When the song finally ended, everybody clapped, Fenton included. In fact, he clapped the longest and loudest. Either it was about karmic balance, or he really liked the way Jeb played BNL.

To Jenx, I said, "The guy who looks like Gil is your leading suspect in Twyla's murder. Right?"

Jenx said she couldn't comment on an ongoing investigation.

"Since when? You drafted me as deputy, remember?"

"Oh yeah." Jenx glanced around the room. I followed her gaze. Most patrons were busy ordering last call or settling their checks. A few were buying CDs from Jeb.

"At this point, we're focusing on the cleaner and the mayor," Jenx whispered.

"You suspect Peg?" I gasped. "I didn't think she even knew Twyla!"

"Our *former* mayor. Gil." Jenx rolled her eyes.

"Isn't the purpose of an investigation to gather facts rather than support suspicions?" Fenton said.

"We follow the evidence," Jenx said. "But Brady only works twenty hours a week, and Roscoe's in a union. So we can't follow it far."

"That's where I come in," I told Fenton. "I work for free."

"Whiskey likes to follow theories, not evidence," Jenx said. "She's no bargain."

Although forty miles and two counties beyond her jurisdiction, Jenx's plan, as she explained it, was to "informally question" a few members of Jeb's audience about the guy who looked like Gil.

I was skeptical. "You're in uniform, and you're carrying your service revolver. You'll scare the crap out of people."

"Watch this," she said, waving to a couple headed for the door. "Yo! Could I ask you guys something?"

To my surprise the couple smiled and came toward her.

"Jenx has the gift of an open heart and mind," Fenton observed.

"That sounds like a psychic reading," I joked.

For the first time since arriving at the Holiday Inn, Fenton grinned at me. "Want to hear my psychic reading of you, Dear?"

"Sure."

"You're in love with your ex-husband."

I recoiled in dismay. "Am not!"

"Yes, you are, Dear. You're as married to Jeb as I am to Noonan."

I shook my head. "Big difference: we got a divorce!"

"A mere formality. Noonan and I will divorce, too. Legally. But in spirit she will remain my *permanent spouse*, just as Jeb is yours."

"I went and got another spouse!" I reminded Fenton. "His name was Leo Mattimoe, and he was the love of my life!"

"Leo was a *transition relationship*," Fenton said. "An emotional and intellectual interlude."

"Interlude, my ass! Leo was my soulmate!"

I said that way louder than necessary. Jeb glanced up from his CD sales.

"I loved Leo the way you loved Noonan," I hissed at Fenton.

He shook his head. "You've confused shock of loss with depth of love. A natural error. Of course you loved Leo, and he was necessary to your personal evolution. But Jeb is your emotional compass, just as Noonan is mine."

Before I could raise another objection, Fenton added, "Here's the rest of your psychic reading, Dear. You tend to assume you have all the facts, while overlooking both the obvious and the inevitable."

"That's Whiskey," quipped my ex-husband, sliding into Jenx's abandoned chair. "Relentless as a riptide. How'd you like my last number?"

I was too rattled to answer. If I'd had Jenx's magnetism, Jeb's electronic equipment would have been arcing all over the stage. Fenton complimented Jeb's music in a way that suggested he actually knew something about music. It turned out that he did. Once upon a time, Fenton had been a music major. He still played jazz piano whenever he got the chance.

"Man, I wish I'd known that," Jeb said. "I would have asked you to sit in."

The conversation turned to when and what they could play together. Magnetic or not, I thought my head might explode. Were Jeb and Fenton rivals or brand-new buds? And what the hell was that nonsense about "permanent spouses"? Did Fenton want to have sex with me or not?

Excusing myself—not that they were listening—I left Jeb and Fenton to offer Jenx my volunteer services. She was now talking with no fewer than six lounge patrons, all of whom looked happy to help. Jenx ignored my arrival, so I pulled up a chair and just listened.

Our police chief was keeping the conversation light by assuring everyone that their comments were "off the record." Her notepad was nowhere in sight. All three couples had seen the man who looked like Gil Gruen. I shivered at their descriptions of his cowboy clothing, which was the main reason they'd noticed him.

Grand Rapids was a long way from Dallas. Maybe the guy in the Holiday Inn lounge was a tourist.

Jenx thanked folks for sharing their observations and wished them a safe trip home. As soon as they left, she whipped out her notebook and pen and wrote furiously.

"Gotta get this down before I forget," she muttered.

A glance back at my table confirmed that Fenton and Jeb didn't miss me. Jeb must have ordered a beer for himself and a diet cola for Fenton. They were laughing and talking. I'd spent enough years on the road to recognize male musicians in bonding mode.

Jenx stuffed her notepad back in her pocket and announced she was ready to check out the perimeter, cop talk for going outside. Since my "permanent spouse" and my date wouldn't miss me, I tagged along.

"One couple spotted Gil when they pulled into the parking lot," Jenx reported. "He was looking in car windows, like he was checking out things to steal. When the guy started toward him, Gil took off fast. Not running, but moving like he had somewhere to go. A while later, he showed up in the bar. He paid close attention to Jeb—but he didn't stay long."

It irked me to hear Jenx of all people call the mystery man Gil. "Talk about theories before evidence! You got zero proof, yet you assume it's him!"

Jenx explained that she was using the official Magnet Springs PD code name for the as-yet unnamed man who resembled our presumed-dead mayor. "GIL" was an acronym for Gone In (the) Lake.

I suggested that "GITL" would be better, but Jenx said it sounded like a character from *Fiddler on the Roof.* I countered by asking how the hell anyone who heard the term "GIL" could tell whether she meant the mystery man or our former mayor.

"Only you would assume GIL means Original Gil," Jenx said. "He has an acronym, too: O-Gil."

I told her that sounded like non-alcoholic beer. To which she replied that I was too stubborn to be a good deputy. Maybe Jenx and Jeb were right. Maybe Fenton's psychic reading was more accurate than I wanted to believe. But not the part about Leo. Or the part about Jeb. No way.

Flashing on Fenton made me think about his missing dog. I asked Jenx if she'd told him about Chester's "interview" with Abra.

"Does Fenton know that Norman might have drowned?"

"We don't make assumptions, remember? Just cuz Abra stopped 'talking' about Norman doesn't mean the dog's dead!"

True, Abra had the attention span of a flea. Norman might well have reappeared later, and she forgot to mention it. Or chose not to. Or maybe Chester got the story all wrong.

"Kids love dogs," I ventured. "There could be a connection between Twyla's kids and Norman. They're all missing."

Jenx wanted to hear what I had to say.

TWENTY-ONE

I DIDN'T HAVE ANYTHING solid enough to be a theory, let alone a trail of evidence. All I knew from my time spent around Chester was that dogs attracted kids the way shiny trinkets attracted Abra. They had to have 'em. Or at least touch them. Thinking aloud, I wondered if a dog—not necessarily Norman—might have lured Twyla's kids away.

"Like the Pied Piper of Hamlet?" Jenx asked.

I was reasonably sure Shakespeare hadn't written that one. The question was whether a dog—by accident or training—might have convinced Twyla's kids to come with him. Or her. Experience had taught Jenx to immediately suspect my dog.

"For the sake of argument, let's say Abra led them astray. Where would she take them?" the chief wondered.

Abra didn't look guilty this time, at least not to me. For once, I actually knew where she was: at home in her room at Vestige. Norman was the one we couldn't find. Better that he was in big trouble than that he was belly-up in Lake Michigan.

"Hey, that's the guy who saw GIL in the parking lot," Jenx said, pointing across the lot to a man opening a car door for his partner. "Let's see if he can show us where GIL was."

Once again Jenx managed not to alarm the nice people—no easy feat when you're in uniform, running toward somebody, yelling. But then Jenx has a nice smile. In fact, the couple remembered exactly where they'd seen GIL and pointed to the far side of the lot.

"He was especially interested in one particular vehicle," the wife recalled. "It's gone now, but there was an ambulance over there. Not a real ambulance. It was a clown car or something."

Jenx said, "Can you describe it?"

"A big old yellow and white striped thing. The sides said Animal Ambulance. Had to be a joke. Or maybe a pet-grooming service."

"It's a joke," I assured her, although Fleggers had no sense of humor.

After the helpful couple pulled away, Jenx said, "I'm thinking maybe GIL was only interested in the Animal Ambulance. He had a history with Dr. David."

True enough. Dr. David had detested O-Gil, and not just because O-Gil was an asshole. The two had a long-standing lease dispute. More important, they disagreed about how to handle vermin. The vet repeatedly blocked the mayor's attempts to poison stray cats that lurked on his properties.

"Looks like the show moved to the parking lot!"

Jeb's cheerful voice rang out. We turned to see my ex-husband and my date striding in our direction.

Although the parking lot was dim except directly under the security lights, I could see well enough to physically compare the two men. Fenton was taller and broader, with better posture. Jeb had a relaxed, shambling style—almost the same as when we were teens. I could have been watching him cross the Magnet Springs High School parking lot after a night football game. To my chagrin, that memory quickened my heart—and a certain other body part.

When they reached us, Jenx announced that she was going back inside to chat with a few hotel employees, just in case they'd seen anything useful. Jeb offered to tag along and play volunteer deputy since he already knew some of the staff.

To Fenton, Jeb said, "We'll talk about that set later."

That left me and the New Age guru under the lights alone. Fenton used his cell phone to summon the Town Car, which quickly pulled up beside us. Where had the driver been while Jenx and I were checking out the perimeter? I reminded myself that most drivers are just drivers. When they're not needed, they probably take a nap or phone their girlfriends or listen to a game.

I declined Fenton's offer of a nightcap from the Town Car bar. We had forty miles to go before dealing with the "Do we sleep together tonight?" question, and I wanted my wits about me. Between the latest appearance of GIL, the revelation of Twyla's murder, and Jenx's magnetic fit, I was rattled. Add to that the déjà vu BNL lounge experience with Jeb, plus Fenton's psychic reading.

When anxious, I like to talk about real estate. It settles my nerves by reminding me I'm good at something. So I ran down the list of Druin's outstanding features, concluding that it had all the elements of a world-class retreat.

"I'm sure it does, Dear," Fenton drawled. "But I may be more interested in a place to live than a place to work. Let's just leave tomorrow for tomorrow." And he slipped an arm around my shoulders.

"Okay, except that, technically, today is already tomorrow. It's after midnight."

"Shhhh," he whispered, and the next thing I knew we were kissing.

This was anything but the chaste good-night peck he'd given me after our dinner at Mother Tucker's. This was a long, deep caress of the tongue. Not too hard, not too fast, not too wet. Just right. Oh, so right. He tickled and teased the inside of my mouth in a way that was almost musical. Like an instrument he played me. And I happily played along. Our duet progressed, involving more body parts and more crescendos. Fenton stroked my face, my hair, my arms, my thighs ... If this was kissing, I had never been kissed before.

Time flies when you're doing it right. Apparently, we kissed for forty miles. When the Town Car pulled to a stop in my driveway, I couldn't believe we were back at Vestige. Discreetly, the driver allowed us a few moments to compose ourselves. I had to disentangle my limbs from Fenton's and rearrange my clothing, which was wildly askew and, in some cases, scattered.

"Dear, may I have the honor of your company all night long?" Fenton said.

"Yes, Dear," I said, repressing the urge to say, "Yes, yes, yes, yes!!!"

I don't remember traveling from the back seat of the Town Car through the front door of Vestige, but we did. And then reality announced itself, in two distinct voices.

First, Abra bounded down the stairs from her room, loudly reminding me that she needed to be fed. She also needed to be exercised, but she could do that herself by exiting through the doggie-door.

Second, Velcro woke up. This was more traumatic, especially for Fenton. When the dog set up his panicked, high-pitched wail, my date covered his ears. Fenton explained that his hearing was painfully sensitive in that upper range.

"What on earth is making those sounds?" he demanded.

When I told him, he couldn't believe it was a canine. Fenton had never met a miniature. Palms pressed to his ears, he squinted at Velcro as I dashed by with the crate.

"Why would anyone breed something like that?" he muttered.

Outside in the exercise pen, I tipped the crate, but Velcro didn't want to leave it. Finally, I succeeded in shaking him out. The plan was to have him do his business on the ground, where god intended. Unfortunately, he had already done some of it in the crate. So I had to clean that—as well as his feet, his splints, and his tiny bottom, too. Another wave of nausea for me.

Not that I blamed the little guy for his limited body-function control. After all, I'd been gone more than six hours. How I longed for the cleaner and that manly way he had with liquid spray and a box of baby wipes…

Speaking of babies, I didn't need to check the nursery to know that Leah, Leo, and their mother were still out. Now that I was used to the twins' presence at Vestige—although I would never grow accustomed to Avery's—the house took on a hollow quality when they were gone. My stepdaughter was apparently still enjoying Family Night Out, ferried by a driver. If the driver was Rupert's cleaner, was he doubling as diaper changer? I couldn't see him as a nanny, but I knew he had at least a few of the necessary skills. The real question would be how did Avery get mixed up with Rupert? And when?

Before I wiped down Velcro and crate in the laundry room, I checked on Fenton. He was perusing my book collection in the library-slash-bar, which used to be Leo's home office. After my husband's sudden death, I had closed up that room. Months passed. Finally, Odette convinced me that I was foolishly letting good square footage go to waste; she suggested a decorator who handsomely converted the space. Sometimes I swore I could still smell Leo in there, fresh coat of paint and new furniture notwithstanding. At least I could now use the room without being daily reminded that my late husband never again would. Odette's "wasted square footage" argument was probably her way of helping me heal.

I had kept most of Leo's books, and Fenton was skimming one now—a slim maroon volume, whose title was something about real estate investment. A sign he was seriously considering Druin? I hoped so. Alas, however, the romantic mood we'd arrived with had evaporated. Fenton barely acknowledged my presence when I explained that I'd need a few more minutes to settle Velcro. In case he couldn't hear me over the persistent yowling from the laundry room down the hall, I slipped off my linen jacket and checked my black lace camisole. Yup. Still as low-cut as I remembered. Hip-rolling my way right up to Fenton, I threw my shoulders back and offered him the best view in the house. He ignored me.

"Diet cola, tea, or me?" I whispered.

Without glancing up from the page, he said, "Dear, that little dog is a mood buster. He's given me a headache, which doesn't bode well for the rest of the night."

I promised to deal with it. After cleaning and re-crating the teacup dog, I had to decide where to stash him. Dr. David had said Velcro needed to be close to me, or close to my personal things. Surely not while I was making love, if making love was still possible. Surely Velcro could be at the other end of the house while that was going on.

No such luck. No matter where I set up a boom box playing *Animal Lullabies*, the shitzapoo yowled miserably. Then I had a brainstorm: I remembered hearing somebody once say that dogs love the dirty underwear of the people they love. Rummaging around my clothes hamper, I came up with my slightly stinky back-up camisole. What the hell. I stuffed it in the crate. Velcro's cries morphed into whimpers of delight. But he was still making nonstop noise. Nothing silenced the little beast . . . until I returned him to my bedroom. Once there, he sighed audibly and thumped his tail against the walls of his crate. The teacup dog had come home.

How would I break the news to Fenton?

"Dear—the shitzapoo will be joining us in the boudoir."

That wouldn't work. Then I had a brainstorm. The man was a spiritual healer. Perhaps he himself was the solution to our dilemma.

"Dear," I began, "you're a pioneer in the field of emotional enlightenment. Have you ever, by chance, guided...an *animal* through visualization to *serenity*? Like you did tonight with Jenx?"

Fenton put down the real estate investment book.

"Dear," he said, sounding none too fond of me, "surely you're not asking me to use my training on that ill-conceived little creature? I did not publish nine books, five of them best-sellers, about personal enlightenment so that I could offer talk-therapy to a dog!"

"Of course you didn't! Dear! The thing is...I'm not sure we'll have a moment's peace if you don't try. In fact, I'm sure we won't. And I really would like to make love with you tonight."

I offered the view of my cleavage again, which didn't seem to tempt Fenton. Was it a PhD issue? Or a Texas issue? Or was it entirely the fault of my headache-inducing dog?

Fenton sighed. "What the hell. You make me hot when you beg."

He excused himself to hold a mini-session with the micropooch. I retrieved the real estate investment handbook that had interested Fenton so much. The title turned out to be *Real Estate: It's an Emotional Investment, Too.* I read the opening sentences:

> A successful real estate investment goes far beyond a financial commitment. It requires the investor to enter into a potentially deep and enduring *emotional* compact with the land and the structures built upon it. Some otherwise qualified investors are rightfully deterred from real estate because they cannot process emotions.

The good news for Mattimoe Realty was that Fenton Flagg was all about processing emotions. The bad news for me, personally, was … that Fenton Flagg was all about processing emotions. I for one believed in stuffing emotions—my own and everybody else's. It hadn't deterred me from doing well in real estate, probably because I balanced my corporate karma with Odette, who didn't give a shit, and Tina Breen, the most emotional person on the planet.

The most emotional person in the house was back in my library-slash-bar with the news that he'd done what he could for "that pathetic puddle of a dog."

"May I remind you, Dear, that I'm an internationally esteemed therapist who specializes in facilitating the spiritual evolution of highly advanced beings. That *shitzapoo* has a brain the size of an almond. He was probably a Doberman in his last life and may well be a Persian cat in his next. In other words, he is not what I have spent four lives learning to counsel."

"*Four* lives …?"

"Three before this one," Fenton said. "I was a starving seamstress in sixteenth-century London, a runaway slave in nineteenth-century Virginia, and Teddy Roosevelt. My memories of being TR cause me pain. That's why, in this life, I'm a therapist."

Fenton stared down my cleavage. "The tiny mutant dog is quiet, and I am hard. What do you say, Dear? Shall we adjourn to the boudoir?"

Why not? I had never gone to bed with Teddy Roosevelt.

TWENTY-TWO

I'M NO EXPERT ON either American history or New Age jargon, but it seemed to me that Fenton had a lot of Teddy Roosevelt *residue*. TR, as he was famously called, exuded masculine vigor. However, I doubt that TR could have out-performed Fenton if faced with a shitzapoo in bed.

I had positioned Velcro's crate on the floor near my bathroom, not far from the boom box that was playing *Animal Lullabies* on an endless loop. The little dog was still blissfully silent when Fenton and I entered, kissing.

Fenton froze. "Is that Jeb singing?"

I tried to explain the efficacy of the Fleggers-produced CD, but Fenton clicked it off.

"Surely, Dear, you can see that it's bad karma for us to make love while your permanent spouse sings—"

To be honest, I had lost track of what was good or bad karma. The only thing I knew for sure was that Fenton and I were hot and bothered and in need of immediate sexual release. Velcro also needed some kind of release. He howled.

Fenton covered his ears. "That runt-dog must have a past-life agenda! Maybe TR shot him on the plains of Africa."

"Maybe you could try another guided visualization?"

"They're not like aspirin, Dear. You can't just double the dosage!"

I had no idea why not. Clearly, our passionate night was doomed unless we soothed Velcro. Dr. David had said that the only way to calm his anxiety was to keep him close to me and my things. What would be closer than in bed with me? Reluctantly, I picked up the crate and set it at the end of the bed. Velcro's yowls faded to a bleating whimper. Fenton removed his hands from his ears.

"You can't be serious. A dog in our bed?"

"He's in a box," I pointed out. "And it's a big bed. You won't even know he's there."

That was almost true until Fenton and I started shaking the bed. Velcro got seasick and barfed noisily.

"Ignore it," Fenton said, aware that I was gagging, too. I'm suggestible that way; I can't help catching someone else's nausea. Fenton pulled me on top of him. That would have been erotic if Velcro's crate hadn't tumbled to the floor. The teacup dog shrieked as if shattered.

"His patella luxation!" I cried, launching myself toward the end of the bed. The shitzapoo sustained his agonizing yowl like a blast on a soprano sax. Hanging upside down, I peered into his bright, frightened eyes. He blinked at me, relieved to see that I cared.

"I know what we need to do for itty-bitty you," I heard my-self say in the Betty Boop voice usually reserved for my stepgrand-babies. "We need to make you feel oh-so-safe."

"Are you kidding?" Fenton said.

He sounded far away because by then I had slid to the floor. Velcro had finally gotten to me, setting off whatever latent ma-ternal instincts I had. Maybe he reminded me of Chester: small, smart, vulnerable.

Next thing I knew, I was holding Velcro, wrapped in my smelly camisole. Yeah, that part was *oogy*, but the little dog insisted on it. Together we snuggled against Fenton's broad chest.

"I'll just hold him till he falls asleep. Okay? Dear?" I whispered. But Fenton was already asleep.

———

At some point, I was aware that Fenton got out of bed and took a shower. Probably not a cold shower because nothing was happen-ing with Velcro between us. I fell asleep and dreamed that I was holding a teddy bear while sharing my bed with Teddy Roosevelt. TR called me "Dear" as he lectured about emotional investments in real estate.

I awoke because Abra was howling. Afghan hounds rarely make much of a racket, but when they do, the ghostly *arrrrhooo* prickles the spine.

"Someone's outside…." I whispered to Fenton. The last time I'd heard Abra make that sound, there had been an intruder.

Fenton rolled toward me. "Is that dog wearing your camisole?"

The shitzapoo had managed to get *inside* my lingerie. He was so content that even Abra's howling didn't disturb him.

"Let me channel TR and do what needs to be done," Fenton said. As he heaved himself out of bed, Velcro kissed—I mean—licked me. On the mouth.

"I'm coming with you, Dear," I announced and dumped the dog back into his carrier. To my amazement, he wasn't whining. Yet. The time was 3:42.

I grabbed my robe and trailed Fenton, who had a bath towel wrapped around his waist. We found Abra in front of the picture window facing Lake Michigan. Frantically she leapt from chair to sofa and back again, using every vantage point to view what was out there.

A shadowy figure, bent in a modified crouch, broke from the cover of my lilac grove and dashed toward Leo's detached workshop. For an instant I thought Abra would crash through the glass after him. Even in silhouette, the man was distinctly Gil Gruen. Clad in a cowboy hat and boots, O-Gil's outline was crisp against the full moon hanging low over the lake. Suddenly my powers of denial were of no use at all.

"It's like when your music teacher came back from the dead!" I hissed.

"It's Norman!" Fenton cried as a large, graceful retriever bounded across my lawn from the direction the shadowy man had just headed.

The Golden hadn't drowned after all.

With Abra leaping straight up and down at his side, Fenton flipped the lock on my patio door. Man and Affie flew through the portal into the night. Abra whooped for joy as Fenton called his dog's name.

That left me standing all alone, wondering what was up. Theoretically, I had a trespasser. I also had one large Texan and two large dogs to protect my property.

Dialing 9-1-1 seemed like a good idea. I gave my name and address and said simply that I had a trespasser—a male of indeterminate age wearing a cowboy hat and boots.

"Gil Gruen?" the dispatcher asked.

"Not O-Gil but probably GIL, as in Gone In (the) Lake. I'm a deputy so I know the code. Could you send somebody over?"

"Probably not," she said. "There are Gil Gruen sightings all over the county. If I were you, I'd lock the doors and go back to bed."

I couldn't lock the doors until Fenton returned. Of course, I was relieved that Norman was back, especially since Abra was the reason he'd vanished. But I still had a prowler. Who was GIL and what was he doing at Vestige? Was it a coincidence that Norman had arrived at the same time?

I decided to turn my home into a giant beacon. First, I switched on every outdoor light—yard, deck, and driveway lamps included. Then I dashed through the house, flicking on light switches in every room. Soon all my windows glowed.

My hope was that Fenton would see the light and hurry back in, and GIL would see it, too, and run for his life. Unfortunately, the illumination bounced back off the glass, making it impossible for me to see out. An invading army could have landed at my dock and made its way up the bluff. I wouldn't have had a clue. That was why, when the phone rang, I yelped, which set off Velcro's alarm. From my bedroom he howled worriedly.

Jenx was calling. "*Who* did you see in your yard, Whiskey?" She was taunting me.

"GIL. As in GITL, not O-Gil," I snapped. "I also saw Norman the Golden."

I could only hope that he and Abra would not run off again. Counting the occasion of Prince Harry's conception and their subsequent two sprees, Norman had been AWOL about a week. No more paid vacation. Back to work he must go.

Jenx announced that she had another reason for calling; there was news about Twyla's kids.

"Did you find them?"

"Not yet. But they're not Twyla's kids. Not even the two she started with."

Jenx explained that her background check on Twyla had revealed no living relatives. Including children, sisters, nieces, or nephews.

"Then whose kids—?"

"Let me finish," Jenx said. "Twyla used to have a Hispanic boyfriend. Name: Efrén Padilla. His last-known address: Chicago."

"Are you suggesting Twyla's ex has eleven kids, and she was taking care of them?"

"Nope. I'm suggesting you didn't know much about your tenant. Also, her ex might be the guy Yolanda saw. I'm following the evidence, Whiskey. You might want to do the same."

"I'm a realtor. I get paid to follow qualified leads."

My doorbell rang. Jenx heard it, too. "Expecting company at 4:15 in the morning?"

"I'm popular," I said and hung up.

Because I'd turned on every light, my front porch was fully illuminated. Through the peephole, I expected to see Fenton with Norman. And maybe Abra, too. Instead I saw only Jeb Halloran.

"What the hell are you doing here?" I said.

"Good morning to you, too. By the way, your robe's on inside-out."

So it was.

"May I help you with that?" he offered.

I declined. Jeb was still wearing the T-shirt and jeans he'd performed in. Grinning, he looked awfully fine for someone who hadn't yet been to bed. Much better than I must have looked with bed-head and an inside-out robe.

"All these lights are attracting every moth in Michigan," Jeb said. "I was driving past and wondered if you were in trouble."

"I'm fine."

Jeb cocked his head, listening to Velcro's cries. "Well, as long as I'm here, how about a bonus lullaby for the little guy—and his mommy?"

I yawned. "You run along and sleep tight. In your own bed. Alone." When I tried to close the door, Jeb blocked it.

"Whiskey, I just saw Gil in your driveway—and Fenton chasing two dogs into the woods. Gil ran toward the lake. I'm going after him. If I'm not back in fifteen minutes, call Jenx."

TWENTY-THREE

"No way you're chasing GIL without me. It's my property, and I'm a volunteer deputy! I can be decent in two minutes or less!"

I was already dashing toward my bedroom. Behind me on the front porch I heard Jeb sigh.

I went for the clothes I could find the fastest—which were in my laundry hamper, where I'd recently found the camisole for Velcro. He stopped crying the instant I entered my bedroom. As I tore through my dirty clothes, I heard his little tail thump hopefully. No doubt he craved another smelly undergarment.

Pulling a rumpled T-shirt over my head and stepping into old running shorts, I tried not to catch a whiff of myself. On the floor near my bed, I found a pair of shoes I wouldn't have to tie because they closed with—you guessed it—Velcro, the miracle fastener. Coincidence?

"See ya," I told the dog by that name and jogged down the hall. When he let loose a heart-breaking howl, I just couldn't take it.

After all, I now knew how to ease his pain. I spun around, ran back into the bedroom, grabbed panties from the hamper, and stuffed them through the grate in his box.

"New perfume?" Jeb joked as we hustled toward the lake. "Don't tell me your week-old sweat turns Fenton on."

"Okay. I won't tell you."

We paused on the highest of the three connected cedar decks that Leo had built. They were lighted, as was the long dock below; tasteful security lamps oozed a yellow glow onto my beach and a tiny portion of Lake Michigan. There were no humans or dogs in sight. I couldn't hear anyone either, just scattered pre-dawn bird-songs and the faint lapping of water on sand. It was a mild, still night about to roll over into a dewy morn. The air was fresh and tangy. Or maybe I was tangy. Cautiously I sniffed my shoulder. Oh yeah, that was me.

"Jeb, do you think it's a coincidence that GIL showed up at the same time Norman did?"

"I'm from Magnet Springs. Our people don't believe in coincidences."

He was right. And a witness had said that GIL was fascinated by the Animal Ambulance. Maybe there was a Fleggers connection.

"GIL, Fenton, Norman, and Abra were here," Jeb mused. "And now they're gone."

"Avery and the twins are gone, too," I told him. "On a date. A driver picked them up, and they never came home!"

"They haven't come home *yet*," Jeb corrected me. "Think of all the nights you didn't go home to Mama."

"I'm not Avery's 'Mama,' and I didn't haul twins around on my nights out."

Jeb feigned a shocked expression. "I didn't even know you had twins!"

When I swung at him, he winced. "Try keeping your arms at your sides. Or go change your shirt."

I figured that GIL had most likely circled back toward the road. Or toward wherever he'd stashed his vehicle—although as far as I knew, no one had seen GIL in a vehicle.

Jeb's cell phone rang; he made a few monosyllabic replies and ended the call.

"That was for you," he said.

"Then why didn't you give it to me?"

"Jenx didn't want to talk to you, she just wanted you to know something: earlier tonight a man fitting GIL's description was seen hitchhiking along Coastal Highway. And guess what?"

I shrugged.

"The guy had a Golden."

So maybe GIL had found Norman and brought him here. How or why, I didn't know. Jeb was willing to help me look for a trail of evidence. He jogged back to his Van Wagon and found a high-beam flashlight. Now we could see what we were doing once we wandered beyond the range of my security lamps.

I was convinced that Abra had seen, heard, or stolen something. For my sake as well as Fenton's, I hoped she hadn't re-nabbed Norman. If she had, I probably owed Fenton a new companion dog—an Abra-proof canine he could count on every day of his life, even if he lived within Abra range.

I hoped that Fenton might decide to live around here, at least part of the year. Granted, his New Age talk put me off. But we did sizzle. Last night had been white-fire hot … till Velcro crashed the party. If we could get beyond the past lives and "permanent spouses"—and keep the teacup dog happy with my old underwear—we could have fun.

Jeb and I made our way toward Leo's old workshop, a detached building the approximate size of a one-car garage. I let Jeb hold the flashlight as I pushed open the not-quite-closed door. That was not as ominous as it sounds; the door never latched. It was one of those things I kept meaning to ask Roy Vickers to fix. Reaching around the door frame, I groped for the switch. When I flipped it, nothing happened.

"Damn," I muttered. "The overhead light's burned out. I forgot about it."

Jeb played his beam over the entire interior and behind the door, too. "GIL's long gone, Whiskey. You're more likely to find your dog."

I didn't want to find GIL. And Abra was welcome only if she returned Norman. I insisted we check my attached garage, which I rarely locked, and the tumble-down barn built back in the day when Vestige was part of a farm. In both places Jeb's beam uncovered only what belonged.

"Now can we call it a night?" he said. "And take a shower together?"

I grabbed Jeb's flashlight and jogged toward the treeline, where my mowed lawn gave way to several acres of hardwoods. I knew my ex-husband would follow, and not just because I had his light. But in the end it wasn't what we saw that mattered. It was what we heard: the insistent bark of a dog coming not from the woods in front of us but rather from behind us. From the direction of the

Castle. Running toward us were Prince Harry, the Pee Master, and his master, Chester.

"What on earth are you doing up at this hour?" I said, shining Jeb's light in their little faces. The beam bounced off Chester's round glasses, and made Prince Harry's eyes glow greenish-red.

"Lower the light, please," Chester said, shading his face. "We're on your side!"

He and Jeb high-fived each other (technically, it was a low-five for Jeb), and then Prince Harry tried to high-five both Chester and Jeb. I repeated my question.

"Prince Harry woke me up because he had to pee!" Chester exclaimed. "That's progress. And when we went outside, I saw the lights on at Vestige. It looked like an emergency, so we came to help."

I made the responsible adult decision not to tell Chester about GIL. No point alarming a child about a trespasser, especially one who looked like a dead man. Instead, I reported that Norman had come back and then bounded off into the woods with Abra.

"Is Fenton with them?" Chester asked.

I didn't know if I had the energy to explain why Fenton would be at Vestige in the middle of the night. It might make me look like, well, like one of Chester's parents.

So I simply said, "Why do you ask?"

"Because there he is!" Chester pointed past us.

I whirled about, and the flashlight whirled with me, revealing Fenton—in full frontal nudity. Apparently, he'd dropped his towel. I hadn't realized how spectacularly well-endowed he was. We hadn't gotten that far. Silently I vowed never to let the shitzapoo foil another night of love-making. Who knew Teddy Roosevelt was hung like a horse?

"You all right?" I heard Jeb ask Fenton.

"Yeah," he panted. "But I lost both dogs."

Remembering my role as hostess, I said, "I didn't really want Abra back."

But Fenton wanted his dog back. Needed him, in fact. He was disconsolate. As he stumbled toward us, Jeb said to me, "Can you give the man some light?"

"I am!" I exclaimed, the beam still on Fenton's best feature.

"Lower, Whiskey," Jeb said. "He needs to see the ground."

As our motley crew moved toward my house, Fenton recounted what had happened. "Norman was glad to see me. God knows I was relieved to see him. Then he spotted Abra, and off they went. At first I thought they were chasing the man who looks like your dead mayor. But I saw *him* turn toward the road. Abra and Norman kept going—straight into the woods. I tried to follow them, but I didn't have a light, and I'm not dressed for the terrain."

"The ground's gotta be rough on your bare feet," I agreed.

"The low branches were a bigger problem."

Once inside Fenton trudged upstairs to dress. I stole a look at the other males; Prince Harry was wagging his tail, Jeb was grinning like a court jester, and Chester seemed utterly unfazed. Maybe Rupert strutted naked around the Castle grounds all the time.

"How about I make a pot of coffee?" Chester suggested.

"Whiskey's out of coffee," Jeb said.

Rooting through a low cupboard, Chester came up with a box of loose tea I was sure I'd never bought. Then he located a teapot and infuser I'd never seen.

"A little Earl Grey makes a good eye-opener," he said. "Of course, Whiskey's out of lemons, but I know where she keeps her honey."

"So do I," said Jeb.

TWENTY-FOUR

AFTER FENTON PUT ON his pants, Jeb offered him a ride back to Red Hen's House. Finally I got the shower I needed. By the time I took Velcro outside to do his duty, it was sunrise, and I had learned how to handle him. His extreme separation anxiety required either *Animal Lullabies*, me, or my scent.

If I couldn't have Teddy Roosevelt in bed, I wanted to sleep alone. So I put Velcro in the guest room with the smelly things he loved and collapsed on my own bed. I woke four hours later to the insistent sounds of my doorbell ringing and Velcro yapping. I couldn't blame him for that. Name a dog who doesn't bark when there's someone at the door. With my robe on right-side-out, I hurried downstairs.

Really, I shouldn't have hurried. I probably shouldn't have answered the door at all. It was Dr. David making a house-call. A "house-modification-call," as it turned out. He literally had a shopping cart full of what he called "assisted-living devices." Not crutches, walkers, or bedpans although these were the canine equivalents. Even so, I let him in—probably because I felt guilty about having let Abra run away again. Dr. David was the dog catcher of last resort in our community. I hoped I wouldn't need his help to find her, and she wouldn't cause too much damage. Lately, my life was all about guilt. And karma. Or were they the same thing?

Dr. David told me to go fetch Velcro while he wheeled in his shopping cart. By the time I returned with the teacup dog, the vet had set up an alternate universe in my living room: graduated-height step stools led to and from every piece of furniture a human might sit on. Clearly this was about making my furniture accessible to nonhumans, even those with bad joints. Velcro required no prompting to demonstrate that the devices worked. He beamed at me from the center of my damask couch.

"Even with his splints on, he can scale your sofa!" Dr. David declared.

"And that's a good thing because—?"

"Because little dogs need to get up off the floor! It relieves their anxiety, Whiskey, by making them feel like equals. And here's another tension reliever."

Dr. David fished around among the items remaining in his cart until he came up with a furry white plush toy that vaguely resembled a lamb.

"Velcro, meet Floozy," he said, placing the toy in front of the dog. To my amazement, the dog immediately humped the toy.

"Very good, Velcro!" the vet exclaimed. To me, he said, "Watch him closely."

I couldn't have looked away if I'd tried. Velcro was going at it with such vigor, I was sure he would damage one joint or another. Suddenly he experienced the relief he was seeking. All over Floozy. And my couch.

"Floozy is washable," Dr. David told me.

"How about my couch?"

My doorbell rang again. I half-expected to find Velcro smoking a cigarette when I returned.

Chester was on my front porch, *sans* Prince Harry.

"I'm here to assist Dr. David," he announced.

Doing what, I couldn't imagine. My living room had already been retrofitted, and the toy *ho* was on the job. In the living room, Velcro was sound asleep, his fuzzy black head resting on Floozy's nicely rounded rump.

"See how relaxed he is!" Dr. David remarked.

I gave silent thanks that my young neighbor had missed the show. "You need Chester's help with something?"

"Yes! He's just in time to help me unload the Animal Ambulance and retrofit the rest of your house."

"Say *what*?"

"Don't worry about the cost of all this equipment, Whiskey. Fleggers is happy to lend it to you in exchange for a modest donation."

Dr. David let Chester push the shopping cart out my front door and down the driveway, where they reloaded it. As chagrined as I was by the sight of a second cart full of stair-step devices, at least there was no back-up Floozy. When Chester was out of earshot, I sarcastically thanked Dr. David for not supplying more than one *ho*.

"Psychologically speaking, a dog should have only one bitch," the vet explained. "Even if that bitch is a lamb, and a fake lamb, at that. If you look closely, you'll see that Floozy is proportioned for maximum canine pleasure."

I would never look that closely, and I told Dr. David so.

"It's science, Whiskey. There's nothing to fear."

"Really? How about losing control of one's home? Most people would fear that."

Which made me wonder if part of my household was still AWOL. I excused myself to check.

"Avery and the twins have gone missing!" I breathlessly informed Dr. David. "And Deely never showed up for work!"

"The twins are fine, and so is Avery," he said. "She gave Deely the day off."

He explained that Avery had left Deely a voice mail message that she and the children planned to spend a long weekend with her "new man."

"Who's her new man? And why didn't I get a message?"

Although Dr. David couldn't answer the first question, he had a theory about the second question: "Because she loathes you."

He announced that he and Deely were now planning a long weekend, too. The only thing that could spoil it would be a Fleggers-related crisis. I gulped, realizing that he must not have heard about Abra and Norman.

"Don't worry about Abra and Norman," he added. "Chester's got that covered."

"How?"

"He's a Flegger-in-training. Too young to run the Animal Ambulance, but he's got a professional driver. So Deely and I can take some time off." The vet came as close to smiling as he ever did in the company of humans.

"But Abra and Norman are *missing*," I reminded him.

"What else is new? If they come back, give Chester a call. And if they don't, they probably will ... someday."

With Chester's help, Dr. David finished retro-fitting the rest of my house, including my bedroom. As I stood in the doorway, surveying the stair-step footstools now in place next to my king-size bed, I wondered if I should even bother inviting Fenton back. Teddy Roosevelt had hunted big game on several continents, but he would have run screaming from a scene like this.

When Dr. David cleared his throat, I realized he was waiting for more than my verbal approval.

"Oh. Right. I'll get my checkbook."

"That would be generous of you, Whiskey," he said. "Make it out to Four Legs Good National Headquarters."

Besides the negative impact on my sex life and my bank account, I quickly discovered another drawback to canine-assisted-living: it created an obstacle course for humans. On my way to my home office, I tripped over a stool and fell flat on my face.

"Why does Velcro need access to all my furniture?" I yelped.

The vet sighed as he helped me up. "It's about relieving stress—on his joints and on his mind."

"Let's just hope *my* joints and *my* mind survive the treatment!"

"Treatment?" Dr. David looked puzzled.

"Therapy. Rehab. Whatever you call this temporary set-up." I waved at the array of graduated stools now cluttering my home.

"This is a way of life, Whiskey. Living with the differently-abled always requires a period of adjustment. In time you'll learn to zig-zag your way around."

"Wait, wait, wait!" Finally I had reached the end of my meta-phorical leash. "If I'm going to make a generous donation, it will be for Velcro's permanent relocation!"

Dr. David gaped. "You're not suggesting we find him another home?"

"No. I'm insisting!"

"But—"

"No problem!" a small voice announced. "I'll take Velcro home with me! Prince Harry needs a playmate."

Chester grinned up at us. I hadn't even realized he was listening.

"You're not allowed to have a dog," I reminded him. "Let alone two. Even Prince Harry is illegal."

Not to mention that Velcro had already been expelled from the Castle, which is how I'd gotten him.

"Not a problem," Chester insisted. "I bribe our new house-keeper to help me hide Prince Harry. He lives in my wing. Cassina and Rupert never go there."

"But Velcro has … special needs," I said, choosing my words carefully.

"You mean, bad joints and anxiety issues," Chester said.

"Yes. And he makes a lot of noise. A lot of messes, too."

Chester shrugged. "We all have our issues, Whiskey."

Okay, but my karma was calling. "Chester, I don't feel right about helping you deceive your mother."

"Trust me," Chester said. "Cassina prefers it that way."

Did that include Rupert's extramarital affair? And, possibly, a shady shuttle service for missing children? I had a bad feeling about the whole arrangement ... until I glanced again at the trail of graduated step stools. Who was I to think that Chester's life at the Castle was more dysfunctional than mine? And the kid really did love dogs. I wrote Fleggers a larger check than I'd intended and promised to help Chester with his dogs any way I could.

After the vet left, I retreated to my office to check my calendar. Fenton was due to tour Druin with Odette that afternoon. Assuming Felicia Gould and her security squad cooperated, it could only go better than our date last night.

Chester appeared in my office doorway. "Whiskey, I've been thinking."

"And a fine job you've done of it, too," I said.

"Thank you. Specifically, I've been thinking about Twyla's missing kids. You're worried about them, and so am I."

I didn't like the sound of that. Chester was a born worrier; he didn't need my encouragement. So I assured him that Jenx was on the case.

"Jenx is overworked," Chester said. "But I know a way to find out what happened to Twyla's kids. I'm going undercover on the North Side!"

Chester had cooked up a *Mission Impossible*-type scheme with a little help from Yolanda Brewster, who probably watched too much TV.

"Kids are more likely to talk to other kids than to grownups. I'm pretty sure I'll come home with some clues!"

I tried to imagine Chester blending in anywhere, let alone an ethnically diverse, economically challenged community; i.e., the 'hood. Still, Yolanda knew the territory and the players. If she thought he could pull it off, who was I to say he couldn't?

All he needed was a ride to Amity Avenue. Expectantly, he looked at me.

"You have a driver," I told him.

"My driver is taking his real estate exam," Chester said, "so he can work part-time for you."

Touché. The more I thought about Chester's idea, the more I liked it. He came from theatrical stock, all the better to play-act his way into somebody's confidence. And I was willing to be his round-trip driver *du jour*. While waiting for him, I would investigate Twyla's house. Now that the coroner had ruled her death a murder, the sheriff's evidence team wouldn't be far behind. I wanted to survey the scene before cops impounded what was left of her stuff.

Chester offered to attend to Velcro while I dressed. He explained that Dr. David had acquainted him with "Floozy, the Personal Canine Trainer," and her "unorthodox" ways. Did I believe that Chester had bought the vet's sanitized version of the lamb's biz? I did not. But the very fact that he could pretend to do so for the comfort of hovering adults, confirmed my high opinion of him as a player. I knew Chester would do well undercover.

I was curious about his "costume," however. That navy blue school blazer was sure to raise suspicion. Just kidding; he didn't wear it in the summer. But his Polo wardrobe wouldn't work, either.

"Don't worry, Whiskey. Mrs. B's got me covered."

Yolanda planned to dress Chester in her grandson's clothes, and then slip him out the back door. We didn't talk much during

240

the short ride into town. At Chester's prompting, I pulled into the alley behind Yolanda's house.

"You're absolutely sure you'll be all right on the North Side?"

"I'm sure," Chester said with confidence. "I have my cell phone. And my natural charm."

He grinned broadly, revealing a few missing baby teeth. I promised to keep my phone on, and we wished each other luck. He jumped down from the front seat and threaded his way between trash cans that were almost as tall as he was. I watched him scramble over Yolanda's chain-link fence, thinking that he was pretty tough for a tiny millionaire.

So as to attract minimal attention, I parked my car inside Twyla's garage and pulled the door closed. It seemed like a good place to start my investigation. Except that Twyla hadn't added anything to the garage, as far as I could tell. It appeared to contain only those sundry tools that either I or a previous tenant had left.

The house was another story. Though stripped of children's things, as Roy had reported, it was not what I'd call orderly. Adult personal items—from clothing to cosmetics—were strewn in every room. I found a hairbrush and curling iron on the coffee table, towels on most chairs, a bra between the couch cushions, and nail polish with toe-separators on the stove. The kitchen table was so littered with tabloid magazines and junk-mail flyers, I could barely see the surface. Twyla's shirts and shorts covered the floor like small asymmetrical area rugs. Either she was in the habit of never putting her own stuff away, or she'd been looking for something. Or someone else had.

I was legally within my rights to be here; I owned the place, and my sole tenant was dead. Still, I felt sick with guilt and apprehension.

What exactly had happened to the woman who lived at 254 Amity Avenue? And the unnamed infants and toddlers she'd claimed were hers and her sisters'? The children had been here, briefly, with their laughter, cries, and dirty diapers. Then they were gone. Spirited away, or so it seemed. Removed under cover of darkness while the ever-vigilant Yolanda Brewster caught a few hours' sleep. Standing here now, I felt as if their essence had been "erased." Only faint traces of hairspray, air freshener, and fabric softener lingered in the air. Innocent and unrevealing.

I drifted back to the cluttered kitchen table where I skimmed tabloid headlines about the latest celebrity couplings, breedings, and break-ups. Had Twyla lived vicariously by reading about the rich and famous? Maybe their melodramas made her feel better.

Several of the tabloids were open, pages scattered. I sifted through the loose piles, remembering much too late that Chester had urged me to wear gloves. By now my prints were on several knobs, doors, and assorted papers … mixed with Twyla's and the kids' and whoever else had visited recently.

A detached tabloid page caught my eye. On it something was hand-printed in bright green ink. I imagined Twyla groping for a pen or pencil and finding only a child's water-soluble crayon. The markers had probably been cleared with the children, but Twyla's note remained. In a short article about Internet billionaires she had circled the name "Vivika Major." Next to it she had written "Call García."

TWENTY-FIVE

GARCÍA? AS IN THE security guard at Druin? Could he be the man Yolanda had seen in Twyla's driveway?

Her wall phone was an older model; it didn't display incoming or outgoing numbers. But it did have a "redial" feature, which might connect me to the person Twyla had tried to reach in her last-ever phone call. I punched the button.

Somewhere a phone rang. Once.

"García," a man replied.

Stunned, I realized I had no cover story. No plan for ascertaining whether this was the García at Druin and whether he knew Twyla.

The man said, "Who's calling?"

"Hello," I said. "I'm … trying to reach … Vivika Major—"

"Not at this number," he said and hung up.

What did that mean? That I had the wrong number, or that part of his job was to block unauthorized calls?

If that was the García who worked at Druin, how did Twyla know him? Maybe he was her old boyfriend. Or her new boyfriend. For all I knew, he—and *not* the travel magazine in the dead dentist's office—could have been the reason she moved to Magnet Springs. She hadn't moved in with him, though. And if the García I'd redialed was in fact the García in Vivika Major's employ, he worked twenty miles from here. There were several small communities closer to Druin.

I didn't speak Spanish or know much about Hispanic culture, but I guessed that García was as common a surname as Smith. Thus, I couldn't be 100 percent sure that the García I'd redialed was the one who worked for Vivika Major. Or could I? If I immediately called the security guard, I should be able to tell whether his voice matched the one I'd just heard.

Unlike the outdated wall phone, my cell phone tracked all calls and contained a directory of currently important numbers, including the number for Druin. I would ask the factotum who answered to connect me to García, the security guard.

"Hello," a young man said. "May I ask who is calling?"

I had forgotten the drill and had failed to prepare.

"Hello…" I scanned the tabloids for a name. "This is… Scarlett… Cruise returning a call to García."

I'd quickly blended two names from two different tabloid articles. If I'd learned anything in my first thirty-four years, it was that you can bluster your way through damn near anything. If you act like you know what you're doing, people tend to assume that you do.

The receptionist said, "I'll put you right through, Ms. Cruise, but you might get his voice mail. If that happens, you can leave a message. Or you can hit zero for Operator. That will ring my phone again, and I'll try to find him for you. Okay?"

"Okay," I said. "What's your name, by the way?"

"Ryan."

I thanked Ryan and waited for him to forward my call. It never rang; García's recorded voice announced that he was unable to answer at the present time. Something had changed in less than a minute. That was the same voice I'd just redialed. Only now García was busy. Was something going on? Something as routine as García's lunch hour ... or as troubling as visitors entering Druin? According to my watch, Odette and Fenton should be arriving at the property. Was Felicia Gould still blocking Mattimoe Realty's attempts to bring Vivika Major a qualified buyer? If so, why?

And that brought me back to my original question: What connected Twyla and García? Once I figured that out, I might just know what had happened to almost a dozen unnamed children.

Without a clear plan, I pressed zero for Operator. Ryan answered promptly and asked me to hold while he tried to locate García. Boring instrumental music played in my ear; then call waiting beeped. Odette was on the line.

"Are you with Fenton at Druin?" I said.

"We're at Druin, where we couldn't get out of the car if we wanted to. And trust me, we don't want to."

Hell of an opening line. I listened to the background noise and made a wild guess.

"You've got a problem with a dog?"

"We've got a problem with a *pack* of dogs. They've surrounded my car and won't let us move." Though loud, Odette's voice was calm.

For my benefit, Fenton shouted, "There are at least twenty attack dogs! Rottweilers and Dobermans! We'll have to wait them out."

"I vote for running them over," Odette told me. "Although it would be messy."

"And very bad for our karma," Fenton said. "We'll wait."

I said, "Do you think somebody forgot to secure the kennel?"

"Ha!" Odette said. "I think somebody waited for us to get here and then opened the kennel. And I think you know who."

"Felicia Gould?" I asked.

"With a little help from the not-so-nice man in the security booth," Odette added.

"García?"

"You're good with names, Whiskey. Yes, García made us wait while he placed a couple calls. No doubt one was about opening the kennel for us. Now—what would you like us to do?"

I groaned. "You're going to make this about *my* karma, aren't you?"

"I'm trying to make this about showing a property," Odette said.

Thinking fast, I asked if she'd called Vivika Major. She had; Ryan the receptionist had told her that Ms. Major was in Australia. And Ms. Gould was unavailable.

"Major may be gone," Odette said, "but I'm sure Gould is here, doing things her way. God only knows why."

"Did you tell Ryan about the dogs?"

"I did. He said he would notify security. Something tells me that won't help."

"Let me see what I can find out," I said. "Sit tight."

"Like we have a choice?" A chorus of snarls sounded alarmingly close to Odette's phone.

"Are you all right?" I asked quickly.

"We're fine. But my sideview mirror is a chew toy."

I clicked back to my other call; on-hold music was still playing. Then Ryan returned to the line.

"I'm sorry, Ms. Cruise, but García isn't answering right now. May I take your number and have him call you back?"

"Actually, it would be simpler if I just spoke with Felicia Gould, so please put me through to her."

Ryan seemed taken aback. After a brief pause, he stammered, "Ms. Gould is unavailable. I could connect you to her voice mail, however."

"Cut the crap, Ryan," I said, my confidence blooming. "This is *Detective* Scarlett Cruise with the Michigan State Police. If Felicia Gould isn't expecting my call, she should be. I know what's going on at Druin, and I'm on my way there now. With back-up. You'd better let me talk to Ms. Gould!"

Another pause. And then a dial tone. Either Ryan was following instructions, or he had choked.

"What's going on now?" I asked Odette, breathless. The dogs' howls and snarls were like the soundtrack of a horror flick. To think I had found Velcro's cries alarming.

"Same old, same old," she replied. "We've lost the exterior mirrors and most of the bumper. Dogs like plastic, you know."

I told her I would call Jenx and the state police.

Suddenly Fenton announced, "The security guy's not in the booth anymore! He's coming straight toward us!"

"That's great!" I cried. "He can round up the dogs and then you can get on with the show."

"Didn't you hear Fenton, Whiskey? García's coming straight toward us—at about forty miles an hour!"

I screamed because Odette didn't. Or maybe she did, and I couldn't hear her over the howls of the dogs. In my terror, I dropped the phone. It clattered to the floor of Twyla's kitchen. Nothing looked broken. How I wished the same would be true for Odette and Fenton. I snatched it up, expecting to hear only my own blood pounding in my ears.

"Are you all right?" Odette asked.

"Am *I* all right?! What do you mean? You're the ones who just got hit by a car!"

"*You* screamed," Odette reminded me. "And then you dropped your phone. We 'almost' got hit, as things turned out. By a Lexus that looks like yours."

"So you're all right? You and Fenton?"

"Our heart rates are a bit elevated, but we're intact. Apparently that was García's way of being heroic. When he came barreling toward us, he terrified the dogs even more than he did us. He's using his vehicle to herd them back to the kennel. Hang on, Whiskey. Fenton wants a word."

"We're fine, Dear," he began. "It looks like Odette will get her chance to show me this property after all."

He sounded good, and not the least bit pissed off about Norman and Abra—or even Velcro.

"About Velcro," he began.

"Gone! History! *Finito!*" I said. "That teacup dog will never bother us again!"

I heard Fenton's startled intake of breath. "Surely you don't mean that you ... Whiskey, that's the worst thing you could do for your karma ..."

"I don't mean *that*," I said quickly. "The little guy's alive! I found a new home for him. Chester wants Velcro."

"I thought Chester wasn't allowed to have dogs."

"That used to be true. It's why I got Velcro in the first place. Then Chester learned to bribe the housekeeper. And now—problem solved!"

Fenton said he didn't like bribes. Bad for one's karma.

"I just had a revelation, Dear," he announced. "I used to prefer big dogs. But now I see their corrupting *gestalt*. Consider—when Abra and Norman are together, she's a wanton hussy, and he's a worthless whore hound!"

"She's always a wanton hussy," I said.

"Udette and I were trapped by a pack of Dobermans and Rottweilers," Fenton said. "Also big dogs. There's a karmic lesson here, Dear. Something we all need to see. And the lesson is ... *small dogs rule.*"

"Small dogs are a pain in the ass!" I said.

Fenton disagreed. "I have to face the fact that Norman may be gone for good. Even if he returns, I'm not sure I can trust him again. Three strikes and you're out, whether you're a ball player or a medical companion dog. It's high time I adopt and train a new canine. And the Universe is telling me that his name is Velcro!"

"But—"

"Think about it! He's the perfect size to go anywhere I go. And he's smart." Fenton's voice turned husky. "He figured out how to get into your camisole, didn't he?"

And the rest of my dirty underwear ...

"He's vocal, too," Fenton went on. "Just what I need to alert me when it's time to take my meds."

"Oh, Velcro's vocal all right."

I detected a new commotion on Fenton's end, not dogs this time, but car doors closing and human voices blending. From the quality of Fenton's voice, I surmised that he had cupped his hand around the phone for privacy.

"Listen, Dear, about last night. I was ... distracted ... by the little guy. That won't happen again, now that my eyes have been opened to his place in our destiny."

I was quite sure that my destiny did not include a camisole-wearing teacup dog with graduated step stools and a stuffed Floozy. Anyway, I had more or less promised Velcro to Chester.

Right now, though, I just wanted to know what was going on at Druin. I asked Fenton to hand the phone back to Odette. She announced that Felicia Gould had personally come out to meet them and apologized for the confusion.

"'Confusion'? Nice euphemism," I said. "I trust her boss will cover the cost of your car repairs, if not your post-traumatic-stress therapy. Did she say why the receptionist had insisted she was unavailable?"

"More confusion," Odette said. "The receptionist is new. Apparently he doesn't yet know all the players. Got to go, Whiskey! The chatelaine is finally ready to show us Druin."

I wished her luck.

Then, through Twyla's screen door, I heard Chester—back from his mission, apparently. Although I couldn't catch every word, it sounded like he was giving instructions, and not to a dog. More like to a human who worked for him. I peered through the screen. Chester was talking to his driver, the cleaner.

TWENTY-SIX

CHESTER WAS STILL UNDERCOVER. It wasn't much of a disguise, but what can you do with a puny, pale-skinned boy with thick wire-rimmed glasses ... and the vocabulary of a middle-aged professional? He was wearing a faded oversized T-shirt, hugely baggy jeans, and high-tops without laces. As he talked to MacArthur, Chester kept absentmindedly yanking up his pants. Oh yeah, he was cool.

MacArthur was standing alongside the Maserati, which must be a very quiet car. Either that or it had arrived while I was on the phone—screaming. After listening to Chester, MacArthur nodded respectfully, said something I couldn't hear, and walked around to the driver's side, where he got in. Chester yanked up his pants again and, attempting some version of ghetto swagger, turned toward the back door.

"Yo, Whiskey! Whassup," he said, when he spotted me on the other side of the screen.

"Yo, yourself. You can cut the act now, Chester. The Maserati blew your cover."

I let him in, and he nearly tripped over his big pants.

"Guess what I used as my alias?" he asked.

"Whitebread Boy?" I was being a smart ass, but Chester's face fell. "Don't tell me I guessed right?"

"It was Mrs. B's idea." He brightened. "If you both thought of it, then the name has to fit!"

Chester recounted how he had quickly found his way into a play circle of kids a few years younger than himself. "The under-seven crowd is the least judgmental. They let me join their game."

When I asked what game that had been, Chester didn't know the official name. Or, for that matter, the objective. "Basically, we were throwing rocks. Turns out I have a pretty good arm!"

Turned out he also had a fair aptitude for being a spy. Chester knew how to get information and then get out before he blew his cover. He'd befriended six-year-old Xavier, who was Puerto Rican. Xavier said he had talked with one of the kids in Twyla's care.

"Are you sure?" I said. "Those kids were too scared to talk to anybody."

"It wasn't about being too scared," Chester said. "It was about knowing the language. Xavier talked to the biggest kid—in Spanish. His name was Pedro, and he knew a little English, but the other kids didn't."

I pictured the bright-eyed boy who had hefted the rock at my Lexus. He'd grinned during my "lecture" while the others stared blankly. No doubt he'd understood some of what I said.

"Pedro told Xavier that all the kids were from Bogotá."

"Colombia?"

Chester nodded.

"What were little kids from Colombia doing at Twyla's house?"

"Waiting," Chester said.

"For what?"

"For Señora García to tell them what to do."

"You mean, *Señor* García," I said, my heart racing. This was proof that the security guard was involved.

Chester shook his head so hard his pants slid down. Hiking them up, he exclaimed, "Señora García is what the kids called Twyla."

I knew my mouth had dropped open because I could feel my tongue getting dry. Was Twyla *married* to García the security guard? Or was that her alias?

Someone knocked on the back door, and I jumped.

"It's just my driver," Chester said. "He got my clothes back from Mrs. B."

Sure enough, MacArthur was holding a brown paper bag. I let him in.

"Since when does the cleaner knock?" I asked.

"Since I became a licensed realtor. I passed the exam this morning."

"Congratulations."

I wasn't sure I meant it. Hell, I wasn't sure I believed a word he said. Whoever he was, though, he was still damned handsome in his crisp, dark suit. When Chester excused himself to change, I decided the time had come to be blunt.

"Are you running a shuttle service for children?"

MacArthur smiled ever so slightly. "Depends on who's asking."

"Me. I'm asking. And here's another question that goes with that one: Did you know Twyla Rendel?"

"Yes—to both your questions."

"Then you know where her kids are! And you know what happened to Twyla!"

MacArthur said, "I know where *your* kids are. And I know Twyla's dead."

"You mean, Leah and Leo?"

"Unless you have other grandchildren I don't know about." His blue eyes twinkled. "I'm taking Chester home to the Castle. Why don't you drive to your office and do what you need to do. I'll pick you up at half past one. There's a property you need to see…"

———

I hate being told what to do by other realtors, especially ones who don't work for me yet. But I was too tired to argue with MacArthur, and of course I wanted to find out what he knew about Leah and Leo. Frankly, I was also intrigued by the prospect of viewing a property.

At Mattimoe Realty, I was surprised to find Tina Breen manning the reception desk—till I remembered that I'd fired the receptionist. With every phone line engaged, Tina looked hassled. Assuming that was my fault, I tried to slip past her. She managed to attach a sticky pink phone message to my sleeve.

By the time I read it, the note was redundant. It said, "Jenx is in your office."

In fact, the chief was asleep in my chair with her steel-toed boots up on my desk. I woke her when I slammed the door.

"Since you started this mess, I figured you owed me a place to rest," she yawned. Jenx explained that she and Brady had been up all night chasing phantom GILs around town.

"I didn't start that," I said. "Rico did!"

"But you drove Noonan out of town. So it's your fault there's nobody around to soothe people."

"Peg's around," I said, meaning our mayor, the kindly owner of the Goh Cup. "She's a good listener."

"She serves *coffee*," Jenx reminded me. "Nobody in Magnet Springs needs caffeine right now."

Jenx looked like she could use some. She couldn't seem to stop yawning. Moreover, her eyes were puffy and shadowed from lack of sleep. Last night she, Brady, and Roscoe had investigated a total of nine GIL sightings.

"You never made it out to Vestige," I complained.

"You had Fenton." Jenx winked. I wondered if she knew he'd been running around naked, and if so, who told her.

"The IRS is back," she added.

Revenue Agent Damon Kincaid had returned with reinforcements. The word on the street was that the federal government suspected O-Gil of faking his own death and then coming back to dig up the fortune he'd buried near one of his properties—the fortune he'd saved by failing to pay his income taxes for three years.

I found that hard to believe. Not the part about Gil Gruen welshing. Despite the sightings, I was still sure the cowboy mayor was dead.

"Why would O-Gil go to the Holiday Inn in Grand Rapids?" I demanded. "And why show up at Vestige?"

In response, Jenx yawned and closed her eyes again. Before she could fall back to sleep in my chair, I spun it. Hard. Hard enough to knock her feet off my desk and get her attention. She was grudgingly interested in my news—or rather, my "evidentiary findings"—about García and Twyla and the kids who spoke Spanish. For once Jenx didn't accuse me of leaping to conclusions, probably because I hadn't come up with any.

I didn't say a thing about the cleaner even though he had admitted knowing Twyla and being involved in some kind of shuttle service for kids. My plan was to play volunteer deputy and find more evidence.

I kept one other fact to myself: that Abra was at large again. Make that two other facts—she'd taken Norman.

Fenton had been right about those dogs being bad. United, they were the canine equivalent of a rogue wave. Speaking of which—Jenx announced that it had been almost forty-eight hours since the last report of riptides. She and other local law enforcement could now relax a little, even if they weren't quite ready to take down the shoreline warning signs. She was heading home to Red Hen's House for a shower and a good meal before starting her next shift.

I managed to send the chief, yawning, out the back door just as the cleaner strolled in through the front door. Juggling a couple calls, Tina brightened at the sight of him. She hit the mute button to ask, "Did you pass?" presumably referring to his licensing exam. MacArthur gave her the thumbs up sign, and Tina flashed him a toothy smile.

MacArthur opened the rear passenger-side door of the Maserati for me—my first time inside a truly fine Italian-made vehicle.

It smelled new—and like the finest leather. Once in the driver's seat, MacArthur addressed me without turning his head.

"Would you care for something to drink, Ms. Mattimoe? In deference to Miss Cassina, I've removed all alcohol, but I could offer you a soda."

I declined. Since there was no partition between the front and back seats, I found his formality oddly amusing.

"Where are we going?" I asked.

"You need to see a certain property," he replied.

"One that you hope to list? Or one that somebody has listed already?"

"One that you're trying to sell right now," he said.

"Why would I want to see that?"

"I didn't say you'd want to see it. I said you need to see it."

Something about this set-up suddenly made me nervous. MacArthur's grinning good looks could put women at ease. Witness how easily he'd soothed Tina. And thus far he'd managed to deflect most of my doubts. But the man was a cleaner.

He cleared his throat. "I hear you're planning to return Velcro." He sounded disapproving.

"Actually, I may have a better solution," I said and quickly explained Fenton Flagg's interest in training the shitzapoo to be his replacement medical companion dog.

"I see. When did you plan to tell Chester?" The driver's voice was stern. Clearly he was in cleaner mode.

"It just happened. But it seems like a good solution. Now Chester won't have to lie to Cassina."

"We all lie to Miss Cassina," MacArthur said. "She prefers it that way."

Suddenly I had a new view of what went on at her cottage: Cassina probably knew about Rupert's trysts and asked only that he deny them.

"We're going to Cassina's cottage, aren't we?" I said, realizing that we were on Coastal Highway, already halfway there.

"You should relax and enjoy the scenery," he replied.

When the door locks snapped down, I tensed.

MacArthur's eyes met mine in the rearview mirror. "I'm just doing my job."

"Which job is that? Driver? Cleaner? Realtor?"

"I'd like to think I'm advancing my real estate career."

"By kidnapping me?"

MacArthur laughed amiably. "You came of your own volition. And you'll be glad you did."

We didn't say much the rest of the way. MacArthur put on a non-Jeb Halloran CD, which was refreshing. I took his advice and paid attention to the scenery, thinking how seldom I left the driving up to someone else. Coincidentally, I had done so twice within twenty-four hours: last night on my date with Fenton and today on my mystery tour. It was really very pleasant—despite the uncertainty of MacArthur's agenda. Cassina and Rupert may have had issues, but they also had a driver; I could learn from them. Assuming I emerged unscathed from whatever MacArthur planned to show me, and assuming I made a boatload of money selling my two high-end listings, I would hire a driver, too.

TWENTY-SEVEN

RIDING IN CASSINA'S MASERATI, I could almost imagine what it felt like to be the music diva herself. Except that I wasn't drunk, high, or swathed in pigment-free fabric. And, unlike Cassina, I hadn't forgotten about Chester. I knew exactly where her son was because I had bothered to ask. MacArthur had assured me that Chester and Prince Harry were safe at the Castle. Chester was busy retrofitting his wing for the return of Velcro.

I felt guilty about that. For two reasons. First, I had failed to bond with the shitzapoo—even though he desperately wanted to bond with me. Second, I had let two different humans think they might have him. Fenton needed a full-time medical companion dog. And Chester needed full-time canine friends.

I, on the other hand, was happiest when the animals in my life, including my stepdaughter, mostly left me alone. Except when I had no clue where they'd run off to. Then I worried. Even now, ensconced in the Maserati's luxurious backseat, watching the rural scenery slide by, I found myself wondering where in all that greenery were Abra and Norman? Prior experience had taught me that they could be enjoying doggie foreplay behind any tree, bush, or barn. Avery and her new man, on the other hand, presumably required more shelter. Wherever that was, I hoped the twins were safe.

"Here we are," MacArthur announced, the burrs in his Rs jarring me back to the present. As he expertly guided the car along the curving dirt lane to Cassina's cottage, I had no idea what to expect.

My cell phone distracted me. Odette was calling; I couldn't wait to hear the result of her tour at Druin.

"The chatelaine came through for us," she began. "Felicia walked us all around, and I think Fenton liked it. He's going to get back to me."

"You saw everything?" I asked.

"Everything but the wine cellar. They're renovating that, remember? Since Fenton doesn't drink, it didn't interest him, anyway. Where are you?"

Odette never cared where I was unless she thought it was going to make her money. Aware that the driver was listening, I said that MacArthur wanted me to take another look at Cassina's cottage. Now I had life insurance: on the off chance that something bad was about to happen, one person knew where I was, and who I was with. I felt better.

"You're not going inside, are you?" Odette asked.

"Why wouldn't we?"

"Remember what happened the last time we were there?"

I remembered that Odette had been more interested in looking over the designer kitchen than in avoiding the noisy lovebirds.

"I'm with MacArthur." Stressing his name, I hoped to trigger Odette's memory that he was not only a driver but also a cleaner. Either he would protect me or … he would dispose of me.

His presence didn't interest her, however. She proceeded to utter a complete non sequitur: "Have you heard from Avery lately?"

"Why the hell would you ask about Avery?" I said—just as my stepdaughter hove into view. She appeared at the end of the driveway, one hand on the twins' double stroller, the other shading her eyes as she stared straight at us.

MacArthur braked gently and turned off the ignition. I said the only thing that sprang to mind, "Avery can't afford this property."

"She's not here to buy it, Ms. Mattimoe," MacArthur said. "She and the twins are here as my guests."

"Pardon?"

Avery was moving toward the driver's side, an actual smile lighting her face.

MacArthur said quietly, "Rupert lets me use this place occasionally. Your stepdaughter and I are enjoying it for a few days."

A voice was coming from my cell phone, which I had allowed to drop into my lap.

"Excuse me," I said hoarsely, and fumbled for the phone.

"I was waiting for the right time to tell you," said Odette. "Now I don't have to."

"You knew?"

There was no chance of MacArthur or Avery overhearing anything I said. He had enveloped my stepdaughter in a passionate embrace.

"It was the reason I stalled the way I did when we were there on Wednesday," Odette said. "I caught a glimpse of Avery in the buff, and I knew you couldn't handle it."

Now I was more confused than ever. "You're saying she was the one with Rupert?"

"No, no! Who cares who was with Rupert? MacArthur and Avery were doing it downstairs while Rupert and whoever were going at it upstairs. You were so frazzled you didn't see Avery grab her clothes and dash out the side door. The Scotsman managed to get himself dressed and back on duty before you got a clue."

"You're sure Avery wasn't the noisy one?" I asked. I didn't think I could handle it if she was.

"As far as I know, she was completely mute."

"What am I supposed to do now?" I hissed. "This is awkward beyond belief!"

"Many moments in your life seem to fit that description. Begin by giving thanks that Avery wasn't the noisy one. Also, that you didn't see her nude. At least you don't have those memories to repress. Then, repeat after me: 'I'm in the business of selling real estate. Screw the rest!'"

Sometimes being all about the money is the best choice. I closed the phone and found my own way out of the Maserati, taking the driver's keys with me. MacArthur was so deep into tonsil-massaging Avery that he'd forgotten the rest of his job. Not a problem. I paused just long enough to kiss both the twins on their soft, sweet faces and then proceeded up the flagstone path into Cassina's cottage. Once inside, I made sure every door was locked. Then, standing in the great room at the floor-to-ceiling window overlooking Lake Michigan, I reopened my phone and placed a strategic call.

I gave Fenton Flagg a virtual tour of the entire house, describing in detail the best features of every room as I passed through it. By the time I'd reached the third floor, someone was trying very hard to access the first floor. Unfortunately for MacArthur, I'd removed not only his keys from the ignition, but also the spare key from under the wood-nymph sculpture. He and my stepdaughter could come in later. When I was good and ready. That would be after Fenton Flagg agreed that this sounded like the home of his dreams, and he wanted to view it. Soon.

So it was that I had achieved an almost unprecedented level of calm by the time I descended the spiral staircase and granted MacArthur and Avery an audience. Of course, it had been Avery's idea to bring us all together. She wanted to rub my face in the revelation that her handsome new boyfriend was someone I'd also found attractive. How did she know that? Either MacArthur had read my vibes and shared them with her—the slime—or she had simply assumed that, since I knew him, I would want him. Following the incident with Nash Grant, Avery might have surmised that she and I tended to be attracted to the same men, the only known exception being my ex-husband, Jeb Halloran. Avery couldn't stand Jeb. Point for his side.

Following Odette's advice, I controlled our meeting, keeping it short and civilized—and all about business.

"I wish you both the very best," I said, thereby sucking the wind out of Avery's sails. "And I have just a few questions." I turned my pasted-on smile toward the driver. "What did you mean when you talked about running a shuttle service for children, and about Rupert becoming a 'father figure'?"

"Isn't it obvious?" Avery interrupted snidely. "Mac already drives Chester and his friends around, so he's available to drive Leah and Leo, too."

"Chester has friends?" I asked. "As in school friends?"

After more than a year of almost daily contact with my young neighbor, I'd rarely heard him mention other kids.

"Chester's friends are mainly the children of people employed at the Castle," MacArthur explained. "I drive the little ones where they need to go while their parents are working. Doctor's appointments, school daytrips, etc. Since Cassina likes to hire and fire, most of Chester's friends don't stick around long."

"That's what Mac meant when he said Rupert was working on being a father figure," Avery interjected. "Rupert's friendlier with kids than Cassina is. He really likes Leah and Leo."

"Did Rupert like Twyla's kids, too?" I inquired.

"Who?" Avery looked blank.

Turning back to the driver, I said, "Tell me how you knew Twyla Rendel. Did her kids enjoy your shuttle service?"

"Twyla García, you mean." MacArthur shook his head. "That's the name she used when she worked at the Castle—with her boyfriend. She didn't have children. And she didn't last long at the Castle. Cassina caught Twyla making too many long-distance calls. The boyfriend got a better offer, anyway, so they both left."

I didn't know if that was true, but at this point, it seemed possible.

"Why were you fighting with Twyla on the day she died? I mean, on the day she was murdered?"

Before MacArthur answered, I stole a glance at my stepdaughter. Her tongue was flicking nervously. I assumed the Twyla connection was news to her. MacArthur didn't like the subject, either. Shifting his weight from one shiny shoe to the other, he seemed to debate answering. Finally, he said, "Rupert sent me to collect some money Twyla owed him."

"Twyla owed Rupert? Are you sure it wasn't the other way around?"

"Part of my job as cleaner is to keep Rupert and Cassina off drugs. Unfortunately, sometimes they get some. The Garcías promised Rupert a score. They took his money but never delivered. I was glad about that. Still, Rupert wanted his cash back. Twyla didn't have it, and she claimed not to know where it was."

Boldly I took a step closer. The cleaner and I were almost eye to eye. "Did Rupert tell you to kill Twyla?"

Avery gasped, her grip tightening on Leah and Leo's stroller.

"Rupert wouldn't do that," MacArthur said. "Even if he did, I would never kill a person. Not even a woman."

I wasn't sure what that meant. Neither, apparently, was Avery.

"Don't you mean 'least of all a woman'?" she said.

MacArthur kept his gaze locked on mine. "Women make the most ferocious enemies. That's why I try not to have any."

"You try not to have any women? Or any women enemies?" Avery demanded.

MacArthur smiled. "Both."

"Good luck with that," I said.

Cassina's living room got a little noisy at that point, without a single additional comment from me. While Avery demanded to know what the cleaner's intentions were, I grabbed the stroller and rolled it out into the sunny fresh air. Leah, Leo, and I followed the path down to the dock, where we watched terns dive and soar.

Moments later Avery and MacArthur appeared. I couldn't read their mood and tried not to care what it was, anyway. God only knew what MacArthur saw in my stepdaughter, besides a challenge, although of course her kids were cute. The Scot didn't strike me as a father figure. More like a man drawn to mystery, money, and risky business; Avery fit the last category.

I suspected that MacArthur needed to be in control. So the driver-cleaner gig was a natural. Selling real estate made sense, too. Nobody got emotionally close to MacArthur, least of all a needy woman like Avery. She was sure to get her heart broken. I just hoped Noonan would be back in town by the time that happened.

Awkwardly, we all five rode downtown together. Avery sat in the front seat, practically in MacArthur's lap, while I shared the back seat with my stepgrandbabies. When she started in on him about past girlfriends and future plans, I serenaded the twins. Thanks to Jeb—and Velcro—I'd recently had a refresher course in lullabies, so the tunes came easily, if not on pitch.

By the time MacArthur dropped me off in front of Mattimoe Realty, I had a plan: to bypass the office altogether, get in my car, and drive home. It was mid-afternoon on one of those nearly perfect late-June days. The sky was azure blue, the winds light, and the humidity low. Best of all, the recent rash of riptides had ended. Or at least we hadn't had one since Wednesday. I wanted to wash the stress of the week away with a quick swim from my own patch of beach. I wouldn't tempt fate by paddling farther than the end of my dock. Just far enough to shake off those landlubber blues and remind myself how good it felt to get wet and physical on a beautiful summer day.

After all, that's why I lived where I did: to swim in the warm months and enjoy the lake view year round. Summers at this latitude slipped by too fast. Invariably, Labor Day rolled around before I realized I'd missed many swimming days in June, July, and August. Maybe Jeb had been right when he said I let a lot of the good stuff get away. Although I wouldn't include our relationship under that heading, I could grudgingly concede his point. I wouldn't concede it to him, of course. Never to him.

I arrived home to find a note from Chester. He had slipped in through the window above my kitchen sink to tend to Velcro. Written in back-slanting, elementary-school cursive and marked "2 PM", the message read:

Whiskey—
I'll be ready to move Velcro to the Castle on Sunday. I fed him and took him out to do his business. He's getting all the exercise he needs from his personal-trainer toy, Floozy. You might want to run her through a wash cycle. —Chester

I groaned. Suddenly the dog that nobody in their right mind would want was the dog that two people thought they needed. And I owed them both: Fenton because my other dog had corrupted and abducted his dog, and Chester because ... well, I was still trying to make up for almost letting him drown.

My overheated brain needed the kind of cooling only a dunk in the lake could provide. After slipping into my basic black swimsuit, I jogged down to the beach and right out into the water.

Anybody familiar with Lake Michigan knows that the wet stuff stays chilly till after the Fourth of July. My skin prickled, especially as the water reached groin level. But I forced myself to push through it almost all the way up to my waist. Then I inhaled and dove under, the liquid cold striking me like a body slap.

In a continuous smooth motion, I switched to the crawl, stroking easily, rhythmically toward the end of my fishing dock, about fifty feet out. There I would tuck and turn back, then repeat. A few dozen brisk laps should clear my head.

I was still on my first lap when the water roared, the sound rolling in like muffled thunder. My first thought was riptide, but I felt no undertow. And riptides, as far as I knew, didn't make noise. Nor did they come in the V-shape of a high-performance speedboat hull. Mid-stroke, I blinked at the gleaming white craft bearing down on me.

TWENTY-EIGHT

My brain required a few precious seconds to process what was happening: I was in the direct path of a speeding boat, and I had nowhere to go.

Swimming parallel to my dock, which stood about a few yards to my right, I was in about eight feet of water. I didn't need a degree in physics to know that the boat was traveling faster than I could, and it was nearly upon me.

Either I was about to be part of a tragic accident, or I was somebody's target. The angle of the sun and my perspective from the water made it impossible to see who was driving the boat. There was a chance that he or she was either sick or distracted. But maybe the captain intended to kill me, injure me, or scare me senseless. If the last option was the goal, the mission was already accomplished.

My first response was to tuck and turn back toward shore, so that's what I did. But not straight back. Crafts like the one racing up behind me were agile enough to swerve easily. And they had at most a three-foot draft, so they could zoom within fifteen feet of the beach.

Stroking and kicking so hard that that every muscle screamed, I angled toward the dock. If this was an attack, I didn't think the captain would risk a collision with all that wood. But my dock lacked a ladder. Assuming I got that far, and assuming the boat was still after me, I would have nothing to grab, no way to pull myself out of the water. I briefly considered diving under the dock and swimming for the other side. But there was no sanctuary there. Skillfully captained, the boat could keep looping until it exhausted me. And if I hovered near the dock, I'd be tossed about in the wake: heaved into a post or sucked under and against the platform. On the other hand, if I swam for shore, I could certainly be run down.

All risks considered, I liked the dock, so that's where I aimed. Gulping air for the energy needed to propel myself, I heard as well as felt the boat veer toward me. So this was no accident. The captain knew exactly how close he or she could cut it. And that point seemed to be where I was now, within a yard of the dock. The roar behind me was like an erupting volcano. Without another thought, I inhaled deeply and dove. I opened my eyes—not recommended amid churning silt, but I needed to know where the dock posts were. Despite sharp pains in my eyes and thick haze in the water, I spotted something vertical and tried to slide past it. As I pushed ahead, a sudden lurch of roiling water flipped me sideways or maybe all the way over. I couldn't tell which direction was up because I couldn't see. And I couldn't control anything but my breath, which I was determined to hold until it burst from me.

I tumbled rather than swam, pebbles loosened from the lake bottom stinging my face. My lungs begged for release. As confusion merged with pain in what seemed like perfect agony, my brain received a dim signal: the boat's roar had become a whine. Or was that something else?

Shards of light, like crystalline teardrops, glittered in the center of my vision. Sunlight sparkling through silt? Or my optic nerve misfiring from lack of oxygen? Suddenly I understood. I was breaking free from under the dock and rising fast toward the dappled surface on the other side. The whine came again, louder—not from a boat engine but from a familiar canine chorus. On the dock, Abra and Norman howled.

I broke the surface, gasping and coughing, but strong enough to stay afloat. When I stopped choking, I rotated in the water to face the pier. Nothing could have prepared me for what I saw: ten feet away was a man in his thirties wearing cowboy boots, tight jeans, a snap-button shirt, and a black Stetson.

Gil Gruen. Our mayor. Alongside whose corpse, five months ago, I had slid into this very lake. He had my dog and her Golden boyfriend with him.

Abra barked at the departing boat; Norman woofed at me. Little did the dogs know that the real show wasn't in or on the water. The real show was Gil Gruen, who miraculously hadn't died. He'd brought home two missing canines. Best of all, he'd arrived in time to ward off my would-be killer.

Incredible? You bet. Since middle school, Gil Gruen hadn't liked one thing about me.

Now he leaned down and extended a hand to pull me out of the water. I stayed where I was, hyperventilating as I kicked in place. No way I was ready to touch a man who'd returned from the dead. Or an optical illusion. My brain was having a hard time accepting this scene.

"Whitney Houston Halloran Mattimoe," the man said in a monotone. "That guy in the boat tried to kill you."

The voice wasn't Gil's. Deep and slow, he spoke like a man waking from a long sleep. A man who'd almost forgotten how to talk. I had to squint into the sun to see him, and my eyes weren't working well after all that silt.

He continued, "My brother didn't like you. But you seem nice. And you got nice doggies."

I smiled. "Only one of the doggies is mine, and she's not the nice one. I didn't know Gil had a brother.... "

"Gil was my half-brother. Same father, different mother. My mother died when I was four. And I went to live at my special school."

Ahh. "I'm so sorry—. What's your name?"

"My name is Hal Gruen. I'm thirty-nine years old. I live at the Hayworth Home. My address is 4156 Donnelly Street, Grand Rapids, Michigan ... "

I was swimming toward him then, suddenly eager to get out of the water and on with my life, which would include wrapping up the Mystery of Gone-in-the-Lake Gruen and his special half-brother Hal. And maybe also figuring out who was trying to kill me before they succeeded.

Hal Gruen liked to talk about TV and the things he'd learned by watching it. For instance, he knew that someone who had nearly drowned would be in shock and need a blanket, or at least a whole lot of towels. He wanted to get me some. So I directed him to the cedar chest on my deck, and he lumbered purposefully away. The two dogs stayed by my side, Abra still fixated on the fading boat, Norman apparently concerned with my well-being. When he sniffed my pulse points, I assumed he'd been trained to check vital signs. But maybe he was just being a dog.

I felt the full effects of my trauma: chills, dizziness, nausea, and general weakness—in addition to the silt that was still scratching my eyes.

Hal concentrated hard on wrapping me in every beach towel he could find. He liked to follow directions. When I asked him to fetch my cell phone from the kitchen, he did so more quickly than I had dared hope.

Still fiercely shaking, I managed to reach Jenx and stammer, "Somebody tried to kill me. Gil's half-brother Hal saved me. Tell Fenton his dog is back. Tell everybody Gil's still dead."

As soon as Jenx ascertained where I was, she said she'd be there in ten minutes. Or less. Within five minutes, Chester had arrived, breathless, Prince Harry bobbing along behind him. My young neighbor had been listening to the police scanner at the Castle and heard that Jenx was on her way here. When he was sure I was all right, he gave Hal his attention.

"Hello. I'm Chester. You look like our dead mayor, but I'm sure you're not."

Hal recited the same introduction he'd offered me. When Chester extended his hand, Hal knew it wasn't because he needed help getting out of the water. This was Hal's chance to demonstrate hand-shaking skills. Although he overdid it, pumping away for a full minute, Chester kept a polite smile on his face. Then Hal asked if he could pet Prince Harry. Even in my post-traumatic haze, I could see that Hal and Chester had something in common: they both loved dogs. And dogs loved them.

———

After Jenx took my statement, she sent me upstairs for a long, hot shower. I emerged from my vapory bathroom to find a steaming mug of tea, brewed and delivered by Chester, no doubt. I was slipping into my robe when somebody knocked on my bedroom door.

"Yo, Whiskey," Jenx said. "Are you decent? Not that I care."

When I let her in, she collapsed in my Morris chair like she was the one who'd been traumatized.

"Yeah, you almost died, but I haven't had any sleep since Tuesday," she yawned. "And this attempted murder won't make my life any easier. About Hal ..."

Jenx flipped through her notepad and ticked off the facts she'd verified by phoning the Hayworth Home. Hal Gruen had been a cooperative, helpful resident until he'd learned of his brother's death. Then he'd begun slipping out after curfew. The administrator's theory was that Hal missed his brother's visits and had somehow got it in his head to go see the people and places Gil used to talk about. Over the years, Gil had bought Hal an extensive cowboy wardrobe, which Hal loved to wear.

"Gil visited Hal?" I echoed.

"Like clockwork, every Monday night."

Our former mayor had never told anyone he had a half-brother, let alone that he cared enough to visit him.

"Back to what happened here today," Jenx said. "Hal got a pretty good look at the boat that nearly killed you."

"How about at the captain? Did he get a good look at him?"

"The guy was sitting down, so it's hard to say how tall he was. And he was wearing sunglasses. But Abra sure didn't like him."

"Maybe because he missed!"

Jenx said, "Chester seems to think Abra recognized the captain."

"Is he translating for her again?" I said. "Don't let him ask her what she's been doing with Norman. They're just into sex."

Jenx explained that Hal had memorized the Michigan registration number of the craft that nearly killed me. She was waiting now for Brady to get back to her with the owner's name.

"Aren't there like eight digits in those licenses?" I said. "How could Hal get all the numbers right?"

"He recovered Norman and Abra and got back to your house in time to save your life, didn't he?"

I lowered my gaze, ashamed.

"Hal never goes anywhere without a notebook and pencil," Jenx said, fluttering her own pad at me. "He writes everything down. That's how he gets where he's going. Hal got the name of the boat, too: VLM 8."

Jenx's cell phone rang. She grunted a few times and disconnected. "Wanna guess what VLM stands for?"

"Don't you mean who?" I felt sick again because I knew those initials; I'd seen them on contracts.

"Vivika Leigh Major owns that craft, and a whole lot of other ones," Jenx said. "Hal said he saw the same boat near Vanderzee Park the morning he talked with a nice lady who was real upset. She was waiting for somebody—the guy driving that boat."

"Hal talked with Twyla before she died!" I suddenly got it. "All those witnesses who thought they saw her with Gil really saw her with Hal!"

"And Hal saw her talk with the cleaner-driver," Jenx said, "like other witnesses claimed. But MacArthur didn't arrive in a boat, and Twyla left with the guy who did."

"Who is he?"

"Somebody connected to Vivika Major."

My mind flashed on García, the security guard and dog wrangler whose phone number Twyla had dialed last.

"Was he Hispanic?" I asked. "Can Hal or Abra tell us?"

Jenx leaned forward, her face deadly earnest. "We don't know. But Vivika Major is your client. Unfortunately, Druin is way out of my jurisdiction. So we gotta make a choice. We can turn this over to County now … or we can turn it over to County later … after we learn a few things. Whatever we do is unofficial. But I'd sure like a crack at finding the guy who killed Twyla."

And I needed to know what had happened to all those kids.

TWENTY-NINE

By the time I threw some clothes on, Chester was concluding Hal's tour of Vestige. He sounded like a seasoned real estate pro.

"This is the kitchen, where Whiskey comes and goes, but never cooks. Note the convenient doggie-door feature. It provides controlled access to and from the exercise pen."

Chester demonstrated by removing the panel so that Abra, Norman, Prince Harry, and even Velcro—with Floozy in his mouth —could exit the kitchen. Velcro's splints slowed him down but not enough to keep him from being part of the group. Or to distract him from his *ho*. As long as Floozy was handy, that boy was calm. No camisoles required. No *Animal Lullabies*, either. For Jeb's sake, I hoped Fleggers didn't sell too many Floozies.

"Show Hal what I usually do next," I told Chester, who took his cue and re-inserted the partition.

"But now they can't come back in," Hal said.

"Exactly."

I smiled at the cowboy-wannabe, who was nervously squeezing his black Stetson. Someone, or some TV show, had taught him to remove his hat indoors.

Jenx, who had stepped out on the porch to use her phone, re-entered, accompanied by Brady and Roscoe. Hal's eyes widened with delight at the sight of one more dog.

"Brady's here to take Hal home to Grand Rapids," the chief announced.

"But we have things to do," Chester objected. "Hal's going to help me retrofit my wing of the Castle for Velcro. And I'm going to show him how I'm training Prince Harry."

"Another time, bud," Brady said amiably.

Hal stroked Canine Officer Roscoe, who had apparently recovered from Abra's back attack. Usually aloof while on duty, the German shepherd wagged his tail. He looked hopefully at Brady.

"You can pet him all the way back to Grand Rapids, if you like," Officer Swancott said. I wasn't sure if that was for Hal's benefit or for Roscoe's.

"Can I come, too?" Chester asked. "With Prince Harry?"

Unauthorized passengers are usually a no-no in a police cruiser, especially ones with four legs. But Brady agreed to make an exception. Chester removed the doggie-door partition, and one by one the other four dogs scrambled back into my kitchen. Eyeing the motley crew with his usual professional detachment, Roscoe seemed particularly disdainful of Floozy. He'd probably busted her type before.

———

After Brady left with his entourage, Jenx informed me that Fenton knew about Norman's safe return. The New Age guru would come by that evening to reclaim him. Since Abra and Norman were material witnesses to my attempted murder, Jenx insisted that we take them with us to Druin.

"Too bad you can't translate canine the way Chester can," the chief sighed. "We'll have to guess what the dogs are telling us."

So our mission was not only unauthorized and illegal but ludicrous. Still, I was up for it ... till Jenx announced that we were taking my car. When I balked, she reminded me that our mission was unauthorized and illegal; we sure as hell couldn't use a police cruiser. She couldn't wear her uniform, either, and changed into the T-shirt and overalls she kept in her trunk. I stared so long at her new ensemble that Jenx jokingly accused me of lust. The truth was almost nobody ever saw her in civvies.

With Abra and Norman together in the backseat, we headed north on Coastal Highway. I cranked up the radio. Not to drown out whining this time, but rather the sounds of two dogs in love loudly sniffing each other's private parts.

Jenx and I didn't have much of a plan. She suggested I pretend to be following up on Odette's earlier visit. That's not how we play the real estate game, but I couldn't think of a better idea.

I would label this a courtesy call. My purpose: to ask Felicia if there was anything I could personally do to make her life easier while Druin was on the market. Meanwhile, Jenx—posing as my intern, if anybody asked—would get the dogs out for a little stretch and see if they pointed her anywhere. Before we left Vestige, Jenx had made sure we had two leashes.

Since it was late Friday afternoon, I drove as fast as the law allowed, hoping to reach Druin before the official start of the weekend. En route, I filled Jenx in on the cleaner's story about how he knew Twyla. Jenx grunted a few times, but showed no real interest. I wondered if she'd already known what I just found out.

At five minutes before five o'clock, I turned onto Internet Way, the private drive leading to Druin. We found the guard house unoccupied and the security gate closed. So we waited. I rolled down my window and smiled patiently at the video camera whose little red light glowed. Finally, the speaker box atop the gatepost crackled, and a voice I thought I recognized as belonging to Ryan, the new receptionist, said, "May I help you?"

This time I told him the truth, more or less. At least I didn't claim to be Officer Scarlett Cruise of the Michigan State Police. I admitted that I was Whiskey Mattimoe from Mattimoe Realty, here to pay a brief courtesy call on Felicia Gould.

"I know she's here," I added quickly. "My agent Odette Mutombo just showed the property, with Ms. Gould's cooperation. I want to follow up on that. This will take only a few minutes."

Ryan was gone so long that Jenx grew antsy. I suspected that she was hatching alternate schemes for accessing the property.

Suddenly Felicia herself was on the line. "To what do I owe this surprise visit on a Friday evening, Ms. Mattimoe?"

I repeated my story about the courtesy call, adding that I was in the neighborhood anyway to check on another listing. Felicia's reply startled me.

"Who's in the car with you?"

"My ... intern. And my dogs. They go everywhere with me—the dogs, not the intern. Although the intern is with me today. She's making a mid-life career change to real estate, so I'm showing her our listings. She won't need to come in with me, though. She can stay with the dogs."

"Don't be silly," Felicia said. "Leave the dogs in the car, and bring the intern in with you. I can give you only a few minutes since I have dinner plans. Pull all the way around the front of the house to the first side entrance. I'll meet you there."

When the security gate swung open, I accelerated; the gate closed behind us.

"'Mid-life'?" Jenx asked. "I'm your age."

"But you're in law enforcement, and that's a high-risk profession."

"So's your biz..."

Since it was Friday at five, I figured García the security guard had gone home for the weekend, wherever home was. Had he loved Twyla? Did he kill her? What was their relationship?

Jenx gasped when the chateau came into view. "Damn straight I'm going inside! I'm not missing a chance to see this joint."

She then shared Plan B: after a brief look-around inside, Jenx would excuse herself to go back out to the dogs while I finished my chat with the chatelaine.

To my surprise, Felicia was waiting for us on the patio alongside the house. And García was with her. Stonily they watched us exit the vehicle, me on the far side. I hadn't quite managed to close my door before all hell broke loose. Abra and Norman bounded out my side, almost knocking me over. García charged Jenx, who—to my astonishment—produced her service revolver, presumably from a pocket in her overalls. I saw why—García had a gun in his hand. Dogs barked; shots were fired; I dropped to the ground. Suddenly I realized that too many dogs were barking. Had someone loosed the attack pack on us?

"Get back in the car, Whiskey!" Jenx bellowed. "Call 9-1-1!"

Crouching on the other side, I shouted, "Are you all right?"

Between the howls and snarls of Abra and Norman, and the aggressive oncoming chorus, I didn't have a clue what was up. Maybe Jenx had been hit.

"Get in the car!" she repeated. "And lock up!"

I did. Once inside, I could see what was happening although I could hardly believe it: Leaping and snarling, Abra and Norman had pinned Felicia against the wall of the chateau; meanwhile, Jenx was holding García at gunpoint on the ground. And coming straight at us, like a low swarm of black flies, was the attack pack.

My sweaty hands fumbled with the phone. I tried twice to hit the three magic digits. The way my life was going, I needed 9-1-1 on speed dial. When I reached the county dispatcher, I gave my name, location, and a one-sentence summary of the crisis. I was relieved she didn't ask what I was doing at Druin because I no longer knew.

Another gunshot rang out. This time it wasn't Jenx or García. Between my vehicle and the oncoming pack stood a young man in a yellow shirt and khakis aiming a rifle at the sky. He needed to fire it only once; the pack of dogs reversed their course, curling away from me in a perfect U-turn. The young man followed them at a trot.

Instantly I relaxed. Even though I didn't understand what was happening, I assumed that Jenx and the good dogs had the bad guys under control. I smiled to think of Abra as one of the "good" dogs.

Within moments I heard approaching sirens. In my rearview mirror I watched two Lanagan County sheriff's cruisers screech to a halt. As the deputies stepped out, weapons at the ready, Jenx pocketed hers and flipped open her badge case. Since Abra and Norman were still barking, I could catch only fragments of what Jenx said: "Realtor … murder … missing children …" I assumed I wasn't really the subject of that sentence.

Abra and Norman had not yet grown tired of cowing Felicia Gould, probably because they were doing it in shifts. One sat howling while the other lunged and snarled; then they switched roles. The sheriff's deputies got García up off the ground and had him spread his arms and legs against one of their cars. I assumed they'd do the same with Felicia Gould as soon as they could figure out how to call off the dogs.

One of the officers got on his radio, and Jenx used her cell phone—to call Chester, as it turned out. Still in Brady's cruiser, he provided the necessary command to "turn off" my dog and her boyfriend. Chester and Jenx decided that I needed practice bossing Abra, so the actual task of delivering the command fell to me. Reluctantly, I left the sanctuary of my vehicle and did my civic duty. The command worked. Instantly the dogs seemed to lose interest in the chatelaine. They yawned, stretched, and sniffed each other's behinds.

Then the side door to Druin opened. The young man in the yellow shirt and khakis emerged, *sans* rifle. Felicia shot him a ferocious glare, which he ignored. Flushed and sweaty, he approached the sheriff's deputies and animatedly told them something I couldn't hear.

Felicia and García were loaded into the cruisers, and the dogs were stowed in my car. Jenx brought me up to speed. Ryan the receptionist was the guy who had turned back the pack of dogs. New to his job, he'd seen a few things that troubled him, and he'd just now shared them with the police.

"Something's going on in the wine cellar," Jenx said.

"Renovations," I offered.

"No. Something illegal. Something involving kids."

My jaw dropped, and I felt the blood rush away from my brain.

"Easy," Jenx said. "The kids are okay. Gould and García have been keeping them there since they removed them from Twyla's house."

Soon the state police arrived, along with a bilingual sheriff's deputy; they headed into the chateau. I didn't leave till they came out again, carrying two infants and escorting nine small children into the slanting evening light. Among them I recognized the smiling Pablo, who had tossed the rock at my car. There was also a fat black Labrador retriever.

I learned that Felicia, and sometimes García, often drove the same make and color vehicle I did. That might explain why Twyla cringed whenever I pulled into her driveway. Or why Pablo wanted to break my windshield. On second thought, Pablo was probably just being a boy.

As for the Labrador ... Jenx explained that he was a good dog used for bad purposes. Used, as I had wildly guessed a few days earlier, to lead and quiet the kids.

The Druin pack dogs were silent now. And my canine passengers were asleep, their silky golden bodies intertwined on the back seat.

If Vivika Major herself wasn't famous, her Internet company was. As soon as the public got a whiff of what had gone down at Druin, Fox News and the entertainment channels couldn't get enough. Their headlines screamed "Dot Com Breeds Kid Scam."

Two days after Felicia's arrest, Chester brought his dogs to Vestige for a play date with my dog, who wasn't interested. Ever the thoughtful guest, Chester provided doggie treats and human treats. The doggie treats did interest Abra, and the human treats were a hit with me. I'd never tried imported pesto potato chips with white-grape soda before. Knowing my kitchen pantry as he did, Chester wanted to ensure we had something to snack on while watching the latest Druin updates on TV.

According to the Fox News reporter, a stunning Asian woman who could have made my grocery list sound dramatic, the Druin scandal had started like this:

"Soon after graduating from Stanford Law, Felicia Gould and Vivika Major launched their first Internet company, a search engine used by physicians and academics. Major expanded their applications and client base, leading to an IPO five years later. Gould's niche was international finance; she found the overseas money they needed to keep growing. For nine more years, they enjoyed an unprecedented boom, expanding into video-editing software, children's entertainment, and foreign language translation."

"Hot markets," Chester agreed. "Cassina's investment portfolio includes them all."

The reporter continued, "Then, in August 2003, Felicia Gould was in a near-fatal car crash and spent eighteen months recuperating."

Chester gasped when the screen filled with images of Felicia lying in a hospital bed, a dazed expression on her face, both arms and legs in traction.

"How sad for her!" he sighed.

"Insiders claim that while Major remained loyal to her cohort, she stopped viewing her as vital," the reporter said. "By the time Gould was able to resume her career full-time, others had been hired to do what she did best. No longer an empire-builder, Gould was relegated to a string of low-stress jobs. The chatelaine post was the last in a long line of professional insults."

"But you said she was a good tour guide, right?" Chester asked me, his eyes shining.

I nodded, signaling with a finger to my lips that I wanted to hear the rest of the story.

"Gould struggled to accept her lesser role in the companies she had built, as well as the fact that she had sacrificed her child-bearing years to a career now in shambles," said the reporter. "In early 2006, she stumbled upon an unlimited growth industry: private foreign adoptions. Facilitating the smuggling of babies and toddlers from South and Central America into the U.S. seemed the perfect marriage of her myriad international contacts and her keen understanding of immigration law. Or how to bypass it. The children she placed were orphans. The parents she served were wealthy and desperate. Were the matches to everyone's benefit? Yes. Were they legal? No."

Chester stared at me. "Why is it a bad thing to help people make a family?"

Since I had no ready answer, I deferred to the Fox News reporter. She went on, "Felicia Gould offered impatient affluent

Americans a shortcut to the family of their dreams. And she made lots of money doing it. Perhaps that was her motivation: to close the gap between Vivika Major's income and her own. Or perhaps her goal was more personal: to build families while secretly running a lucrative business right under Major's nose. Inside her heavily armed fortress."

Chester and I listened intently as the reporter explained that Felicia Gould hired young women like Twyla to pose as mothers and act as mules. In fact, the reporter profiled Twyla and her boyfriend Efrén Padilla, who got her into the business; he knew people who knew people, folks who made good, if illegal, incomes doing things "on the side." Padilla went by the name García, and sometimes Twyla did, too. García, who already had a history in the court system, proved more than willing to talk to the cops as part of a plea bargain.

The reporter then cut to an interview with García, whose lawyer was conspicuously absent. García may have been unwise to grant the interview; apparently, he couldn't resist media attention. On TV he looked exactly as he had when I saw him at Druin—except that, instead of a security officer uniform, he now wore prison orange.

García explained that Twyla's part-time cashier gig at Food Duck was just a cover to establish credibility in Magnet Springs; her real work was taking care of kids in transit and assisting with their pick-up and delivery. She wasn't supposed to have more than two or three children at a time.

"But Twyla never could do math. She misscheduled and ended up with eleven kids," García said.

The camera cut back to the reporter directly addressing her audience. "And eleven children was too many in an unfortunate and conspicuous setting, where landlord and neighbors paid close attention."

I gulped.

"When Twyla Rendel reported to Felicia Gould that she was on the verge of eviction, Gould took radical action," the reporter said. "Rendel had been known to say too much to outsiders, and Gould didn't trust the young woman's emotionalism. So she ordered García to move the kids to Druin, where—as chatelaine—she could ensure their temporary seclusion."

Now the camera returned to the interview with García, who said, "Felicia told Twyla to pack the kids' things in trash bags and bring them to a meeting place near Vanderzee Park. The belongings would go to the kids, she said, and Twyla would have a new assignment in Chicago. I met them there and drove off in Twyla's car, still loaded with the bags. Felicia was dressed like a man. She told Twyla to get into her boat, VLM 8. The plan—or so she said—was to ferry Twyla to a rendezvous with some guy who would take her to Chicago."

The reporter told her viewers, "For Twyla Rendel, the only rendezvous was with death. In a shallow, tree-sheltered inlet near Thornton Pointe, Felicia Gould struck Rendel in the back of the head with a shovel and then strangled her with nylon anchor line. She tossed the body overboard. Meanwhile, García followed instructions to strew the contents of several of Rendel's trash bags along the nearby beach, which was devoid of swimmers due to a riptide alert. Gould intended to simulate the aftermath of a riptide. As she had planned, Rendel's body rolled in to shore near the scattered trash."

Back on camera, García explained that he had been sent to Twyla's house to remove all evidence connecting her to Druin. I knew he'd missed the tabloid note that I later found.

But Felicia Gould had made a bigger error: she forgot to check Twyla's pockets before disposing of her body. The reporter speculated that panic must have seized the chatelaine when she realized Rendel's corpse could offer damning evidence. That was why she later drove to the beach and checked the body herself.

Chester said, "Felicia underestimated Abra and Norman! They can recognize and remember a human female, especially one who's up to no good!"

I nodded. Disguised or not, Felicia remained connected in the dogs' minds to the new-dead woman on the beach at Thornton Pointe. Although Chester was a fine canine translator, we would never be sure we had the whole story; after all, we had a species gap. Apparently, Felicia was nasty to the dogs, and that's something they never forget. Being a sight hound, Abra recognized HF, even in a speeding boat.

Vivika, herself, posed almost no threat to Felicia's operation, despite the kids being stashed in the wine cellar. The mogul didn't wander around Druin, let alone enjoy its myriad rooms and features. A pathological workaholic paranoid about business security, she had no emotional investment in her real estate.

Felicia, however, had everything at stake. She tried various means to discourage Odette and our client from viewing the property, including letting loose the dogs. It all backfired, and in the end Abra and Norman looked like heroes. Hell, they *were* heroes.

———

Chester convinced me to host a modest holiday bash at Vestige. It was the Fourth of July, and I had a lot to celebrate. Fenton was slated to close next week on Cassina's cottage. He was still interested in Druin, too, as a retreat center. But he wanted to postpone that decision until his "permanent spouse" returned to Magnet Springs. In the meantime, Odette would no doubt find additional qualified prospects to drive up the bidding.

I hadn't yet been back to bed with the reincarnation of Teddy Roosevelt, although Fenton had offered several invitations. The more I thought about it, the more married to Noonan he still seemed. And that couldn't be good for my karma.

Avery and the driver were still dating. I would have let MacArthur work for Mattimoe Realty even if he hadn't taken her off my hands. On my most cynical days, I wondered if Avery was blackmailing him. Maybe MacArthur had dirty secrets that only Avery knew. Or maybe he liked his women big, loud, and nasty. More work for the cleaner...

The sun was setting over Lake Michigan, and I was sitting on my top deck, a Killian's in my hand. Chester had just replaced Hal Gruen's black Stetson with a brand-new white one "because Hal's one of the good guys." My diminutive neighbor was showing Hal how to serve hors d'oeuvres.

A horn blared, and Fenton emerged from his pickup, accompanied by Norman, who bounded toward Abra. She lay at my feet, munching Hal's newly discarded black hat. On the deck below us, Prince Harry yipped happily and chased splint-free Velcro in circles. Now a resident of Chester's retrofitted rooms, the shitzapoo was making an amazing recovery. Holding his little head high, he carried his personal trainer, Floozy.

Jeb plopped down in the deck chair next to me and flashed his famous dimpled grin, the one that used to make my heart melt.

"Life is good, isn't it, Whiskey?"

He didn't wait for my answer. Instead, he picked up his guitar and strummed the opening bars of a very dangerous tune by Barenaked Ladies.

Somebody gasped. Somebody else pointed at the horizon. I kept my eyes on Jeb. It was the Fourth of July, and fireworks were starting. Real ones. And the other kind, too.

~ The End ~

If you enjoyed reading *Whiskey and Water,*
stay tuned for Nina Wright's next Whiskey Mattimoe Mystery

Whiskey with a Twist

COMING SOON FROM MIDNIGHT INK

ONE

"SHE BREEDS AFGHAN HOUNDS? Then why the hell would I want to meet her?"

I was drinking with my ex-husband, who looked good in the sunlight slanting across Mother Tucker's oak bar. So good that I strained to remind myself of the pain that must have surrounded our divorce. At the moment I could recall none at all.

"Uh, I already have an Afghan hound," I said. "One is too many."

Jeb Halloran sipped his scotch, a single malt that he could only recently afford. "Susan Davies has connections."

"Will she take Abra?" My voice rose in hope.

"She sells dogs, Whiskey. She doesn't collect them. But she might introduce you to her husband."

"Will he take Abra?"

"No, but he might help you make money. Liam is a builder."

"The real estate market sucks." It was my turn to drink. But unlike Jeb, I didn't sip. I gulped. The Pinot went down way too easy.

Jeb signaled the barkeep to pour me another. "It's not that bad."

"Not if you're a buyer with financing. If you're one of them, you've got plenty to choose from. Thanks to all those foreclosures…"

Real estate values were in the toilet, even in Magnet Springs. A downsized job market and mortgage-lending crisis had tightened screws on homeowners everywhere. Michigan and other industrial states were especially hard hit. Locally, though, we had an advantage: ours was a resort region, scenic and sports-oriented the whole year round. We were a playground for the Midwestern rich. Particularly those from Chicagoland, a mere one hundred miles across the Greatest Great Lake.

Jeb said, "Knowing Susan and her husband might help. He's negotiating with the Shirtz Brothers. Money will be made."

I knew about Susan Davies' husband and his builder-developer machine. Rumor had it that Liam Davies, Ltd., was conferring with a local farm family to purchase an eighty-acre parcel at the north end of town.

"No real estate commission to be made on that transaction," I said.

"Ah, but what happens next?" Jeb tossed me a teasing look. The kind that usually led to action in the boudoir.

"What?"

He grinned maddeningly. "Meet Susan. You know how things work."

I knew this much: During economic downturns, the poor get poorer, the middle gets squeezed, and the rich scoop up real estate bargains. Chicago-based Davies had built his fortune turning land in Illinois and Indiana into industrial compounds, office parks, and subdivisions. His plan for the land along Uphill Road remained a mystery. Although the property was zoned agricultural, anything was possible.

"Start pouring. The drinks are on me!" announced a voice rich with Tongo accent and real estate commissions. Odette Mutombo, the best realtor on this side of the state, slid onto the bar stool next to mine. Ignoring me, she fixed her sparkling black eyes on Jeb. "Don't let Whiskey sing you sad songs. I'm here to change her tune."

"I leave the singing to Jeb," I quipped, referring to my ex-husband's rising career. "You've got good news that involves real estate?"

"I have amazing news. Opportunity knocks for those who can hear it: Me."

Folding her manicured hands on the bar, Odette smiled languidly. "I just took a meeting with Liam Davies' people. They want Mattimoe Realty as broker of record for their new development."

Before I could gasp, Jeb's cell phone sang out his own version of "Itsy-Bitsy Spider," now available wherever music was sold. He turned away to take the call.

"She'll need something stronger than that," Odette informed the barkeep when he presented a fresh glass of Pinot Noir. "Pour her what her boyfriend's drinking, and make it a double."

"He's not my—" I protested. Odette made the rude raspberry sound she favored when calling my bluff. "Okay, but I can't drink whiskey."

"For this news you will require sedation. Liam Davies' people want me to handle the project, start to end. And it's a whopper. Will you sulk!"

Once upon a time I would have. Back when the market was stronger than my ego. Before I'd accidentally absorbed enough New Age wisdom to sort out my priorities. Now I accepted both my own limitations and Odette's astonishing strengths. The woman could sell saltwater to sharks. Ergo, she could make money in a down market. Although I owned and operated Mattimoe Realty, sales wasn't my forte. Which was why I gave thanks every day that Odette worked for me and not the competition. Anything she brought in the door fattened my company coffers.

"I should buy *you* a drink," I told her.

"Oh, you will. Plus dinner and assorted high-end gifts of gratitude. Not to mention the colossal commission checks you'll sign. But tonight I'm buying. Drink up."

The barkeep slid a double Glenfiddich my way. I would have preferred to stick with Pinot Noir. Hard liquor got me into trouble, especially trouble of the sexual sort, which I didn't want to risk. My engine was already revving too high. Seven mostly happy years after divorcing Jeb—which included my brief but blissful marriage to the late great Leo—I was seeing Jeb again. Translation: we were having sex. Hot sex. Frequent sex. Better-than-ever sex. And it was scaring the shit out of me. I must have had plenty of reasons for divorcing him way back when. Yet, in the throes of renewed passion, I couldn't remember a single one.

When the short-term lease on his house ran out at the end of July, Jeb had suggested I let him move in with me. Instead, I found him another rental. But now, two months later, he hardly ever went home. He spent most nights with me at Vestige, the lakefront home I had lovingly built with Leo. The lonely, horny part of me wanted to give Jeb his own key. But the sane, self-protective part wanted him to hit the road on another music tour while I cooled my jets. After a whole season of intense sex, I needed to separate my brain from my libido and decide which one was my friend. Even in the midst of Odette's thrilling news, I caught myself eyeing Jeb's ass.

"You'll love Davies' plans for developing the property," Odette purred. "A two-phase, two-income-level *super*-subdivision: Little House on the Prairie *and* Big House on the Prairie—Little House for the common people, Big House for the rich. Separating the two will be a manmade lake. And in the middle of the lake will be an island with tall, thick trees."

"So the people in the big houses don't have to look at the people in the little houses?" I guessed.

"You're catching on!" Odette clinked her chocotini glass against my tumbler of scotch. "Mattimoe Realty will be the listing agent for fifty homes that sell for under two-hundred-thou, and fifteen homes that sell for more than one-point-five million. Cheers!"

I clinked back and chugged my scotch. It was alarmingly smooth. "But the economy—"

Odette made the raspberry sound again. "The rich always have money! Davies will start on *that* side of the lake."

"Did you say 'Davies'?" Jeb rejoined the conversation.

Odette summarized her latest coup. My ex congratulated her and told me to expect a call.

"From who?"

"The other Davies. She phoned me, looking for you."

"Did you ask her to take Abra?"

"Not yet," he said as my cell rang. "But you can try. That's Susan now."

The first zing from my free scotch hit me the instant I opened my phone. I was pretty sure I slurred my greeting. "This is Whiskey."

"Hello, Whiskey," said a warm female voice. "This is Susan Davies. I believe we're both fans of Jeb Halloran. He's told me so much about you and your Afghan hound. I hope you don't mind that I asked him for your number."

Scotch buzz notwithstanding, I had three instant questions, none of which I asked out loud. First, which horror stories had Jeb shared about me and my diva dog? Second, when and where had he shared them? Third, and this was related to Second, what did Susan Davies mean by claiming that she and I were both "fans"? As Jeb's former wife and current lover, I was way more than a fan. Was she? I suddenly remembered one painful reason for our long-ago divorce: Jeb liked to stray.

I took another slug of scotch. "How do you know my ex-husband?"

"He didn't tell you?"

"He didn't." I glared at Jeb, who was leaning on the bar, laughing with Odette.

"Liam and I caught his act at the Holiday Inn in Grand Rapids. That was in August. Since then, my husband has been too busy to go back, but I've heard Jeb at least five more times."

"Five *more* times?"

"At least. Fabulous, isn't he?"

"That's one word for him." My voice was calm although my diction lacked crispness. Since I rate peace of mind higher than clarity of speech, I drank some more. "What keeps bringing you back to Grand Rapids, Susan? Surely not Jeb's music…"

"You're right. Hearing Jeb sing is a treat, but that's not why I'm in the area. He didn't tell you why?"

"Again—no, he didn't." I frowned at my ex-husband, who was having too much fun to notice.

Susan said, "Besides my kennel in Schaumburg, I co-own three dogs in Grand Rapids. The other owner and I started a breeding program. Our bitch is in heat."

"How nice for you!"

"It is, actually. Which brings me to the reason I called. I have a request, Whiskey. It's unorthodox, not to mention short notice, but I'd like to stop by your home. Tonight. My co-owner, Ramona Bowden, is with me, and we want to meet your dog."

"My *dog*?" I blinked. "You don't want to meet *my* dog."

"Oh, yes, we most definitely do."

"Why not meet a nice Afghan hound? Mine is a convicted felon."

"We know that."

Susan Davies didn't seem to get it. So I spoke slowly. "Abra steals things. Expensive things. She consorts with thieves and kidnappers. My dog has a criminal record."

"Her criminal record is why we want to meet her!" Susan said. "It's why we are inviting her—and you, too, of course—to participate in next week's Midwest Afghan Hound Show."

At least that was what I thought she said. Since it made no sense, I blamed the scotch, set my empty glass on the bar, and waited for Susan Davies to try again.

"Are you there, Whiskey?"

"We must have a bad connection. It sounded like you want Abra to be in a dog show. Because she's a criminal." I giggled.

"That's right. Ramona and I are in charge of Breeder Education. We believe that the most effective way to teach grooming and training is to show how *not* to do it. Abra is the worst example we've ever found."

ABOUT THE AUTHOR

Nina Wright loves big dogs and beaches. A former actor and a playwright turned author, she writes for adults and younger readers. This is her sixth published novel. Nina also leads entertaining workshops on writing and the creative process.

To contact her, or for more information about her workshops, see Nina's website and blogs:

www.ninawright.net

http://whiskeymattimoe.blogspot.com

http://ninawrightwriter.blogspot.com

http://mrfairlessrules.blogspot.com